"COOKIES. THAT'S WHAT I WANT."

"My sister bakes these cookies that are basically just sugar and lard. I can eat about a hundred in two days."

"Somehow I don't think you're exaggerating," she told him in a teasing tone of voice.

"You calling me fat?" Christian grinned as he eased down the exit ramp and stopped at the light and turned to look at her.

Her eyes rolled up and down the length of him. "Hardly."

Oh, he knew that tone.

And he liked it.

"It's my one weakness," he told her, his whole body registering the fact that despite the cold outside it was suddenly very hot inside his car.

"The only one?" she asked, her tongue slipping out to wet her lips.

Christian wanted to groan. There was something about the way she held his gaze, the way she moved, so sensual and erotic, yet there was nothing in-your-face or tacky about her. It was like she just had an inherent sexuality and he found that really smoking hot.

"No, I can definitely think of one more."

And if he could get it, he wouldn't even miss the cookies.

from "Blue Christmas"

BOOK YOUR PLACE ON OUR WEBSITE AND MAKE THE READING CONNECTION!

We've created a customized website just for our very special readers, where you can get the inside scoop on everything that's going on with Zebra, Pinnacle and Kensington books.

When you come online, you'll have the exciting opportunity to:

- View covers of upcoming books
- Read sample chapters
- Learn about our future publishing schedule (listed by publication month *and author*)
- Find out when your favorite authors will be visiting a city near you
- Search for and order backlist books from our online catalog
- Check out author bios and background information
- Send e-mail to your favorite authors
- Meet the Kensington staff online
- Join us in weekly chats with authors, readers and other guests
- Get writing guidelines
- AND MUCH MORE!

Visit our website at
http://www.kensingtonbooks.com

DONNA KAUFFMAN

Unwrapped

ERIN MCCARTHY

KATE ANGELL

KENSINGTON BOOKS
http://www.kensingtonbooks.com

KENSINGTON BOOKS are published by

Kensington Publishing Corp.
119 West 40th Street
New York, NY 10018

All Kensington titles, imprints, and distributed lines are available at special quantity discounts for bulk purchases for sales
promotion, premiums, fund-raising, educational, or institu-
tional use.

Special book excerpts or customized printings can also be created to fit specific needs. For details, write or phone the office
of the Kensington Special Sales Manager: Attn. Special Sales
Department. Kensington Publishing Corp., 119 West 40th
Street, New York, NY 10018. Phone: 1-800-221-2647.

Kensington and the K logo Reg. U.S. Pat. & TM Off.

ISBN-13: 978-0-7582-5133-6
ISBN-10: 0-7582-5133-5

First Kensington Books Mass-Market Paperback Printing:
October 2012
First Brava Books Trade Paperback Printing: October 2011

10 9 8 7 6 5 4 3 2

Printed in the United States of America

Contents

Contents

Blue Christmas

ERIN
McCARTHY

Chapter One

"Santa can suck it." Blue Farrow kept an eye on the highway and tried to hit the buttons on the radio to change the station. She was going to grind her teeth down to nubs if she had to listen to Christmas songs for another twelve hours. It was like an IV drip of sugar and spice and it was making her cranky.

Was she the only one who thought a fat dude hanging around on your roof was a bit creepy? And why were those elves so happy in that Harry Connick Jr. song? Rum in the eggnog, that's why. Not to mention since when did three ships ever go pulling straight up to Bethlehem? She wasn't aware it was a major port city.

Yep. She was feeling in total harmony with Scrooge. "Bah, Humbug," she muttered when her only options on the radio seemed to be all Christmas all the time or pounding rap music.

Blue had never been a big fan of Christmas, never having experienced a normal one in her childhood since her flaky mother (yes, flaky considering she'd named her daughter after a color) had done Christmas experimental style every year, never the same way twice, disregarding any of her daughter's requests. The trend on feeling tacked onto her parents' Christmas had continued into Blue's adulthood, and this year she had been determined to have a great holiday all on her terms, booking herself on a cruise with her two equally single friends. She had turned down her mother's invitation to spend the holiday with an indigenous South American tribe and her father's request to join him with his barely legal wife and their baby girl, and instead she was going to sip cocktails in a bikini.

Maybe.

The road in front of her was barely visible, the snow crashing down with pounding determination, the highway slick and ominous, the hours ticking by as Blue barely made progress in the treacherous conditions. Planning to drive to Miami from Ohio instead of flying had been a financial decision and would give Blue the chance to make a pit stop in Tennessee and visit her old friend from high school, but the only thing heading south at the moment was her vacation. It was Christmas Eve, her cruise ship departed in twenty hours, and she'd only made a hundred miles in six hours, the blizzard swirling around her mocking the brilliance of her plan as she drove through the middle of nowhere Kentucky.

She was going to have to stop in Lexington and

see if she could catch a flight to Miami, screw the cost. Not that planes would be taking off in this weather, but maybe by morning. If she flew out first thing, she could be in Florida in plenty of time for her four o'clock sail time. All she had to do was make it to Lexington without losing her sanity from being pummeled with schmaltzy Christmas carols or without losing control of her car in the snow.

When she leaned over and hit the radio again and found the Rolling Stones she nearly wept in gratitude. Classic rock she could handle.

But not her car. As the highway unexpectedly curved and dipped, she fishtailed in the thick snow.

Blue only managed a weak, "Oh, crap," before she gripped the hell out of the wheel and slid sideways down the pavement, wanting to scream, but unable to make a sound.

She was going to die.

If there hadn't been anyone else on the road, she might have managed to regain control. But there was no stopping the impact when she swung into the lane next to her, right in the path of an SUV. She wasn't the only idiot on the road and now they were going to die together.

Blue closed her eyes and hoped there were bikinis and margaritas in the afterlife.

Santa was the man. Christian Dawes sang along to the radio at the top of his lungs, the song reminding him of his childhood, when he had listened carefully on Christmas Eve for the telltale sound of reindeer paws. Tossing the trail mix out for the reindeer to chomp on, putting the cookies on a plate for Santa, the magic and wonder and awe of waking up to a ton of presents, those were some of his best memories.

Someday when he had his own kids, he'd create all of those special moments for them, but right now Christian was content to play awesome uncle, arriving on Christmas Eve loaded down with presents for all his nieces and nephews. His trunk was stuffed with spoils, and he'd brought enough candy to earn glares from his two sisters and potentially make someone sick. But it wasn't Christmas until a kid stuffed his face with candy then hurled after a session on the sit and spin. That's what home videos and infamous family stories were made of.

Unfortunately the lousy weather was slowing him down on his drive from Cincinnati to Lexington. He'd left work later than he'd intended anyway, then by the time he'd hit Kentucky, he'd been forced down to thirty miles an hour because apparently the road crews had taken the holiday off and had decided not to plow. He hoped his family wasn't holding up dinner for him at his parents' house.

If he wasn't gripping the steering wheel so hard he would call someone and let them know he still had a couple of hours ahead of him, but he had no intention of reaching for his phone. A glance to the right showed a car next to him, but other than that, he could barely see the road in front of him. He needed Santa to dip down and give him a lift in his sleigh or it was going to be midnight before he arrived.

What he didn't need was a car accident.

In his peripheral vision, he saw the car next to him slide, spinning out so fast that Christian only had time to swear and tap his brakes before he hit the car with a crunch and they went careening toward the guardrail. When his SUV stopped moving a few seconds later, despite his efforts to turn the skid, he had the other car pinned against the railing.

"Shit!" Christian turned off his car and leaped out, almost taking a header in the thick snow, but terrified that he'd injured someone. "Are you okay?" he asked, yelling through the howling snow as he peered into the driver's side window.

The major impact of his SUV's front end had been in the backseat and trunk, so he hoped if there was an injury it wasn't serious. But with the snow smacking him in the face and the window plastered with wet flakes, he couldn't really see anything.

He knocked on the glass and when it started to slide down, he sighed in relief.

"Are you okay?" he said again now that the person in front of him could hear him.

"Are you okay?" she said simultaneously.

He nodded.

She nodded.

And Christian became aware that he was staring at the most strikingly beautiful woman he'd ever seen in his whole life.

Chapter Two

Blue sat in her car, chest heaving, nodding rapidly to the man staring at her in concern as she tried to calm down. She was alive. Not dead. Everything on her body was intact and she had no pain.

"I'm fine. God, that was scary. I'm sorry, it was my fault, I skidded."

He leaned forward into the window, his face coming inches from hers. "Say that again, the wind is really howling."

"I said I'm sorry," she repeated loudly, suddenly aware that the guy she'd collided with was damn cute.

Wearing a knit winter hat and a camel colored jacket, he looked very rugged and outdoorsy, his chin sporting some scruff that matched the color of his coat. He had deep brown eyes and when his mouth spread into a grin, he had a warm, crooked smile.

"Well, you don't have to yell at me," he said, tone teasing.

Blue felt her heart rate returning to normal and at his words she felt her shoulders drop in relief. She laughed. "Okay, I'll leave that to your wife."

It was a comment she would have made to any man under the circumstances, but she had to admit she was a little curious what his answer would be.

"No wife. No girlfriend. No one at all to yell at me."

Yes. Not that it mattered. At all. But she could hear the flirt creeping into her voice. "Then I guess this was a thrill for you."

He laughed. "Totally. I'm going to move my car then we'll just have to back yours up, okay? Let's see if we can get you back on the road."

Right. The car accident. The fact that he was standing in the middle of a blizzard. Her crunched vehicle. Those were relevant. Not his dimples or broad shoulders.

"Okay."

"Wait for me to move before you try to back up."

Blue became aware that her teeth were chattering. "Got it." As soon as he walked away, she rolled her window back up and turned up the heat. She wasn't wearing a coat and it was finger-numbing, nipple-raising cold outside.

For a split second as he pulled his SUV back onto the road in front of her, heading in the correct direction, Blue wondered if he would just take off and leave her there. But her cynicism, while well honed, didn't even last a full minute before it was obvious he was walking back to her car, pulling gloves onto his hands. His bottom half, which hadn't been visible before, was just as hot as the top. Those were nice jeans, hugging in the right places.

Blue hoped there would be a multitude of smoking hot guys on the cruise because her sex drive had kicked into high gear for whatever reason.

"Okay, try to back up and I'll guide you," he said when she rolled her window back down.

She did, and her tires just spun in the snow. "Damn." She leaned her head out. "How deep is it?"

"Pretty deep. And you can't rock it because you're halfway through the guardrail. If you accelerate too hard you could go off the cliff."

Yeah, no thanks. Blue frowned at her steering wheel. This complicated things. She tried to reverse again, but her car spun ominously to the left.

"You need to get out of the car. This is looking dangerous. We'll call you a tow."

Leave it to her to screw up a vacation by nearly driving off a cliff. Turning her car off, silencing John Lennon midlament, she grabbed her purse and her jacket and pushed the door open. She wasn't wearing appropriate shoes. She had wanted to be comfortable so she was wearing zebra print ballet flats with jeans, a vintage Mötley Crüe T-shirt, and a funky red scarf. Her jacket was a thin black velvet designed for indoor use more so than out. This was going to suck. A lot. Much more than listening to Santa and his ho ho hos.

The wind slapped her in the face as she pulled on her jacket and tried to button it. After a few seconds, she realized it was futile and tried not to whimper as snow cascaded over her mostly bare feet.

Her nose instantly froze, her shoulders hunched in revolt, and her jeans decided at that moment to slide down, allowing her midriff to be pummeled by wet fat flakes.

At least her companion was looking at her in sympathy. "Come sit in my car while we call somebody."

By the time they hiked the twenty feet to his car and Blue slid into the passenger seat, her mouth was stuck open as little gasps of horror escaped. Her entire body felt like someone had repeatedly stabbed her with a million sharp pins. Her companion had turned his car off in the interim so it wasn't really any warmer than it was outside, but at least there was no wind and no snow smacking her in the face and torturing her feet. She stomped her shoes to remove the excess snow and tried not to whimper.

He cranked on the car and the heat and looked at her. "Is that the only jacket you have?"

She nodded.

"Shoes?"

"This is it unless I want to change into flip-flops. I'm going on a cruise. I didn't want a bunch of winter stuff with me." Blue touched her nose. It was still there, despite her not being able to feel it.

"Here." He leaned into the backseat and rifled through a bag. He emerged with two wool socks. "Put these on."

They were like crack to the addict, dangling in front of Blue, as tantalizing as a winning lottery ticket. But it seemed really weird to take socks from a stranger. "Don't you need these?"

"They're just socks. I can get more." He gave

her a look of amusement. "Just put them on. You look like a Popsicle. But a cute one."

That made a certain body part unthaw slightly. "Thanks." As she kicked her ballet flats off and bent her knee so she could drag on one of the thick socks, she added, "I'm Blue, by the way."

"What?" He looked at her, his expression one of confusion. "Don't worry, you'll warm up. I don't think you're at risk for hypothermia yet."

Blue laughed. "No. I mean, I'm Blue. That's my name." She abandoned the sock for a minute and stuck out her hand to him. "Blue Mariposa Farrow. Pleased to meet you."

Understanding hit Christian and he felt like a first-class idiot. "Oh, shit, sorry. I'm Christian Dawes. Nice to meet you too, though I wouldn't have minded better circumstances."

"No kidding. And don't worry about not catching my name. I'm well aware it's unusual. My mom was going for unique and lovely territory, but she just landed in weird."

Blue went back to struggling with his sock, and as Christian watched her long and elegant fingers, and took in that wide smile below her high cheekbones, he thought that the name actually suited her. She had black hair with blunt bangs, the sides angling down past her chin. Her eyes had dark shadow on them and her fingernails were painted a deep blue. There was something very edgy yet playful about her appearance and her expressions. He'd only spent ten minutes with her and he could already see that she emoted with exaggerated facial expressions. She did the eyebrow arch, the head tilt, and a whole variety of movements with her lips.

Lips that he wouldn't mind being on his.

"It's definitely a unique name, but it's actually very pretty. Mariposa is butterfly in Spanish, isn't it?"

"Yes." Blue finished with the socks and sighed. "Ah, that feels good. And if you think Blue Butterfly is a pretty name for a grown woman you're smoking something and I don't mean a Marlboro. It's a corny name. But I'm used to being Blue." She did a fake drumroll on her knees and grinned. "Ba dum dum."

Christian laughed. "Well, I guess my parents went for the obvious. My sisters' names are Mary and Elizabeth. I think if they could have gotten away with naming me Jesus they would have."

"See, my mom would have just gone for it. So be grateful."

He was perfectly content sitting in his warm car staring at her, but Blue pulled her cell phone out of her purse.

"I better call someone if I hope to ever get out of here."

Right. Her wrecked car. Christian picked his phone up out of the cup holder, figuring he should call his family and warn them of the delay. Except he had no bars on his cell phone. He tried to call his mom anyway but it didn't do anything. "Is your phone working?"

Blue was frowning at her own cell phone and holding it up in the air. "No. Damn, this could be a problem."

"It must be the hill messing things up." They

had slid to a stop nestled in a curve where the highway had been carved out of a steep hill. Given the curve and the incline, it was no wonder Blue had lost control in the piled-up snow. Christian rolled down his window and stuck his phone out, hoping miraculously it would start working. It didn't.

"Where are we? Are we close to an exit? I guess I'll have to walk."

Christian dropped his phone back down and hit the button to put his window back up. Then he shot the woman next to him an incredulous look. "Are you crazy? You can't walk in this. And if you think for one minute that I would let you walk in this, then you have another thing coming. It's probably two miles to the next exit and you're half-naked."

"I'm not half-naked!" Her face scrunched up.

Okay, maybe that had been melodramatic but he was appalled at the thought of her walking in a blizzard with a velvet jacket without gloves and those stupid girl shoes that exposed the tops of her feet. Sexy, yes, practical, no.

"Well, you're certainly not dressed for taking a stroll in a snowstorm. And I would be a complete jerk if I let you do that. I can drive you to the exit, it's no problem."

Her mouth opened like she was going to argue, but then she just nodded. "Okay, thanks, I appreciate it."

"I'm going to run back and grab your suitcase. You might be stuck in town in a motel overnight before they can tow your car." Seeing her about to protest, Christian argued, "And before you say you can do it, just let me do it. I'm wearing boots."

She sighed, but she nodded. "Thanks." She handed him her keys. "The suitcase is in the trunk. I guess there goes my cruise. I'll never make it to Miami in time to board. This sucks."

"I can't believe a cruise leaves on Christmas day." The last thing in the world Christian would want to do on Christmas would be to spend it in the airport or boarding a cruise ship. Christmas day was for eating way too much food with family and chasing his nieces and nephews around. It was the one day a year the outside world completely disappeared and the only thing that mattered was family.

"I'm not big on Christmas. I'd rather just skip the whole thing."

Christian tried not to gape at her, but man, it was like she was speaking in tongues. Who the hell didn't like Christmas?

The gorgeous woman sitting next to him apparently.

Not sure what to say that wasn't being intrusive and pushy, Christian just settled for nodding. "Well, I'm sorry that you might miss the boat. We'll see what we can do to get you south as soon as possible."

"Thanks." She smiled, but it was a little forced.

Christian opened the door and hustled to her car. In the trunk was a hot pink suitcase with a pink and black plaid scarf tied to the handle. He grabbed it and ran through the snow, hoping he didn't wipe out and fall on his ass. But if there was any possibility of getting her to Lexington and on a flight to Miami, he wanted to help her. It occurred to him he could just drive her to Lexington himself once the tow was on the way and that would save her a hell of a lot of time. She could deal with retrieving her car on the way home after her cruise.

He tossed her suitcase in the trunk and jumped in his car, shaking the snow off his hair. Blue laughed and reached out and dusted the shoulder of his jacket off. "Sorry, I should have gone and gotten it."

"Which again, would make me a total jerk." Christian knew he couldn't actually feel her fingers through the fabric of his coat and his sweatshirt, but he certainly appreciated her closeness. When she pulled back, he was disappointed. There was something so dynamic about her, so sensual, that he was suddenly thinking about unwrapping her instead of any presents, which made him a total goofball jackass. Just because he carried her suitcase through the snow did not mean she was going to fall into his arms.

Damn, he needed to start dating again. A few months dry spell, and he was getting weird.

Putting his car into drive, he glanced back at the empty highway and pulled out. "It's almost eerie how no one is on the road."

"I know. I guess I should be less worried about my cruise and more grateful for the fact that you were out here too. Otherwise, I'd be totally stranded."

Out of the corner of his eye he saw her shudder. Then she shook it off and grinned. "No food and a constant barrage of Christmas songs. Talk about a nightmare."

He actually didn't even want to think about what

might have happened if she had been out there alone with a nonfunctioning cell phone. He suspected she would have tried to walk and that would have been a disaster. "Not having my Black-Berry working would drive me insane."

"Where are you heading, by the way?"

"To Lexington, to my parents' house. My whole family is in Lexington and I grew up there. I moved to Cincinnati for college and I'm still there. Guess they'll be carving the turkey without me tonight."

"I live in Cincinnati too. In Clifton."

"I'm in Hyde Park. We're practically neighbors." Though they weren't exactly the same kind of zip code. Not surprisingly, Blue lived in a city neighborhood where a lot of college kids and coffee shops were. Christian lived in an upper middle-class family area, with some young professionals thrown in. It was safe and he was close to work, but sometimes he glanced around at all the strollers and wondered if he was missing out on the nightlife of a hipper neighborhood. Then he realized what he really wanted was a family, not the opportunity to hit the bars every night.

"Is your family going to worry?"

"Definitely. My mom is probably freaking out already. Hopefully I can call her when we get to a gas station. She panics, but hell, that's what moms do, right?"

"Not mine."

The tone was so matter of fact that Christian risked taking his eyes off the road and glanced over at her. Blue didn't look upset, just resigned. "What do you mean?"

"My mom doesn't worry about anything. She prides herself on being zen."

"Is she going on the cruise with you?"

Blue snorted. "Oh, please. I had to endure a lecture on the frivolity and social irresponsibility of cruise ships. My mother is actually in South America with an indigenous tribe. She wanted me to go, but eating bugs isn't my idea of a good time."

Yikes. "And I thought eggnog was disgusting."

Blue laughed. "Yeah, well, all I wanted was a mai tai or two but it's starting to look doubtful."

"Cookies. That's what I want. My sister bakes these cookies that are basically just sugar and lard. I can eat about a hundred in two days."

"Somehow I don't think you're exaggerating," she told him in a teasing tone of voice.

"You calling me fat?" Christian grinned as he eased down the exit ramp and stopped at the light and turned to look at her.

Her eyes rolled up and down the length of him. "Hardly."

Oh, he knew that tone.

And he liked it.

"It's my one weakness," he told her, his whole body registering the fact that despite the cold outside it was suddenly very hot inside his car.

"The only one?" she asked, her tongue slipping out to wet her lips.

Christian wanted to groan. There was something about the way she held his gaze, the way she moved, so sensual and erotic, yet there was nothing in-your-face or tacky about her. It was like she just had an inherent sexuality and he found that really smoking hot.

"No. I can definitely think of one more."

And if he could get it, he wouldn't even miss the cookies.

Chapter Three

Blue was flirting. She was stranded in the middle of nowhere Kentucky with a broken-down car and a cruise ship pulling out of port the next day most likely without her and she was flirting with Christian, her knight in a white SUV.

She supposed she could tell herself it was her amazingly sunny disposition finding the silver lining, but the truth was it wasn't her cheerful self calling the shots right now, but her undersexed one. It had been months since she had dated and Christian was cute with a capital C. He had dimples and a grin that made her want to grab his cheeks and kiss the hell out of him. He was sweet and funny and she knew beyond a shadow of a doubt there were some serious muscles hiding beneath his many layers of clothing.

So she was flirting. What of it? She deserved to after nearly dying in this bitch of a snowstorm.

"What weakness is that? Fast cars or loose women?"

Christian pulled into a gas station right off the exit. "Neither. I like beautiful women, not loose ones."

At the moment, Blue thought she was probably out of the running then, because she felt pretty damn easy sharing this small space with him.

"Beautiful women like you."

She almost blurted out a very middle school "You think I'm beautiful?" but she managed to contain it and be cool. "Thanks. Though I prefer gorgeous."

Laughing, he put the car in park in front of the gas station. "Okay, gorgeous, let's go in and see if we can make contact with the outside world."

There was only one truck in the parking lot and the gas station looked like it had seen better days. As they entered, the bell tinkled over the door and the smell of stale cigarette smoke smacked them in the face. A thin guy in his forties with two full-arm tattoo sleeves glanced up from the magazine he was reading. He scratched his scraggly beard. "Hey, what's up? I didn't expect to see anyone tonight."

"Hi," Blue said, coming up to the counter, her feet feeling weird and overstuffed in Christian's wool socks and her ballet flats. "We had a car accident on the highway and I can't get cell phone reception. Can we use your phone to call a tow?"

"Sure." He shoved a chunky cordless phone over to her. "But I doubt you're going to have much luck. It's snowing and it's Christmas Eve."

Well, thanks, Captain Obvious. Blue fought the

urge to roll her eyes. Fortunately, Christian stepped in, preventing her from saying something seriously sarcastic.

"Yeah, I know, bad luck, huh?" Christian said with an affable smile. "We have two cars. We were thinking of just leaving the one here and heading on to Lexington."

They were? That was news to her.

"Do you think that's our best bet? You know the towing companies around here and you know the roads. What's the word?"

"You can't drive to Lexington," he said, shaking his head. "The highway south of this exit is closed. Guess it iced over bad at the curve and they declared a snow emergency. Only emergency vehicles allowed on the road. It was on the news."

"Are you serious?" Blue asked, slightly stunned. Did they really just close roads? Was that allowed? "Is there another way to go south?"

"Well, there's always Route 43, but I wouldn't recommend that. It won't be plowed and if you get in trouble, there's nowhere to go for help. I suggest you sit this one out tonight and start over again in the morning."

"But . . ." She was speechless. Absolutely speechless. This sucked. Really bad. Like if there were the definition of suck in the dictionary this would be it.

Christian put a hand on the small of her back and rubbed gently. It was an unexpected reassurance. Thank God she'd hit him and wasn't doing this on her own. Not that he would probably appreciate that fact, but she was damn grateful.

"Is there a motel hereabouts?" Christian asked. "I'm not digging the idea of sleeping in my car tonight. I've stopped at this exit before and I seem to remember there's a motel just on down the road."

Noticing that the longer they stood there the more Christian's Kentucky roots surfaced, Blue was amused. "On down the road?" she asked, grinning.

"What?" He looked bewildered.

"Nothing." Blue squeezed her lips together as she glanced at the gas station attendant. He looked equally confused.

"Well, yeah, there's old Roy's place, but I'm not sure if he'll be open tonight. It's called the No-Tell Motel."

Fabulous. They might as well call it Serial Killers and Hookers Sleep Here. Blue tried not to make a face, but given the grin Christian shot her she wasn't successful. What could she say? All her thoughts were always splashed across her face, an unfortunate gift her emotional mother had given her.

"It's about a half mile east."

"Is that right or left?" Blue asked. Men always spoke in terms of north-south-east-west and it just made it more complicated than it needed to be.

They both raised an eyebrow like this was the dumbest thing they'd ever heard.

"I got it," Christian said. "Don't worry about it."

"O-kay then," Blue said, the eye roll slipping out before she could stop it. "But shouldn't I call for my tow first?"

Ten minutes later she was gritting her teeth and glaring at the yellow pages in front of her. "I've called every tow service in the county and not a single one has answered their phone."

Gas station man shrugged. "Told ya."

"Don't people need to work? Aren't we in a recession?"

Another shrug. "It's Christmas Eve."

Whatever. Blue slapped the book closed and turned to Christian. "What are you doing?" she asked, irritated beyond belief with the whole situation. Even Christian's cuteness couldn't make up for the fact that everyone else's obsession with Christmas was ruining her vacation.

Christian had a shopping basket loaded with bottled water, soft drinks, and a surely illegal quantity of snack foods.

"We have to eat. And I doubt this particular motel has room service."

The guy behind the counter snorted. "You'll be lucky if you get clean sheets."

Lovely.

"Do they rent by the hour?" Christian asked, his tone joking.

"Oh yeah, definitely." The guy cleared his throat. "Not that I'd know anything about that. Though be careful, if you go over even a minute, Roy charges for a whole 'nother hour."

Eew. "Anyway," Blue said, determined to steer this conversation away from the gas station guy's fond memories of sixty-one minute hook-ups. "What snacks did you get?"

"Chips. Peanuts. Ho Hos. You know, in honor of Christmas. And a premade margarita mix and a bottle of tequila so you can close your eyes and pretend you're on the cruise."

That was sweet. Really sweet. Even though all

the tequila in the world couldn't fix the fact that she was freezing her ass off with swollen feet from cramming them into her shoes with socks in the middle of the boonies of Kentucky in a motel that probably had Magic Fingers beds.

But she was willing to give it a shot. "Thanks. Let's get some cups and napkins then too. And could you please change the radio station in here?" she demanded, whirling to the gas station guy as the fifth Christmas song assaulted her ears and took her over the edge.

"To what? It's Christmas Eve. I like Christmas songs."

"Well, I don't."

His eyebrow shot up. "That's un-American."

Blue debated using her scarf to strangle him. "What does being an American have to do with Christmas?"

"We invented Santa."

"We did not!" Blue opened her mouth to launch into a recap of all the cultures who had a Santa figure in their lore, but Christian shoved in front of her and dropped the basket on the counter.

"Go on and get the napkins, gorgeous. We should head out before the roads get worse." He nodded at the gas station attendant. "It's been a long day."

"Tell me about it."

Was she really being dismissed? To go get napkins? Blue narrowed her eyes. Okay, she realized Christian was just trying to prevent a confrontation between her and the guy behind the counter, but she still didn't like it. She was cold and tired and now that Christian mentioned it, she was hungry. The fact that it was extremely likely she was going to miss her cruise had her suddenly feeling like she wanted to cry.

This was all just further proof that she and Christmas didn't mesh.

"Did you change your mind about napkins?" he asked when she didn't move. "And hey, look what I got for you."

Christian slid reindeer antlers onto her head and grinned. "Now that's adorable."

She stood there, seething just a little. A lot. She was wearing reindeer antlers. With jingle bells. "Are you fucking kidding me?" she demanded.

"Not in the least." Then he leaned forward and kissed the tip of her nose.

Just like that.

All familiar and comfortable and sexy and cute.

Blue was so caught off guard that by the time they left the gas station five minutes later, Christian whistling a Christmas song as he carried the bags, she hadn't managed to spit out a single word.

And she was still wearing the antlers.

Christian beeped his car open and tossed the bags in the backseat, pleased that he had managed to catch Blue off guard. She had clearly been on the verge of losing it big time, and he knew she had good reason to. But hell, it was Christmas Eve, and they might as well make the best of it, so he had wanted to snap her out of her bad mood. Plus she'd looked so cute and pissed off in the antlers, he hadn't been able to resist kissing her.

He wasn't sure he'd cheered her up, but he had definitely silenced her. That was a start. She had just stood there dumbstruck while he'd paid for everything in his basket, plus two travel mugs for their makeshift margaritas.

When they got in the car, she finally spoke. "Where are your antlers? If I have to wear these dumb things you should be wearing them too."

"Mine's even better." Christian dug around the bags on the backseat and pulled out a headband with a giant felt Christmas tree on top and shoved it on his head. "See?"

Her mouth twitched, but she held back her laugh. "Very nice. How long do we have to wear these?"

"Until midnight on Christmas Day."

"Good luck with that."

"I don't need luck. I have charm." Christian shot her a grin and made his Christmas tree bounce.

"Is that what you call it?" But she did smile at him, even if her arms were still crossed over her chest. "What do you do for a living, by the way?"

"I'm a toy engineer."

"Are you serious? Now why does that not surprise me?"

"I admit it. I'm a big kid at heart. Or a total nerd. Whatever you want to call it. But I like my job. I work mostly in sports themed toys for the toddler and preschool set." As he headed east, he glanced at her. "What do you do?"

"I'm a hairstylist."

"That seems like a natural fit." It did. She had that funky, edgy vibe that women in the salon always had. They were always on top of the current trends and changed their hair color constantly. Not that he could picture her with anything other than black hair. It suited her, as did the way the cut framed her striking face.

"Yeah, I like it. It's a creative outlet and I like working with people. I didn't have the patience to go to a four-year college. My mom hates it, though. She has issues with all the chemicals we use."

"It sounds like your mom has some issues in general." Then he realized that sounded totally rude. "No offense or anything, I'm sure she's a great person."

But Blue just snorted. "She's unique, that's for sure. And totally disappointed in her hedonistic chemically processed daughter."

Christian could hear the underlying tone of hurt in her voice. She was trying to mask it with nonchalance and a snarky expression, but it was clear it bothered her. Having a great family himself, he couldn't even imagine what it must feel like to essentially be alone on Christmas. "Well, we have Doritos and Slim Jims and she's eating bugs, so it's all good."

"True that." Blue pointed. "Look, there it is. The No-Tell Motel. God, I can't believe that's really its name."

Turning into the lonely parking lot of the low-slung motel, Christian eyed it through the raging snow. "There are probably worse. Like The Hell Motel. I wouldn't want to stay there."

"Or The Sleep and Peep."

Christian laughed as he parked the car. "The Hills Have Eyes Inn."

"Bubba's Bed."

"Pappy's Shack."

"The Resting Place."

"Hot Brown Haven."

"What the hell does that mean?"

"Hot brown. The sandwich. It's turkey." She clearly hadn't grown up in Kentucky.

"Oh. I've never had one."

"Well, I'd get you one, but I don't think they're to be found at the No-Tell Motel."

"There's no telling what's at the No-Tell."

"We're getting good at being corny."

"You're drawing it out in me." Blue grinned and shoved her feet back into her shoes. "Corny is part of your charm."

"So you admit I'm charming."

She made a face and opened the car door. But then she turned to him, one foot already in the parking lot. "Hey, thanks for hanging with me. This sucks a lot less with you."

You'd have thought he won the freaking lottery the way he was grinning as he climbed out of the car and headed for the No-Tell.

He wasn't sure how big a leap it was from her saying her day sucked less with him around, to convincing her they were meant to get naked together but he was damn sure going to try.

Chapter Four

Blue stamped her feet in the forlorn lobby of the No-Tell, the air not much warmer than it was outside. There was no one at the desk. "Great, no one's here."

"The door was open. There must be someone here." Christian leaned over the desk toward the back room. "Hello? Can you help us?"

Pulling her cell phone out of her jeans with nearly numb fingers, Blue scowled at it and shook. "I still don't have reception. God, being cut off like this sucks."

"Think of it as an adventure."

All that cheerfulness must be exhausting. "Thanks, Dad." Blue glared at him as he stood there in perfect nonchalance, clearly convinced this was all going to work out just fine.

She, on the other hand, was starting to think she might die before this was all over.

"Where the hell is the employee?" She paced

and tried punching buttons on her phone again, just in case something had changed in the last sixty seconds. It hadn't.

"Just relax, they're just not expecting us, but someone is clearly here. I can hear the TV."

"Did I mention I don't have a lot of patience?"

"You're also a little cranky, too, but it's all part of *your* charm."

And he lightly punched her on the arm.

Blue blinked. He should be exactly the kind of guy that drove her insane. She could only take so much optimism. Normally she went for moody artist types who spent large quantities of time on their hair and ridiculous amounts of money for vintage band shirts and designer jeans. They also tended to disappear for a week or two at a time without warning then reappear with whiny requests for attention.

Which when put like that made her wonder what the hell she saw in them.

Christian had managed to make her smile in the midst of a really suck-ass situation and he had never once complained, or God forbid, asked if he could lay his head down in her lap for solace. Yeah, she'd had that happen before. Scary moment.

"Did we leave the Doritos in the car?" she asked, feeling the need for comfort food. Suddenly it felt like her whole concept of dating and the perfect partner had tilted *Titanic*-style and was slowly starting to sink.

"Yeah. You want me to go get them?"

Oh. My. God. And he was willing to just go fetch chips for her? Without her asking or without bitching or without demanding a blow job. Blue's face went hot and she definitely felt off-kilter. "No, no, that's okay. I can wait five minutes. I just wish I'd eaten dinner."

Christian was about to respond, but just then a man who looked approximately a thousand years old shuffled in through the door to the back room.

"What do we have here?" he asked them, adjusting his glasses and craning his neck to see them from his hunched over position.

"Hi," Christian said, sticking out his hand. "How are you tonight, sir? Merry Christmas."

The man shook Christian's hand. "Thank you, thank you. Merry Christmas to you, too. Like those hats you're wearing, very festive. Are you kids traveling in this weather? Doesn't look very safe out." He gave them a look of concern.

Blue smiled. "Unfortunately, it's not. We had a bit of an accident and now the road is closed for travel, so we're kind of stuck here for the night. Do you have two rooms available?"

Not that she was opposed to bunking with Christian, because she was pretty sure she wanted to shag his brains out, but he was going to have to make the first move. She did have some standards with men she'd just met who weren't her type.

"Two rooms? Nope, can't do it. We don't get much business here and I'm semiretired and well, I haven't kept things up as good as I could have and the place needs a new roof. With all the snow, seven of the eight rooms have leaks with buckets in them. There's only one that's fine and it's the one closest to the office here where my grandson did a patch on the roof."

"You can take that," Christian said, looking at her. "I'll take the one with the least leaking, I don't mind."

Was there a pause there? Was he waiting for her to say something? Blue wasn't sure, but she realized he wasn't going to throw it out there in front of the old guy, and he was clearly trying to be a gentleman. Blue hadn't been aware that those still existed, but apparently she'd been wrong. Maybe about a lot of things.

"Christian, you don't have to take a leaky room. You can just share mine, it's not a big deal."

"Are you sure?" He smiled and it wasn't a "gee, thanks" kind of smile. It was a "I'm going to ignore my bed and be in yours" kind of smile.

Perfect. "Yes. I have to warn you, I'm kind of a slob, though."

"I wouldn't have believed anything else." He turned back to the motel owner. "Okay, we'll take the good room. How much will that be, sir?"

"Oh, I don't take credit cards," the manager said, when he saw Christian pulling his out of his wallet. "But don't worry about it, I'm not going to charge folks who are stranded on Christmas Eve."

"It's no trouble," Christian insisted, pulling several twenties out of his wallet. "We're just grateful you can put us up."

"Put your money away." He waved his hand and looked offended. "I'm not having none of that."

"Well, thank you," Christian said. "We appreciate it. I'm Christian, by the way, and this is Blue."

"What did you say?" He scrunched his eyes up at Blue. "Did he say your name is Blue?"

"Yes." She shrugged. "My mom was trying to be unique."

"Huh. I knew a fella named Red once, but that was his nickname. Never met anyone named after a Crayola crayon before. But my grandson's name is Rock so I guess if you can be named for something no one ever wants to be as dumb as, I guess you might as well name someone after a color in the rainbow. Not sure what happened to Sarah and William though."

"My sister's name is Sarah," Blue told him, rocking on her heels, amused by his assessment of the randomness of name choices. "I think my father saw the error of his ways."

He nodded. "I can see that." Then he winked behind his thick glasses. "Though I reckon you're the prettier one anyway. I'm Roy, by the way."

"It's a pleasure to meet you, Roy."

"Is there any chance I can borrow your phone, Roy? I just want to call my friend and let her know what happened to me."

"Sure, sure, no problem." He pushed the phone over to her.

Blue dialed Emily and left her a voice mail explaining the situation when she didn't pick up her phone. She handed the phone to Christian, who called his parents. Curious, she half-listened to his conversation, noting that he was both respectful and comfortable in tone.

"Where were you headed?" Roy asked Blue.

"Florida. I was supposed to be going on a cruise."

"Oh, boy. Mother Nature can be a bitch, can't she?"

That made Blue nod grimly. "Yes, she can be, Roy."

As Christian hung up the phone, Roy got them a key and handed it to him. "If you all are up and hungry in the morning, come on over to the office here and have some breakfast with me. Doesn't look like my grandkids will be able to collect me until the afternoon with the weather like this, and I'd enjoy the company."

"We'd love to," Blue said, knowing instinctively that Christian would be on board with that. A glance over at him showed he was nodding in agreement.

Which was something most men Blue had dated would not have been happy about.

That odd little unsettling feeling hit her again. "Have a good night, Roy. Stay warm."

Christian gave him a wave and they headed out to the car. Blue leaned in the backseat and gathered up her purse and the bags from the gas station. She was about to go to the trunk to get her suitcase when she saw Christian already had both her bag and his and was opening the door to Room 1.

"Ladies first," he told her with a smile, the doofy Christmas tree on his head bouncing.

She swallowed, trying to recover her earlier crankiness. Pissed off was a better place to be than unsure of herself. That was a feeling she couldn't stand and with Christian, she definitely felt off-balance. He was a breed of male she didn't understand. The good guy who got married and bought a suburban house and mowed his lawn. It was freaking her out how much she was attracted to him.

Slipping into the room, she dumped the plastic bags on the tiny table and tried to ignore the fact that it smelled like old socks. "At least it's warm."

"And snow free." Christian put their suitcases against one wall and peeled off his coat. "So your sister's name is Sarah? How did that happen?"

"My father recently married a girl twenty-four years younger than him—exactly half his age, not that I'm doing the math—and they just had a baby they named Sarah Jane. I guess the nearly three decades since my birth mellowed him into a traditionalist." She grinned. "After all, having a midlife crisis and marrying a pretty young thing is fairly traditional for men."

"I don't even know what to say to that," Christian said. "You're handling it much better than I would. I think I would yak if my dad married some chick younger than me."

Blue kicked off her shoes and sat on the edge of the bed, wiggling her toes. "Yeah, well, I saw it coming. Over the years as his hair got thinner, his girlfriends got younger. My parents split when I was two, so it's not like I knew anything different. Seeing him with girlfriends was no big deal. But I have to admit, I had a cringe moment when he actually went and married this one and had a baby. But Sarah is a pudgy cutie and it's not her fault her parents' marriage is doomed to failure any more than it was mine."

His eyebrow arched. "Cynical?"

"Who, me? Never." Blue peeled off her coat. "My God, it's like a thousand degrees in here. Where's the thermostat?"

"Too cold . . . too hot . . . there's just no pleasing some people." He grinned when she threw her scarf at him, even as he was already readjusting the thermostat. "Ready for a margarita, Scrooge?"

"I thought you'd never ask." She stood up and emptied the plastic bags of their dubious spoils. "Is it gross to eat Doritos with margaritas?"

"Yes. But that's not going to stop us, is it?"

Blue ripped open the bag and popped one in her mouth. "Hell, no."

She turned to hold the bag out to him and almost bumped into him. He was right behind her and he had peeled off his sweatshirt, leaving him only in a T-shirt. Yep. Those arms had some serious muscles. "Oh! Sorry," she said, immediately wanting to kick herself for sounding so stupid and flustered.

But damn it, she was flustered. He was close. Cute. Sexy. Generally speaking, she dated men who were skinnier than she was, and the way he sort of towered over her, his chest like twice the width of hers, was . . . hot.

Christian didn't back up. He just stuck his hand in the bag and grabbed a handful of chips. "You're right, it's burning up in here. I wish I had shorts."

And with that, he tossed the chips in his mouth then stripped off his T-shirt, revealing a chest worthy of a skin calendar. Drool pooled in Blue's mouth. Holy crap, she was as vulnerable to a pair of biceps as the next woman and had never known it.

"It is hot in here." Stupid, lame ass thing to say. Turning back to the table, annoyed with herself, she twisted the cap on the tequila bottle hard. "But unlike you, poor sap, I have a whole suitcase full of summer clothes. Maybe I'll just put on a sundress and make you jealous."

"I've never once wanted to wear a sundress."

"Ha ha."

"Do you have a bikini in there?" He reached around her, his bare arm brushing hers as he popped the lids off the travel mugs.

"Yes."

"Black?"

"How did you know?" she smirked, dumping a boatload of tequila into both cups.

"Lucky guess." He picked up the bottle of mixer, his eyes challenging her. "If you put on the bikini I'll really be jealous."

"Is that right? Are you sure this isn't just some kind of guy trick to get me almost naked?" One she didn't really mind. The particular warm and increasingly wet sensation between her thighs had nothing to do with the overactive furnace and everything to do with wanting him on her, in her. All of the above.

"It totally is," he admitted. "But if we grab a towel from the bathroom it has the added benefit of making you feel like you're on vacation."

She snorted. "Yeah, right. This is so far from my idea of a Caribbean cruise it's not even funny. But if I put on a bikini I get to take off these stupid antlers."

"Hey, don't hate on the antlers. They're cute and festive. Roy said so. But yes, you can take off the antlers."

"Where did yours go, by the way?" She crossed

her arms and glared at him. Somehow he'd managed to ditch his tree hat without her noticing.

"I couldn't get my sweatshirt off with it still on."

"Uh-huh. Likely excuse." But nonetheless, Blue backed up, taking in the sight of him in his jeans and socks and nothing else. After a second of digging around in her suitcase, she found her bikini and her travel bag. Time to brush her teeth, while she was at it. Dorito breath was not hot.

"But when I come back out here, I think you need to be my pool boy." She snapped her fingers and pointed. "A drink, please."

Christian's eyes lifted from the bikini in her hand to meet her stare. "Yes, ma'am."

Blue strolled into the bathroom, making sure she put a little roll into her gait since she knew he was checking out her butt. Once the door was closed, she did a little victory dance. So no cruise for her, but she was going to have sex, and sometimes that was better than a vacation. Sex and a vacation would be ideal, but she was going to take what she could get, and if Christian's biceps were any indication, the getting would be good.

When Blue opened the bathroom door, Christian had already downed half his drink, feeling very hot and thirsty. Partially from the overly warm room, but mostly from anticipation. He totally dug Blue and if he was reading the signs right—please God, let him be right—she was on board with a little horizontal shuffle.

Not exactly how he had pictured his day going when he'd left the office today, but when Blue strolled back into the room, he almost fell to the

ground in gratitude. Holy shit, she was smoking
hot. As all the blood rushed from his brain south
and his erection swelled to unmistakable propor-
tions, Christian just stared at Blue. Her body was
exactly as he'd pictured it, small, perky breasts and
a flat stomach above lean, long legs. Legs he could
perfectly picture wrapped around him.

She had a towel over her ass and she wrapped it
over her front, knotting the fabric so that he could
no longer see her thighs, which was damn disap-
pointing.

"I have your drink ready for you," he told her.
"Like a good pool boy."

"Excellent." She pulled a pretentious pose then
sat on the edge of the bed, crossing her legs.

He handed her the plastic mug and said, "Do I
have permission to sit next to you?"

"I don't know if that's appropriate," she said
breezily. "But fine. It's your job on the line."

"I'm willing to risk it. Besides, my boss is on
break." Christian sat down next to her and there
was a moment of silence between them. He'd
swear he could practically hear their sexual energy
crackling in the air between them. "This isn't so
bad, huh? We have all the important things."

"We need music though," she said. "And I don't
mean Christmas carols."

Christian glanced around but there didn't seem
to be a radio or anything. "I have my iPod but I
didn't bring the speakers." And he'd be damned if
he'd let her plug into it and tune him out. He
wanted to talk to her, among other things.

"That's okay. I guess I shouldn't bitch. This is
about as good as it gets under the circumstances."

Hmm. That wasn't exactly a glowing review on time with him. Not that he should blame her. This wasn't how she'd planned her Christmas to go down. "Hey. I'm really sorry about your cruise," he said in a soft voice.

"Thanks." She shrugged, but her smile was a little forced. "Sorry, I don't mean to be a downer, but it suddenly hit me that I just spent a thousand dollars, which took me an entire year to save, on a trip I won't be taking. That sucks. A lot."

"That does suck. And I won't give you a pep talk, I know how annoying that is."

"You're a smart man."

"But I really think I should sing for you." He nudged her arm, very much aware of how little she was wearing and how close they were sitting.

Blue turned and gave him an incredulous look. "What about that is a good idea? Can you even sing?"

"No. But that's not the point. You want music." He stood up and cleared his throat. "And I shall provide it." He had to admit, this was a gamble. She might just get totally annoyed, but he thought that he was just awful enough that he'd get a laugh out of her, which was his goal.

"You're a nut, you know that, don't you?" Beneath her towel, she adjusted herself until she was sitting on the bed cross-legged. "And you're scaring me."

Christian grinned. "You so don't look scared."

"I am. I'm terrified of what is going to come out of your mouth."

"The King, baby." He stuck his hip and his hand out. "Isn't it obvious?"

"No." She tucked her hair behind her ear and frowned in confusion.

"Blue Christmas," he sang in an off-key, warbly attempt at Elvis. "I'm having a—"

"Oh, my God." Blue held her hand out, her lips twitching. "Stop. That's not going to happen."

"Why not? It's the perfect song because your name is Blue, obviously as you know, and it's Christmas, which again you know, and you're well, blue, as in feeling blue, so see, isn't that a great irony?" He gave her a cheesy Chesire grin.

"I was thinking more like it's awful, but really isn't irony just another word for awful?"

"Basically. Well, if you don't like my Elvis, there's always the Porky Pig version. B-b-b-b-blue C-c-c-christmas."

Blue burst out laughing. "You're insane."

So he kept going, spouting the whole song in the infamous pig's voice, adding hand gestures where it seemed appropriate. By the time he was halfway through, she was laughing so hard she was clutching her sides.

"Stop. Oh, my, God, stop, you're literally killing me."

"See? Doesn't that make you feel better?" He got close to her and bent over so that his face was level with hers. "B-b-b-blue. What's so funny?"

"Did I mention you're insane?" Her laughter petered out, but she was still grinning. "Thanks for distracting me and replacing 'Santa Baby' in my head with the grating sounds of Porky Pig."

Her lips were temptingly close to his and Christian dropped his eyes to them. "I could distract you from that too."

The remnants of her laughter disappeared as she caught his intent. Her head tilted slightly and her eyes widened, the blue in them darkening. "How so?"

"By kissing you."

"That would definitely work."

Oh, yeah. Christian put his hands on the bed on either side of her and moved closer until his mouth claimed hers.

The remains of her laughter disappeared as she caught his intent. Her heart effectively skipped a few as she watched the blue in them darkening.

"I—"

"Be calm, love."

That wasn't the least work...

Oh, well, Christian put his lips to the top of either and...his mouth against his mouth remind...

Chapter Five

As Christian's lips had descended on hers, Blue had experienced a brief second of panic that maybe the kiss would suck, and then she'd be stuck here with Christian in awkwardville. But then he touched her and that silly little doubt vanished in a kiss that she felt from head to toe, and mostly in between.

It was total perfection. His mouth moved over hers with confidence and skill and it took all of two seconds for her to reach up and place her hands on his bare biceps. Muscles. What a novelty. The way he surrounded her, the smell of his aftershave, the roughness of his chin under the delicious softness of his lips, was perfect. After a long minute of him taking her mouth and her surrendering, Blue pulled back, her breathing heavier than normal.

"What's wrong?" he asked, voice husky and low.

"Nothing." She shook her head before lying

back onto the bed on her back, holding her hand up for him to join her. "I just wanted to do this."

To surrender. To take the kiss vertical, him over her.

"Oh, damn," he said, his Adam's apple moving as he swallowed hard. "You are so unbelievably sexy."

"Thank you." She'd had a moment of doubt, since after all she was in a bikini, but as he moved up the length of her on the bed, and settled his man bulk down onto her, Blue was glad she was barely dressed. Besides, everything always looked seriously better when it was flat instead of when she sat and her stomach made that funny little roll. Not that she wanted to think about any of that. She really only wanted to think about him. Banishing all stupid insecurities, she sank back onto the bed and relaxed.

God. His body was so hard and warm and overbearing. She reveled in the pleasure that sensation and novelty brought. His hardness made her feel feminine, soft and small and seriously aroused. Who cared about a potential stomach roll when she was downright skinny next to his masculine bulk?

"You're pretty hot yourself," she told him in all seriousness, running her hands across his chest. She had to pause a second and close her eyes just to take it in, that smooth skin pulled taut over rippling muscle.

Most men she'd been with had only been smooth and hard in one place, and as Christian's erection nudged her bikini bottoms, she was amazed that all of him was as exciting to touch and stroke as that part. This was a whole new education in the male form and she was definitely enjoying the lesson.

Especially when he started kissing her again, his hand sweeping back her hair, his lips doing delightful things to her mouth and to her insides. When his tongue swept across her lips, Blue gave a soft sigh and without thought or intent, shifted her legs apart so that his body settled more fully on hers.

"I don't want to crush you," he said, trying to move back.

She grabbed his butt—and was so glad she did—to hold him in place. "No, I like it, your weight on me." And now that she had been forced to brace her hands on his ass, she might as well explore that fine behind while he went back to kissing the corners of her mouth, her neck, her shoulders.

Her greedy hands rushed over the denim, searching out all the contours of his muscles and squeezing. Wow. Just wow. Even his ass was hard. Blue felt her desire shifting, kicking up a notch from aroused to seriously ready to feel him inside her.

"Babe, you're driving me crazy," he murmured, as his tongue slid down over her bare flesh between her breasts.

"I could say the same for you."

"Really?" Christian lifted his head and gave her a satisfied smirk. "Good."

He lightly sucked her nipple through her bikini top.

"See, like that, right there?" Blue fought the need to pant. "Driving me crazy."

"That's good information." He proceeded to do

the same thing to her other nipple, sucking and lightly nipping through the thin fabric.

As he drew on the tight bud she felt a responding tug between her thighs and out of instinct and desire opened her legs even more. Christian gave a low moan.

"You know where this is going, right?" he said, looking up at her, his brown eyes intense.

"Uh, yeah." She smacked his butt for emphasis. "Hopefully sooner than later."

"Just checking, and giving you a chance to bail if you want to."

While that was the right thing for him to do, she also thought he was clearly insane if he thought she wanted to just make out and stop when they were stranded in a motel room in a snowstorm with tequila. "I don't want to bail. At all."

He gave a satisfied smile and returned to her nipple, pulling the fabric down this time and swirling his tongue over her tight bare flesh. That was more like it. Just as she was relaxing and letting arousal spread out in her body, he lifted his head again.

"I have a question."

"Can it wait until later?" He already knew her middle name and what the hell else did he need to know?

"Is there like an angry crazy ex-husband or boyfriend with tattoos and a mohawk that I should know about? Or worse, a crazy current husband?"

Blue smacked him again, much harder this time, feeling fairly insulted. "Don't you think I would have mentioned that before now if I did?"

"Not if you wanted to have sex with me."

"Well, then how do you know if I'm telling the truth if I say no?"

His head tilted. "Huh. I guess I don't."

"Then just shut up and kiss me." It wasn't that hard to figure out, seriously.

"Aren't you going to ask me if I have a girlfriend or wife?"

"I already did on the highway." Blue grinned up at his cute face. "Besides, I'd know if you were lying. You have no game."

"Excuse me? I have game." On his knees between her legs, he lifted his arm and flexed, showing off a Celtic cross tattoo. "And guns."

Blue fought the urge to laugh. He really was just so freaking cute. She should be miserable tonight, yet he had her constantly grinning. It was weird and unnatural. Didn't he realize she was a cynic?

"You do have guns. Very nice ones." She trailed her finger across his impressive bicep. "But game? No, sorry. You're clearly frighteningly honest."

Giving a grin, he shrugged. "Well, that's true. I'm sorry, I can't help it. I just can't bring myself to be an asshole. But I can try if you want to."

Now she did laugh. "No, that's okay, thanks. I kind of like that you're a good guy." Though she would like it if he were a good guy removing her bikini top even better.

He leaned down and surprised her by kissing her, then biting her bottom lip in a sharp, unexpected aggressive move that had her body reacting immediately. Everything on her went tense, from her shoulders to her gritted teeth, to her nipples, to her clenching inner thighs. "Oh, God," she murmured.

"No more talking." Christian slid his fingers behind her neck and undid the tie to her bikini. He peeled it down, baring her breasts.

Normally Blue didn't love getting naked in the dead of winter, but the room was as warm as a sauna and Christian's appreciative gaze heated her up equally as the furnace. Then his brown eyes disappeared as he lowered his mouth to her nipple, and there definitely was no more talking as he licked and teased her sensitive flesh. She'd never really considered herself easily aroused by breast play, but whatever he was doing, however it might be different, she was really enjoying it.

Letting her fingers skim across his amazing biceps, Blue let her eyes drift closed as he moved to her other nipple. When his thumb began to slowly brush up and down over her clitoris, running along the smooth fabric of her bikini bottoms, Blue sighed in both pleasure and anticipation. The motion, the soft barely there contact, repeated over and over, while his tongue laved and wet and sucked at her nipple, until the tightening deep inside her was aching and she shifted her ankles restlessly on the bed.

"Christian," she murmured, opening her eyes and staring down at his light brown hair.

"Shh."

Blue was about to protest that even spoken in that languid tone, she was not a woman to be shushed. But she forgot to worry about it when he obliged what had been her original complaint and moved his thumb from outside the fabric to inside. That slick slide of the pad of his thumb in a firm, confident stroke over her swollen clitoris made her groan.

She just lay there, more passive than she usually was in bed, and enjoyed the sharp arousal he drew out in her, reveling in the satisfaction when he finally plunged his finger inside her and hooked it.

Oh, my God, he'd found her G-spot in under two seconds. Without benefit of her coaxing, visual aids, or a GPS directional system. Just like that. He was in and on it.

Blue was so unprepared she couldn't control her body and her response and lifted her hips as she burst into a very unexpected and very powerful orgasm. Gripping his shoulders, she rode it and his finger hard, a shocked burst of pleasure leaving her lips.

Stunned, as her body quieted down, she felt her cheeks pinken. She had felt that orgasm in every inch of her and she was actually mildly embarrassed. Now who was the one who had no game? That had taken him less time than it had to stammer out b-b-b-blue in his Porky Pig accent.

That off-kilter feeling was back big-time. Something weird happened to her around him and she wasn't sure she liked it. Or she did like it. Which embarrassed her. So when faced with mortification there was only one thing to do. Call on her inner-sass.

"You suck," she told him, her chest rising up and down in a heaving cliché.

His eyebrow shot up. "Excuse me? I don't think you can deny you enjoyed that, so how do I suck exactly?"

"Oh, I did enjoy that. That's the problem. You

should not be allowed to get me off that easily." It made no sense and was totally contrary and made her sound pretty bitchy and ridiculous, but his smile, his easy temperament, his muscles . . . it was all a little too appealing and that was freaking her out.

Christian burst out laughing as he stared down at Blue, her dark blue eyes meeting his unflinchingly. Her cheeks were pink from her orgasm and her hair was spread out on the bed in exotic black strands. Never in his entire life had he been criticized for bringing a woman to the point sooner than later.

But then again, he'd never made love to a woman like Blue.

It wasn't hard to figure out that she had a bit of a wall up in the form of eye-rolling sarcasm. Given her parents it wasn't any big surprise. But he found her intriguing and sexy and adorable. There was a vulnerability hidden beneath the cynicism and he couldn't believe how hard he'd fallen for her in the space of just a few hours.

"I'm about to get you off again," he told her, kissing the corners of her mouth and enjoying the sharp exhalation of air she gave. "So you're going to be really pissed at me in five minutes."

"It'll never happen," she murmured, her eyes hooded as he lazily ran his thumb over her firm nipple. "That had to be a fluke."

"Oh, yeah?" Christian knew he had a certain class clown quality to him, but he knew what he was doing in bed. He could make her come again, no question about it. "Are we placing bets?"

"Sure. If I win, which I will, you have to promise never to sing that Porky Pig song again."

"Deal. And if I win, which I will, you have to wear the antlers all night." He could make it so much worse, but they didn't know each other well enough yet. He wasn't sure how far her tolerance of pranks extended.

"Fine."

"Five minutes," he told her. Reaching over for his cell phone he put it next to her head. "Time starts now."

Then without waiting for her answer, he moved down the length of her body, pausing just long enough to flick his tongue over her breasts, and trail a line down to her belly button. Christian peeled her bikini bottom off, his mouth watering and cock throbbing. He wanted her so damn bad, more than he could remember wanting anyone in a very long time. He'd never really experienced this sort of instant attraction and it had him a little thrown at the same time he was enjoying every second with her.

Brushing his hands over her inner thighs, just barely touching the warm skin, he murmured, "Open your legs for me."

She made a sound, maybe of shock, he wasn't sure, but her gasp was followed by spreading her legs wide for him without hesitation. Christian teased his fingers over her flesh on either side of her sex, blowing on her clitoris at the same time. The tangy scent of her arousal was intoxicating and he closed his eyes briefly, reining in his own throbbing need, before refocusing on her.

It was all about the tease, just barely touching her, skimming over her with first his finger, then his tongue, then back to a finger, barely sinking into her wetness before retreating. Her clitoris was swollen and enticing, but he avoided it initially, just barely flicking his tongue over it. Blue's breathing had altered, growing heavier, anxious, and her body started to shift restlessly.

Almost time, but not quite. Christian slid his tongue down her inner thighs, while his fingers were just a soft whisper over the small strip of hair she had. He moved to the smooth folds on either side of that perfectly groomed rectangle and licked the soft skin.

"Oh, damn," she said. "Do something, please."

That's what he needed to hear. Shifting, he opened her with his fingers and moved his tongue from top to bottom and back again. The jerk of her thighs and the sudden grip of her hands into his hair were satisfying as hell and he started a quick, smooth rhythm, devoting most of his attention to her clitoris.

Sliding a finger inside her, he sought out the sponginess of her G-spot at the same time he gently sucked on her clitoris.

Blue's hips bucked and she gave a gasp, her orgasm intense and beautiful, the climax of her inner muscles, the burst of slickness, and her heady cry all surrounding Christian. It was so sexy that as soon as she quieted down he was shoving his jeans and boxers down and digging in his pocket for his wallet, hoping there was still a condom in there.

She rolled her head to the side, gasping for air and picked up his phone. Squinting, she said, "Shit. Four minutes. You win."

As if he cared at this point.

All he cared about was getting this condom on as fast as possible and burying himself in her.

When Blue started to sit up, he held her down by her hips. "Where are you going?"

Smirking, she said, "To get my antlers."

"Later. Later I'll make you dance naked in them."

Another one of her priceless expressions flashed across her face. "I don't f—"

He cut her off. "Later. Right now, I just need to be inside you."

Her mouth fell into an O and her eyes darkened.

Christian took her knees and pushed them up and out, leaning down to give her a hard, demanding kiss. She had him so tight with hot need he suspected his earlier accomplishments getting her to orgasm were probably going to be trampled under his desperate pounding, but hey, she had to know how sexy she was and what that did to a man's restraint.

Then he lost the ability to form words when he pushed inside her.

Swallowing about a garbage can full of spit, Christian closed his eyes and paused, his cock throbbing inside her slick heat. Shit. Nothing, no woman, had ever felt this good in his entire life. She commanded every ounce of his attention, every nerve ending in him strumming, his thoughts scattered, his senses overwhelmed.

When she said, "Oh, that's just the best thing ever," Christian couldn't have agreed more.

Staring down at her beautiful face, brushing his lips over the softness of hers, Christian began to move inside her. With each slow stroke he took, she gave a soft moan of approval, and he moved a little faster, pushed a little harder. Blue lifted her hips to meet his thrust, and that was all the encouragement he needed. Hands on either side of her head, he braced himself and went at her, taking and pounding and gritting his teeth in agonized ecstasy.

Her moans got louder, her nails dug into his skin. His muscles tensed, his blood rushed past his ears with a buzzing, his body totally focused on that intimate, hot, wet connection with her.

When her inner muscles contracted around his erection and her cries froze and her eyes rolled back as she came for a third time, Christian let go of the tight hold he'd had on himself and crashed completely and totally out of control.

He yelled.

He shuddered.

He lost all rational thought as he came inside Blue.

And when he finally settled back down into his body and could process what he was seeing as hearing as well as feeling, he realized Blue was grinning up at him.

"Wow," she said and laughed, the sound so free and joyous that Christian laughed breathlessly with her.

"That," he told her. "Was epic."

"Epic?" She ran her satin fingertips over his back. "I like."

Christian sighed, his cock still pulsing a little inside her. "I like, too."

He liked it, her, all of this, a whole lot.

Chapter Six

Blue lay on the bed, legs tangled with Christian's, lazily running her fingers over his chest. The muscles were addictive, truly. As could be the sex. He hadn't been exaggerating when he'd called what had just passed between them epic. She had never been that aroused, that out of herself, yet so completely aware of every molecule in her body.

Amazing. Plain and simple.

Now she just wanted to yawn and laze on the bed like a satiated cat, but somehow she already knew that she had about thirty seconds before Christian started talking. He was a verbal guy, something she wasn't really used to, but found she liked. There was something about his constant chatter that made her feel like he was a genuinely well-adjusted guy happy with his life.

What a concept.

"You know, if you're really, really nice to me I won't make you wear the antlers."

"Well, forget it then. I'll wear the antlers." Blue grinned as she nuzzled closer to him.

He chucked softly. "Then you don't want to make love again in a little while? Because that's what I meant by being really nice to me. Letting me touch and taste and pleasure you all over again."

Christian had a way of taking her standard sarcasm and turning it so that she didn't immediately have a quippy response. She had expected him to make a crack about getting him a drink or the chips and not only hadn't he done that, he'd referred to sex as making love. She could honestly say never in her entire life had a man said that to her. It was always sex or any wide variety of crude nicknames, and that had never bothered her. In fact, she'd preferred it. Using the term making love had always seemed so cheesy to her, but right now, it seemed . . . natural.

That thing was happening again.

That weird swelling bubbly kind of feeling in her chest, like indigestion, but in a good way.

"Oh," she said, without an ounce of cool. "I definitely want to do that again later."

"Good." He kissed the top of her head and shifted on the bed. "God, I'm starving. I need to eat something. You want a drink, babe?"

"Sure." Blue leaned down and pulled on her bikini bottoms. For some reason, lounging topless was totally acceptable, but having a margarita on top of the bedspread buck naked was too much for her.

Christian didn't seem to have the same reservations. He strolled around the room completely bare-assed, which was fine by her, because it was a damn good ass.

While he dug his hand into the Doritos bag and helped himself to a fistful, he said, "I wonder if there's an ice machine? These margaritas would taste better with ice. I should look."

"You should probably get dressed first," Blue said, rolling onto her side and propping her head up with her hand.

He made a face at her at her mock innocent tone. "It's a good thing I have you around, otherwise I'd be strolling outside into a blizzard naked."

Blue laughed. "You should try sarcasm more often. That was pretty good."

"Why, thank you." Retrieving their cups from the nightstand, he poured more liquor into them, followed by mixer. Then taking the two bottles he opened the motel room door and plunked them down out in the snowdrift that had accumulated outside. "That will cool them down for later."

Giving an involuntary yelp as the cold air wafted over her, Blue grabbed a bed pillow and plunked it down over her mostly naked body. "Are you crazy? Close the door! It's cold and you're naked! Someone will see you!"

He turned his head and shrugged. "Who the hell is going to see me? There is no one else here, Roy is asleep I'm sure, and there isn't a single car out on the road. Besides, you said this room was too hot."

All of which made total sense. "Nothing phases

you, does it? You're just chill all the time. That kind of freaks me out."

Christian cocked a brow and slammed his fists together to crack all his knuckles. "It freaks me out that that freaks you out."

"So we're just a couple of freaks?"

"Seems that way."

"Are you going to close the door?"

"Eventually. After I've proved my point that no one will ever see me—"

Christian's words cut off and he started laughing.

"What?" Blue sat up and tried to look out the open door. Not that she wanted to get too close to it. It was damn cold and the wind was howling, kicking up snow. Christian actually had snowflakes on his feet.

"Someone just drove past. A female cop. She waved." With that, he shut the door. "That was funny."

"You're lucky she didn't ticket you for indecent exposure."

He just shrugged, rubbing his arms. "Man, it's cold out there."

Really? Men could be just totally baffling. Blue balled up his T-shirt and threw it at him. "No kidding, Einstein."

Catching the shirt, he said, "I'm not going to wear a shirt with no pants. That would really toss me into the pervert at the door category. Besides, it's just hard to feel sexy with a shirt on and no boxers."

"Then put on your boxers," she drawled. "That seems a little obvious."

He did step into his boxers then took a swig of his drink. "I'm too sexy for my shirt, so sexy it hurts." Then he did an impromptu strut, a sort of macho frat boy version of the catwalk, swinging his T-shirt.

Blue didn't want to laugh. She really didn't. But by the second pass when he had stuck his hand out and switched to "Do Ya Think I'm Sexy?" by Rod Stewart, she totally lost it.

"Oh, my God, you're ridiculous." She was laughing so hard it hurt, especially when he morphed into doing the sprinkler dance move, then did some hip thrusting in his boxers. "Stop."

He did then pulled an innocent expression. "Stop what?" He handed over her drink and took another sip of his. "Want any of this food?"

"Sure. Bring the chips to bed and we can get under the covers since this room is, ahem, freezing now from having the door open for twenty minutes. Maybe there's something on TV we can watch."

They settled back into bed, Christian propped up against the headboard, pulling her against him. It was a nice position, all that warm naked man chest behind her, strong enough and broad enough that she just felt relaxed, not like she was crushing the life out of him.

"The temperature's just right in here," he told her in a teasing voice as he started channel surfing.

"Uh-huh." Actually it was, but she wasn't going to admit it.

"Cool. *It's a Wonderful Life* is on." Christian set down the remote on the bed.

Blue sat up and turned to search his face. "Are you *serious?* I am not watching this schmaltzy crap."

"Of course I'm serious. This is a great flick. I mean, the dude changes his life and gets a grip on what really matters."

"That never happens in real life."

The minute the words were out of her mouth, Blue wanted to retrieve them with a fish hook. Damn it. Now he was going to psychoanalyze her. Or worse, not even care that she'd said something so boo-hiss.

But all he said was, "Sure it does. Happens all the time. And the point of the movie is not to make a totally lost soul find himself, but to remind people who are mostly doing it right to keep on doing it right."

Blue folded her arms over her bare chest as she frowned at the TV, leaning on his chest. "I still don't want to watch it."

"Fine. But if *Charlie Brown's Christmas* is on we're watching it."

"You do realize that all those Christmas specials are horrible? I mean, something awful happens in every single one. The island of misfit toys, Charlie Brown's pathetic little tree, Cindy Lou Who watching the Grinch steal all her presents, Frosty melting . . . they're depressing."

"They all have happy endings."

Blue snorted. "Yeah, after everything sucked, anything even remotely okay seems brilliant."

"Though I could never figure out why Frosty didn't just toss a chair through the windows. I mean, he was melting in a glass greenhouse. He totally could have busted himself out."

"You've put a lot of thought into it." Blue picked up the remote, but somehow found herself not pushing the buttons, just staring blankly at Jimmy Stewart.

"So have you, obviously." Christian brushed her hair off her shoulder.

She shrugged.

"Was Christmas really that awful for you?" he asked in a soft voice that made her shoulders stiffen.

Her throat felt tight and she wanted to laugh it off, blow him off, deflect the question with wit or sarcasm. But she couldn't. She nodded. "Yeah. For most kids, aside from the religious aspect, Christmas was about them. For me, it was like the one day that made it really, really clear that I was an afterthought in my parents' lives."

She was glad he was behind her so he couldn't see her face. She knew she didn't mask her emotions well and she was feeling really vulnerable. But at the same time, she was actually relieved she'd spoken the truth. She had never admitted that out loud to anyone in her entire life and she instinctively knew that she could trust Christian with something so personal. Maybe it was even easier because she'd just met him. She didn't know exactly what it was about him that instilled such confidence, but her heart did pound a little faster than normal as she waited for his response.

He kissed the top of her head. She'd never really had a man do that, and Christian had already done it more than once. It made her feel . . . protected.

"I'm sorry, Blue," he said, brushing his lips across

her temple. "That's a raw deal and you deserved better than that."

She turned her head slightly, trying to see his expression. "You're not going to tell me that I'm whining? To suck it up. That everyone's family is dysfunctional and I should get over it?"

"Of course not. Those things *hurt* when you're a kid and you carry it with you to adulthood. What was Christmas at your house like? Describe a typical day."

Blue chewed her lip and leaned forward a little so she could see him. "Are you sure you want to listen to all this? It's not like I was abused or anything."

But he just nodded. "Yes, I want to hear it. Get it out. Rant if you want. You're entitled to your feelings."

She hesitated, but then she leaned back against his chest and played with the edge of the bedsheet. "Well. My dad only saw me a few times a year, and he never wanted me for Christmas. He always went skiing. Sometimes he would send me a present, sometimes he would forget altogether, and most years I got a five dollar bill in the mail. Which, let me tell you, five bucks didn't go very far even twenty years ago, and it's not like my dad was hurting for cash. But it wasn't the dollar amount, it was like I said, being an afterthought."

Christian laced his fingers through hers and squeezed.

"My mother was all into social justice and charity, which was great. I mean, I think it's awesome that she's dedicated her life to helping others, but when you're six and your friends are all getting

Barbies, being told your mother donated money in your name to the Red Cross just makes you resentful. She'd lecture me about starvation in Africa and I'd just wonder why it was *me* who had to give up toys so they could eat when no one else had to. It wasn't like my mom gave up buying clothes or spending a ton of money on airfare to exotic locales or on her yoga classes."

"So she didn't give you presents at all?"

His voice sounded so appalled, Blue instantly felt better.

"Not unless you count hemp mittens as a legit Christmas gift."

"That's it? That's all you got?"

"One year, yeah. Some years I got nada. We didn't have a Christmas tree either. Environmentally unsound, obviously."

"That is fucking cracked."

Christian's vehemence amused her. "So now you know why I don't dig Christmas. It was something everyone else had and I envied them at first, then just resented the holiday altogether. For other kids, it was the best day of the year. For me, it was . . . lonely."

"That sucks. And your parents should be ashamed of themselves. They were both selfish. And your mother has wonderful ideals but she did you wrong. I bet my ass when she was six she wanted a goddamn Barbie too. She expected you to be a mini-adult and that was cruel."

Hearing someone else say the things Blue had always felt lifted a gigantic weight off her shoulders. She'd always felt like she was the one lacking, like she was horrible and petty to feel the way she had as a kid, when she knew in her heart her feelings were legitimate. And somehow, having spoken them out loud and having them validated by Christian, she felt decidedly less bitter.

"Thanks," she said softly, turning and giving him a kiss. "I appreciate that."

"Did you ever get a good gift? Anything at all?"

She didn't even hesitate on that one. "Yes. Just once. I was eight, and my dad had been to New York for Thanksgiving and he bought me a glass snow globe. He gave it to me for Christmas, and it was even wrapped and everything. And I loved it . . . it was like magic. You shook it and the beautiful little flakes danced around the high rise buildings. They had wreaths on them for Christmas and I imagined that in a big city like that, with all those people, you would walk down the sidewalk in the snow and never feel lonely ever . . ."

The image of the cityscape dissipated in her mind and Blue cleared her throat, wondering what the hell she was doing. She was just going to shut up now.

"Have you been to New York?"

"No." Because what if she walked down the sidewalk in the snow at Christmastime and still felt lonely? She didn't want to ruin the magic, the hope.

"You should . . . it would be like embracing Christmas, hope, a different life for yourself than what your parents created."

Or be crushed. One or the other. It freaked her out that he had used the word *hope* as well, that he could somehow pinpoint her emotions, that he hadn't just shut this whole conversation down with an ill-timed joke five minutes ago. She didn't know how to deal with him, with any of this, so she just said, "You're quite the philosopher, you know that? Not what I expected."

"Nah. Just a guy who is content and wants amazing people he knows to feel the same way. And you have a choice now, you know. You can keep Christmas as a time of year that makes you unhappy, or you can decide to let it in and make some of your own traditions."

"Like margaritas in bed in a cheap motel?" she said, mustering up a sassy smirk. This was all too raw. She needed to retreat.

Part of her figured he would argue or sigh that she was ditching the serious tone of the conversation. But he didn't. After a second, where he searched her face with an intensity that was unnerving, he nodded.

"Exactly. Margaritas in bed on Christmas Eve. I like it."

"Then I'll get you another one." Blue popped up out of bed and took their empty cups off the nightstand. She went to pour them refills, but first she lifted the lid of her suitcase and pulled out a T-shirt and a pair of pajama pants, and not because it was cold outside and she was about to open the door.

She wanted to be covered up.

Christian watched Blue dragging on a shirt and cotton pajama pants and tried to make some sense of his complicated thoughts and emotions. If he didn't know better, he'd swear to God he had fallen head over ass for this woman.

He liked everything about her, from the sound of her voice to the way she tilted her head, to the vulnerability she buried beneath sassiness. The way she had readily agreed to breakfast with Roy, the ancient motel owner, said a lot about her heart, and he liked her sense of humor, the way she was determined to remain aloof and always cracked.

When they left this motel, he didn't want to never see her again.

He wanted to date Blue out in the real world and everything about that stunned and excited and scared the shit out of him. Never having had this instantaneous response to a woman, he had no freaking clue what to do with it.

So he tossed back the bedding and got out of bed. The one thing he could do was brave the cold himself instead of having her do it. "No, Blue, I'll get the bottles. I'm the one who stuck them out there. And you're a freeze baby, while I'm clearly not."

"A freeze baby?" She stopped with her hand on the doorknob and smiled at him in amusement. "I've never heard that expression before."

"Where the hell have you been hiding?" Christian didn't bother to put his shirt on, and he was already wearing his boxers. Good enough. Two seconds of cold wasn't going to kill him. A glance behind the curtain of the window to the parking lot showed it had actually stopped snowing. "Stand back, miss," he joked in a country drawl. "This is man's work."

The eye roll from her was expected, but she did back up and ripped open a pack of peanuts on the table. "I do have one Christmas tradition," she said unexpectedly.

"Yeah?" He threw open the door and waited for her to elaborate as he grabbed the tequila and the mixer, ignoring the biting wind that cut into his flesh. He couldn't exactly complain that the cold hurt after pulling the macho act.

"Before the big Christmas party at the nursing home, I go and do the ladies' hair for free."

Christian paused, half bent over, touched beyond belief, and forgetting all about the icy chill seeping into his feet. God, he was falling hard for Blue. Crazy, out of control, illogical, wanted to write a goddamn love poem falling for this gorgeous woman.

"I mean, it's not a big deal, it's just they like to feel good about themselves when their families show up for the party and I . . . I like to talk to them. They're very sweet."

He could almost hear the blush on her and as he stood up, Christian turned slowly with the bottles in his hands. "I think that tradition rocks, Blue."

She put her hands on her hips and she nodded in conviction. "You know what? It does. It totally does."

Christian kicked the door closed with his foot. "You rock."

She took the tequila out of his hands and grinned. "I do, don't I?"

It was that moment that he lost himself in a haze of tequila, lust, off the chart attraction, and the spirit of Christmas giving.

Plunking the mixer down on the table, Christian grabbed Blue and kissed her, a wild, tongue plunging sweep of domination and desperation, wanting to show her how completely awesome he thought she was and how she rocked all right. She'd rocked his world to the very foundation in one night.

Christian lifted Blue right off her feet, his hands on her ass as she wrapped her legs around his waist.

"Yes," he managed between kisses, the feel of her body so close to his electrifying. "You definitely rock."

Chapter Seven

"You're really strong," she murmured between kisses.

Christian ground her hips against his and breathed in the fresh scent of her skin. "You're tiny, it's not hard to hold you. And I'm hopped up on adrenaline. I could probably lift a car right now." Or have sex again after not much of a break to refuel.

That definitely wasn't going to be a problem. His erection was knocking on her door already and he turned and sat on the edge of the bed, Blue still in his lap.

They kissed each other with a wild abandon, her nails digging into his back, his fingers tangling in her dark hair. Christian yanked up her T-shirt to her armpits and covered her breast with his mouth, tugging at the taut nipple.

How he was so frantic after they'd already made love, he had no idea, but he was. He was every freaking cliché there ever was about a man in the desert being offered water, and it didn't make sense. Nothing made sense about the fact that every inch of his body was desperate, compelled, irrational to be against Blue, to possess her, claim her, fill her.

"Get on your knees," he urged her, skimming his palms down into the waistband of her pajama pants.

"What?" she asked breathlessly, her head lolling back, nipples displayed invitingly in front of him.

"On your knees. Now." The tone was rougher than he intended but he wasn't going to wait.

She did, her eyes hooded, lips cherry red and glistening from his kisses.

When he yanked her bottoms down, panties included, she gasped.

A little determination and some hard tugs had them off both ankles and Christian freed his erection from his boxers right before she settled her thighs on either side of his and her warm flesh collided with him.

He was willing to say the hell with foreplay and just slam her down onto him, but Blue took his cock in her hand and slowly stroked it. It was Christian's turn to gasp, and he dug his fingers into her hips. She moved her lithe touch over him up and down, a feathery tease of a touch, her lips brushing against his neck in a similar barely there contact.

That was only damaging his control, but when she took him and slid him up and down in her wetness, using the tip of his cock to stimulate her clitoris, he was almost destroyed. "Oh, damn," he said, teeth gritted, grip on her so tight that he could see the whiteness of his fingers. "What the fuck are you doing?"

"You know what I'm doing," she whispered in his ear, her tongue flickering out to lick his lobe. "I'm getting off with your cock."

Oh, yeah, he definitely knew that's what she was doing. Christian tried to breathe, realizing she had turned the tease around on him. This was torture.

"You like that, don't you?" he asked her, enjoying each slick slide up and down her, almost being allowed access to push into her, then being denied as she pulled him back up again. Definitely torture.

"Uh-huh." Blue's breath came in short staccato bursts and she was concentrating intently, her free hand on his shoulder to brace herself.

He realized she was actually going to be able to come and he stared at her in fascination, amazed that she was so gorgeous, so sensual, so in tune with her own body.

"That's it," he told her. "Take it, take what you want."

She did. She moved him into position and let her hips drop so that he filled her in one motion. Christian exhaled sharply, his grip on her waist brutal. It was a tantalizing position, her body resting on his, her breasts teasingly close, her hands on his shoulders, her hair falling in her face as she leaned forward and kissed him.

He knew she couldn't really get the leverage to set the rhythm like this, so he did, pumping his hips so that he went deep inside her. The way she enclosed him, her slick sweetness stroking at his cock, was insanely good.

Obviously she felt the same way, because he was barely in her and Blue was coming, her lips parted, eyes wide in shocked ecstasy, her orgasm the result of all that teasing she had done with his cock. It had the same reaction on him. Christian gave one last thrust then gave in and exploded with her.

Being there together increased his intensity, both of them shuddering and pulsating together, sexy and intimate and exciting.

They stared at each other, gazes locked, and Christian saw something in Blue's eyes that he knew was in his, a hope, a surprise, a depth of emotion that was illogical but was there.

He wanted to say something brilliant and poetic that would sweep her off her feet and make her certain that she wanted to be with him.

But he didn't have those words, didn't know how to be that guy.

So he just said, "I'm having a Blue Christmas and damn, it's good."

She laughed softly. "Don't start singing."

He cupped her cheeks with his hands and kissed her slowly, savoring the taste of her. "No singing, I promise."

Blue gave a satisfied sigh and extracted herself from him, untangling her legs from his and crawling up the bed.

"Where are you going?" Christian couldn't resist running his hand over her bare ass since it was presented so enticingly in front of him.

"To lay down under the covers. You wore me out."

He grinned. "You did do a lot of work this time, all that using my—"

She cut him off with a fake prime expression. "I don't know what you're talking about. And if you don't stop, I'm not going to let you cuddle with me."

"Oh, cuddling was on the table?" He'd already figured out Blue wasn't much of a cuddler, so if she was offering, he was going to take it. Hopefully he could convince her to sleep naked too. "Then I'm on it. I'll shut up."

He could move fast when he wanted to and he was up next to her, settled under the covers, in a blink. Hauling her onto his chest, he sighed in contentment. "Don't let me fall asleep."

"How am I supposed to do that?" she murmured, her own voice lazy and slumberous.

"Talk to me."

But she didn't, just gave a yawn, her fingers tracing a pattern over his chest in a soothing manner that had Christian's eyes drifting closed.

He fell asleep in less than two minutes, comfortable and content with Blue in his arms.

Blue woke up warm and cozy, momentarily disoriented as to why her bed was so comfortable and the bedding so soft on her skin, until she remembered she was in a motel room with Christian. Sometime during the night she had slid off of him, but her leg was still over his and her hand was on his chest. His naked, very hard chest.

The muscles were nice. She was amazed at how nice they really were.

And how nice Christian was.

So nice it scared her. She was waiting for the minute it turned and his asshole nature finally revealed itself. For the moment he proved he was as selfish as the next person.

His hand covered hers and he yawned. "Merry Christmas, Blue."

Her heart squeezed in a way she both liked and was terrified by. His voice was scratchy and still sleepy.

"Merry Christmas," she managed, even though she had the sudden urge to bolt out of bed, get dressed, and run as far from him as she possibly could.

This man had the power to hurt her when he finally disappointed her and that was scarier than any snowstorm.

"Mmm," he said, turning and kissing her forehead. "I would give anything for bacon and eggs and some big old pancakes."

"Maybe Roy can hook you up."

"Maybe. But that would mean I have to get up and I'm comfortable just lying here forever."

She was too, which was precisely what had her unfurling herself from him and throwing back the covers.

"Ahh," Christian said. "It's cold out there. Where are you going?"

"The bathroom." Without looking at him, knowing if she did, she might just embarrass herself and wrap her arms around him, or worse, get weepy, Blue picked up her discarded pajama pants and pulled them on, along with her T-shirt.

A peek out the window showed that it had stopped snowing and it looked like the plow had made at least one pass on the main road, though the parking lot was buried. With any luck, she could get a tow arranged and then . . . do what?

She wasn't sure. Getting a rental car on Christmas was bound to be dicey, but if Christian could take her to the airport in Lexington, she would have options. Fly south, rent a car, get a hotel. She could do something.

Which would be better than staying here feeling like she might hyperventilate from emotions she didn't altogether understand.

Rummaging through her suitcase, she found a pair of jeans and the only shirt she'd packed that had sleeves. Along with undergarments and her toiletries bag, she headed for the bathroom to take a shower.

Well aware of Christian's eyes following her, she didn't dare look at him.

"Is there a fire?" he asked.

Yes. "What do you mean?" she asked nonchalantly.

"What's the hurry? I doubt we're going to able to find a tow truck this morning and the longer we linger, the easier our drive to Lexington will be. Give them time to clear the roads. We don't even know if the highway has been reopened."

"Well, we're not going to know if we stay in bed, are we?"

She dared a glance at him and he was sitting up, studying her carefully. "Is something wrong?"

"No, of course not. I just can't fix the problem and get to Miami if I don't get out of bed."

He threw back the covers and revealed his naked body, his penis partially erect in what she hoped was just a sleep erection. She couldn't handle another round of amazing sex without saying something stupid or needy or vulnerable. She'd already blathered on too much last night, telling him about her family.

"What are you doing?" she asked, fighting the urge to back up. That much muscular man was more than she could resist if he came on to her.

"I'm getting out of bed so we can see what's going on out there. Fix the problem. Get you out of here."

He didn't sound belligerent or upset. He looked calm, like he always did. But there was something in his expression that told her he wasn't entirely pleased with the situation. Neither was she.

"I figure at least if I miss the cruise I can hang out for a few days in the sunshine, right?" Not that she could afford either a plane ticket to Miami or a hotel, but that's what a credit card was for. She just couldn't face driving back to Cincinnati in a rental car and spending the night alone in her empty apartment.

"Or you could spend the night in Lexington with me. Have dinner with my family. Then tomorrow you can go to Miami. You don't want to spend Christmas at the airport."

No, she didn't. But it didn't matter. Why should Christmas be any different now than it had been her whole life? Part of her wanted to say yes, she'd love to spend the night with Christian and his family, but it would be like playing house. He wasn't hers and his family was going to think it was weird as hell for her to be there.

And she didn't think she could sit there in that kind of family togetherness knowing she wasn't part of it, knowing that she didn't belong. "I seriously doubt your family wants a total stranger invading their Christmas."

He scoffed, standing up. "Please. They're always telling me to bring someone, and there are so many people there, one more will hardly be noticed."

"I don't think it's a good idea."

There was a long pause where he stared at her so intently she wanted to squirm, but she stood her ground, head up.

Then he just said, "Alright."

Part of her was relieved. Part of her was disappointed. Maybe in some way she had wanted him to try a little harder to coax her. Not that there was anything fair about that. He had offered, it had been a generous offer, and she had refused. Why would he twist her arm?

Because he wanted to be with her, that's why. That's what she wanted him to say. But that was a stupid expectation. Christian had a family to go to and he had just met her.

Blue beat a path to the bathroom before she said anything else and before he offered to join her in the shower. Any more intimacy would undo her.

She locked the door and turned on the water. She would shower alone. Be alone.

Just like she was every day.

Chapter Eight

Christian watched Blue across the table in Roy's kitchen, wondering what was going through her head. She was animated enough with their host, smiling and laughing as he told her stories, but she was not meeting Christian's eyes, and she seemed nervous.

Maybe not nervous. Remote. She had retreated from him. That was obvious. He didn't know why.

Or maybe he did. He just didn't want to acknowledge it.

He was too much of a goofball for Blue. She was a cool chick, into cool guys. He was a toy engineer who got off on family dinners, playing with kids, and singing off-key while doing the sprinkler. Not her style.

How could he expect her to prefer coming to his parents' house for dinner when she could be on the beach in Florida? He couldn't.

"So I got out of the navy in '51 and settled down here and took over this place," Roy was saying. "Ain't exactly the Ritz but I did alright. Thought about changing the name, but it always gave me a chuckle and people around here knew the No-Tell."

"We were so glad to find you and this place last night," Blue told him, piling egg on her fork. "I don't what we would have done without you, Roy."

If Christian wasn't mistaken, the old guy blushed a little. "Hope it was comfortable enough for you all."

"*Very* comfortable," Christian interjected, willing Blue to look at him and remember what had passed between them.

She did, but her look was definitely one of disapproval. Oh, so now not only was she not coming to dinner with him, she was going to pretend that the night before hadn't happened? The hell with that.

His goddamn world had been rocked by this woman, and she was going to have to hear about it.

"You can call on my house phone to get your tow, though I don't know how soon they're going to be able to dig your car out." Roy said. "I checked on the Internet and it looks like the highway is re-opened so you can get south if you want in your good car. If I were you, I'd just book a tow truck and go on and enjoy your Christmas and worry about getting your car from the garage in a few days."

"That's what I was thinking," Blue said with a nod.

Christian was still stuck on the fact that Roy had checked road conditions online.

"That is, if Christian doesn't mind me hitching a ride with him to Lexington."

That was the stupidest thing she'd ever said and he was actually a little bit offended. "Of course not. I'll take you wherever you want to go."

His bed would be preferable but if that weren't an option he would make sure she was safely wherever she wanted to be.

Suddenly feeling gloomy, Christian bit off a piece of his bacon and chewed it hard, watching Roy stare at Blue with no small amount of admiration as she smiled at him. Is that what he looked like? Moony? He felt kind of moony and he wasn't sure he liked it.

After another twenty minutes of eating and small talk Blue indicated they should be heading out. "If that's okay with you?" she asked politely.

What was with the sudden solicitous manners? It didn't suit her. He liked it better when she just said what she was really thinking, not this tea party attitude.

"Sure," he said easily, reaching down to get the second unopened bottle of tequila he had bought at the gas station. He handed it to Roy. "Just a little thank you for putting us up."

Roy's eyes lit up. "Tequila. Alright, sir. Haven't had a worm since I don't know when." He got up and shuffled over to a kitchen cabinet where he stowed it away. "I won't be sharing that with the grandsons. They can get their own liquor."

After handshakes and Blue giving Roy what seemed like a spontaneous hug, they headed out into the parking lot. Christian had already loaded up the car with all their stuff.

Blue started walking in the direction of their room.

"Where are you going?"

"To the bathroom if you need to know," she said testily. "And no, I don't need help."

That was it. He didn't deserve the cold shoulder. Bending over, Christian packed some snow together. As Blue stomped off, back to him, he launched a snowball at her. It smacked right between the shoulder blades, bursting on the velvet of her jacket. She came to a grinding halt and whirled around, face furious.

"Did you just throw a snowball at me?"

"Well, I doubt it was Roy," he said, fighting the urge to grin. She looked so outraged.

"You're a jerk."

"Come on, lighten up. It's Christmas. Throw one back at me. You'll be amazed at how good it feels." Christian held his arms out. "I won't even duck."

Blue hesitated but then she bent over and scooped some snow up, packing it quickly. She hurled it at him and he took it right in the face. Fortunately her packing skills sucked so he didn't break a tooth or his nose, but it was damn cold when it burst in powdery wetness all over his face.

"Lucky shot," he told her.

She was laughing, wiping her hands off on her jeans. "You're right, I do feel better."

That was more like it. He hated seeing her so aloof. "Run, Farrow, or it's on."

When he launched another snowball at her she shrieked and ducked.

Then they were engaged in full-out combat,

Christian landing five snowballs to every one she managed. She was having trouble getting them to stick together and half of hers fell apart in the air, but they were both laughing, snow falling off their coats, hands red and raw, snow kicked up all around them as they dodged each other's missiles.

He stalked toward her, a ball in each hand ready to launch as she frantically tried to scoop up more snow, her cheeks pink, eyes bright. When he was two feet away, she slipped and went down on her ass, laughing, hands up.

"Ack, shit! I give up. Don't hit me."

Christian pretended to throw one and she screamed even louder. "Just kidding."

Grabbing a handful of loose snow, she tossed it at him, but it just blew back all over her, coating her hair, her eyelashes, her lips. "Crap!"

"Ah, poor baby." She looked so cute and cold, Christian squatted down and brushed her hair and shoulders clean. He leaned in to kiss her.

And ate snow instead. Her eyes danced as she laughed, and Christian blinked at her, a mass of snow crammed into his mouth.

"It was just too easy."

Christian spit out snow and shook some off his nose. Damn, he loved her sass. "Good one. Now get in the car before I throw you in the snowplow pile. You'll sink to the bottom and no one will find you for a week."

As he helped her to her feet, she said, "Liar."

"Only on Christmas."

She laughed. "That's ridiculous."

"I'm pretty ridiculous." Christian smacked the bottom of Blue's jeans.

"Hey." She swatted at his hand.

"I'm getting the snow off."

"Uh-huh."

"We should have made a snowman," Blue said, glancing around the parking lot.

Christian didn't want to make a snowman. He was suddenly understanding her earlier sense of urgency. If this was it, it almost seemed better to walk away now, before it got worse. He was afraid the more time he spent with her, the more he was going to argue with her about why she should spend the night with him.

"We should go."

"I've never made a snowman before," she said, looking back even as she started following him to the car.

Shit. "Never?"

"No."

Christian fell just a little bit harder for this beautiful badass woman who had never gotten presents and had never made a snowman.

"Then let's make a snowman. But first . . ." Christian reached into his car and pulled out some gloves. "Put these on. Your hands are beet red. Then we'll make a killer snowman."

Blue was constantly amazed at Christian, how thoughtful, kind, easy to be with he was. She had expected he would ignore her request, given that she had been rushing him out before, but he just gave her one of those searching looks then agreed. Just like that. Even dredging up gloves for her. Maybe it wasn't that big of deal, but it more than anyone had done for her before.

As she followed his lead as he rolled a ball of snow across the parking lot, accumulating more snow with each roll, she blew her hair out of her eyes and promised herself she would just enjoy the moment, not feel sorry for the future. Right now, she just wanted to feel the snow on her face, and appreciate what Christian had done for her, that she hadn't spent the night alone.

"By the way," she told him. "Thank you."

"For what?" He brought his ball to a stop. "Here, roll yours over. It's about the right size."

As she struggled to maneuver the ball of snow three feet, her shoes slipping, she told him, "For everything. For not leaving me on the side of the road. For driving me to Lexington."

"You're welcome."

Her ball of snow reached his. She stopped and looked up at him from her awkward half-bent position. "And for last night."

But he shook his head. "You don't need to thank me for that. It was definitely my pleasure." He worked his jaw, glancing out at the road. "Blue, are you sure you don't want to come to dinner?"

She wasn't sure at all of anything, really. But she knew it wasn't fair to him to pretend that they could be something they weren't. It wouldn't be fair to disrupt his Christmas with his family, and God knew, she didn't want to feel like the holiday orphan everyone felt sorry for.

"Yeah," she whispered. "I'm sure. But thank you for offering."

He just nodded. Then he picked up her ball and settled it on the bigger one. Another five minutes they had the head on, with mulch from the flower box hidden under the motel awning as eyes and a nose.

"Wait." Christian went into the car and emerged with the half empty bottle of tequila. "I think he needs it more than we do." He settled it at the snowman's feet.

"Good call. What should we name him?"

"Bob."

"Dick."

"Jane."

"Herman."

"Parson Brown."

"Beaver."

"Beaver?" Christian raised an eyebrow. "You dirty girl."

Blue laughed. "I never claimed to be as pure as the driven snow."

He grinned. "For which I'm grateful."

"Hold on." Running over to the car, Blue pulled her camera out of her purse. She'd had it at the ready for the cruise, but now she took a few shots of the snowman. The motel. Dashing back into the lobby, she snapped a shot of a grinning Roy.

And then Christian. She took a picture of Christian, his arm around the snowman. Then pretending to steal the liquor bottle back from Bob, the snowman. Maybe they hadn't officially named him, but she liked Bob.

"Come here," Christian said. "Get in the picture."

"How are we going to do that?" But she handed him the camera when he reached for it.

"Not on that side," he told her with a headshake

when she tried to pose on the opposite side of Bob from Christian. "On this side."

Seeing where he was going with this, she let him. She put her arm around Christian and smiled as he held the camera out and took their picture. It was a moment she wanted to capture. Happiness.

But after Christian took three shots, she told him. "Alright, that's enough. Let's go."

With each picture she shifted from joy to regret, like she had been all morning, and it was time to leave.

Christian glanced over to see Blue waking up as he pulled into the airport. She had slept the nearly two-hour drive to Lexington, which had been a disappointment. He had wanted to have every minute with her, to savor their time together. Then again, she had been in a weird mood when they'd left the motel and he didn't think the conversation would have been comfortable anyway.

She had asked him to take her to the airport before she'd fallen asleep so here they were. Blue rubbed her eyes and yawned. "Are we here? That was fast."

"For you, sleeping beauty."

"Sorry. How was the drive?"

"Not too bad. Could have been better, could have been worse."

Christian swung into short-term parking.

"You don't have to park. You can just drop me off."

"If I was a jackass," he told her. "You don't even have a flight. I'm going to walk you in." And he didn't want an argument. She was going to take his company and his concern whether she liked it or not.

She sighed, like he had suggested something really burdensome for her. "That's really not—"

"Ah," he cut her off. "I don't want to hear it."

"But you—"

"No. Forget it. I'm parking the car."

"Jerk," she muttered.

"Yes, I'm a total jerk for wanting to make sure you're safe," he said calmly, swinging into a parking spot.

She made a face. Christian laughed. He leaned over and gave her a soft kiss. "Punk."

"Thanks." Blue gripped the lapel of his jacket and stared into his eyes. "Thanks."

He knew she wasn't talking about calling her a name. "Yeah," he told her. "Blue . . ."

But that was enough to send her bolting. She was out of the car and standing at the trunk waiting for him to open it.

With a sigh, he popped the trunk and got out too. She was putting her purse over her body crosswise so her hands would be free and reaching in to get her suitcase out of the trunk.

"Wow, look at all these presents," she said in amazement.

"Six nieces and nephews, six adults, it adds up." Christian stared at all the gifts, poorly wrapped by him two days earlier. "And maybe I overdo it with the kids. Just a little."

"Nah," she said softly. "I think that's great."

"Blue, I want your number," he told her, pulling

out his phone. "I want to call you when we both get back to Cincinnati."

"It's not a good idea . . ." She bit her lip and stared down into the trunk. "I'm not the right woman for you . . . you have traditions, a family, a different kind of life than I do."

He understood her feelings, but he'd be damned if he would agree with them. "Why don't you let me decide if you're the right woman for me?"

"Christian."

"Let me have your number. Please. That's all I'm asking for." God, he was sounding pretty close to begging. But he couldn't let her walk away with no way to contact her. He just couldn't.

Blue gave him her number, though she wasn't looking at him, but at the concrete floor of the parking garage.

But he had it, that was what mattered. He sent her a text to give her his number, and to make sure she had given him a legit number. Her phone chimed in her purse and she pulled it out.

"I have a text that just says 'Bob.' I take it this is you?" she asked ruefully.

"The one and only." Then Christian took advantage of her distraction and leaned down and kissed her, pouring all of his hope and want and attraction to her into the kiss.

She responded immediately, her hands resting on his waist, her breath soft and satisfied. But after a minute, she broke away, and he let her.

Christian reached into the trunk and rummaged around, finding the small gift he knew was there. It had been meant for his eight-year-old niece Caitlyn, but he'd also gotten her a nail polish kit, so she'd never even miss this side gift. He pressed it into Blue's hands.

"Merry Christmas, Blue."

"But . . . this is someone else's present. I can't take this." Her face was stricken.

"I got my niece another present too, and this is something I want you to have."

To his horror, tears pooled in her eyes. "Oh. Thank you. I . . . I . . . have to go."

She grabbed the handle of her suitcase on the ground and started walking toward the airport entrance. What the hell? Was she really going to just leave like that?

"Blue."

Christian started to follow her, but she swung around and he saw she was crying for real, tears streaming down her cheeks.

"Don't follow me! Please." She clutched the little wrapped box he'd given her, then whirled around and walked off so fast she was practically jogging.

Christian stood there in the silent gloomy garage and watched her disappear, feeling like something amazing had just slipped out of his hands. As he got into the car, he decided it was a blue Christmas after all.

Chapter Nine

Blue burst into the airport, sobbing so hard her vision was blurred, clutching the present Christian had given to her. It was probably nothing special, after all, it was essentially a re-gift, but that he had thought to give her something, well, God, it had just caused her to come undone.

She wasn't even sure why it had affected her so strongly, but she had just known she needed to get the hell out of there before she threw her arms around Christian and found herself on the way to the Dawes household for dinner. Which was something she wanted so bad she could practically taste it, a normal relationship with a normal man, with a normal family, and that was dangerous. So very dangerous.

Picking her way past several ticketing counters to a coffee shop, she plunked her purse down on the table and reached for a napkin to wipe her tears and blow her nose. Her purse was buzzing again and she figured it was Emily looking for a status update on her travel.

But when she sat down and pulled out her phone, it was from Christian. It just said, "If you change your mind." Then he had included his parents' address.

Blue set her phone down, staring at the open message.

Pulling out her camera, she viewed the pictures of her and Christian posing next to the snowman. God, he was cute. Damn, she looked happy. She scrolled back and forth through them three times, before setting the camera down.

She stared at the present, wrapped in Barbie wrapping paper. It was a lousy wrap job, which meant Christian had done it himself, not had the mall employees do it. That was definitely his style, taking the time to do it himself.

Almost afraid to see what it was, she suddenly reached out and tore off the paper. Opening a little box, she pulled out a snow globe.

Oh, my God. The tears came again, so loud and wet and raw that an older woman sitting at the table next to her patted her arm and asked her if she was okay.

"I'm fine," Blue choked out, picking up the snow globe and shaking it.

It was a Christmas scene, a snowman in front of a decorated tree, the fake flakes dancing around them. It wasn't anything particularly amazing, but that he had heard her meant more than she could ever imagine.

Clutching the snow globe to her chest like she might lose it, drop it, or have it stolen, Blue glanced down at the text message. What the hell was she doing?

Any man who gave her a snow globe was a man worth pursuing. Worth dating. How many times in her life was she going to meet a guy like that? It had taken a freaking snowstorm and a car accident to find this one and the odds of having another opportunity like this weren't likely.

Putting the snow globe back in the box and into her purse, along with her phone and the camera, Blue wiped her eyes and stood up. Heading for the exit, she scanned the signs for the taxi queue. She was going to dinner.

Christian bounced Alison on his back, her six-year-old shrieks splitting his eardrums. Normally he loved playing with the kids, but he had to admit, he was going through the motions right now. All he could think about was Blue, tearing off like that. He was never going to see her again. He knew that. She had made her mind up that it wouldn't work.

That sucked. Big time.

He couldn't believe that he had found someone so amazing, so special and intriguing and sassy, and all he got was twenty-four hours. It was damn hard to swallow.

Kids were running around the living room and his mother and sisters were in the kitchen, putting the finishing touches on dinner. His two brothers-in-law were watching TV with his father, grateful for Christian's role as climbing post for their kids for the night. The tree was blinking, the house was warm and smelled fantastic, and Christian just wanted to stomp his foot like his nephew Cole.

"Did you think you were going to *die* out there in the blizzard?" Alison asked him.

"Not at first. But then . . ." He bounced her on his back for effect. "I saw the abominable snow-man."

"Really?"

"Really. It was awful. He was huge and had mas-sive teeth and big claws and this horrible roar. But it turned out his name was Bob and he was just lonely, so we had a drink together and sang songs."

Alison ran her fingers through his hair, making it stick out in multiple directions. "I don't believe you!"

"It's all true."

The doorbell rang. His father and his brothers-in-law didn't move or react, transfixed by the TV. His mother yelled from the kitchen, "Sam, get the door!"

"I got it," Christian told his father, who looked loathe to stand up.

He gave Alison a horsey ride on the way to the door, wondering if one of the neighbors was stop-ping by with more cookies. They had enough for the entire state already, but Mrs. Morris next door did some rocking raspberry bars.

But when he flung open the door, he froze. It wasn't Mrs. Morris. It was Blue. Standing there on the stoop in her velvet jacket, her hair dusted with fresh falling snow, her eyes wide, phone clutched in her hands. A taxi sat in the driveway, still run-ning.

"Blue. Hi," he said, bending down and shaking

Alison off his back, his heart pounding. She had shown up, proving him completely wrong, and hope started to swell inside him.

"Hi," she said. "I . . . I came to say thank you for the snow globe." She rubbed her lips together nervously. "It's beautiful, Christian."

"You're welcome. I wish I could have given you more." He wanted to reach for her, but at the same time, knew this was her move.

"You've given me more than you can imagine." She swallowed, hand nervously tucked into the front pocket of her jeans, other hand clutching her phone like a lifeline. "And, I would like to see you again if that offer still stands."

Hope burst into full-fledged glee. Christian nodded. "Hell yes."

"Okay. Good. That's good." She stood there, still looking awkward. "I wish I had something to give you for Christmas."

Christian burst into a grin. "This would be a perfect time to kiss me," he told her. "That's something you can give me."

Blue shocked him by suddenly launching herself into his arms, like she'd just been waiting for the invitation. Arms around his neck, she kissed him relentlessly, both of them pouring their emotion into the hot and passionate embrace.

He only came to his senses when he realized Alison was tugging on his leg.

As they managed to pry themselves apart, Blue whispered in his ear. "I want to be with you. Is that insane or what?"

"Totally insane. And I'm crazy desperate to be with you, so I guess that makes us a good fit." He patted Alison's head absently and stared intently at Blue. "So are you going to Miami tonight or are you going to send that taxi away and come into the house?"

He'd gotten more than he'd ever expected, a possible future with Blue and he was thrilled, but damn, he wanted her to come into the house and make his Christmas complete.

Blue stared at the man in front of her, a little girl clinging to him like a monkey, and felt things she'd only ever dreamed she could feel. Hell, yes, she was coming into the house. She wasn't stupid enough to walk away from him twice in one day.

Turning she waved off the taxi then grinned at Christian. "What's for dinner? I'm starving."

Leaning down, she smiled at the little girl. "Hi, I'm Blue. What's your name?"

"Alison." She looked up at her uncle. "What did she say her name was?"

Blue laughed, knowing she was about to spend the next ten minutes hearing that from a whole round of relatives.

A middle-aged woman appeared in the doorway behind Christian, wiping her hands on a kitchen towel. "Christian, who's at the door?"

Christian glanced back, grinning. He reached out and took Blue's hand and pulled her into the house. "Mom, this is Blue. My girlfriend."

And Blue decided maybe Santa didn't suck so much after all.

Santa in a Kilt

DONNA
KAUFFMAN

Chapter One

Finally, she was his to claim.

The doors of the ancient abbey were opening and everyone was waiting, with collectively drawn breath, for the bride and groom to make their exit as man and wife. But Shay Callaghan's attention wasn't on the heavy, weather-beaten doors, creaking loudly as they were dragged the rest of the way open by two of his fellow islanders. Nor was it on the couple who were due to pass through them at any moment.

Instead, his attention lay across the wide, cobblestone path . . . on the maid of honor, Kira MacLeod. In fact, he found it impossible to look anywhere else.

"There they are!" someone shouted.

The abbey bells began to peal as Shay's best mate stepped through the doors and, in a move that was purely Roan, swept his bride up into his arms and shouted, "Please, everyone, make way for Mr. and Mrs. Roan McAuley!"

"And the crowd went wild," Shay murmured beneath his breath, though his lips twitched in a hint of a smile, and he clapped along with everyone else as a cacophony of shouts and cheers went up. Shay stood alongside his other best mate, who was also the best man, Graham, each of the men decked out in their formal clan tartans. Shay in the Callaghan forest green and deep blue, and Graham sporting the MacLeod brighter green and blue, shot through with red and gold.

Shay was sincerely happy for Roan, as he had been for Graham, when he'd tied the knot but a few months past. Shay simply didn't see that same future for himself. As a divorce attorney, he knew where that trail ended, more often than not, and it was not a path he was willing to embark on.

Roan carried Tessa down the stone steps and past the wedding party. As it had been with Graham's wife, Katie, Tessa also made a stunning bride, with her vivacious red curls and expressive face. A face that she turned toward her best friend, Kira, as she passed by, mouthing something Shay couldn't see, before swinging her gaze back, and aiming it, surprisingly, toward him. Despite Tessa's perch aloft in her husband's arms, she managed to pin him with her bright blue gaze for a brief but very specific moment as she bounced past. Shay couldn't tell if it was a look of gauging . . . or warning, not that either made any sense.

But before he could sort it out, the couple had passed by and everyone in the party filed in behind them. Everyone but himself. He stood back, and apart, as he often did, his gaze easily tracking Kira in the crowd.

Roan had had a thing for her once, which was why Shay hadn't made his own interest known. Or so he'd told himself. Not that Roan had ever done anything about his attraction. Kira had been back on Kinloch for almost two years now, and Roan had been content to keep things platonic. But everyone knew he'd been interested.

No one had known of Shay's interest. But then, very few knew much of anything that crossed Shay Callaghan's mind. Or resided in his heart. He was a man who chose his words carefully and spoke when it mattered. He was also a loyal friend, a trusted confidant, and a calm head in any crisis. And that was all anyone truly needed to know, aye?

But, the thing was, watching Roan and Tessa together now, their smiles, their laughter, simply the way they looked at one another, he understood. Kira hadn't been the one for Roan. And, quite simply, Tessa had. Roan certainly hadn't wasted a moment once he'd met her. He'd known Tessa less than a few months and not only had he immediately gotten involved with her . . . he'd married her!

And now, without the friend code of honor standing in his way, Shay was clear to pledge his case. He was quite good at pledging cases.

But he remained where he stood. Because looking at her, as he was now, seeing her eyes shining so brightly, smiling with such sincere joy, her heart so open, so readily apparent to anyone who wanted to know what lay inside . . . he knew, deep down, in that place that made no rational sense, but was all the more truthful because of it, he knew. Kira MacLeod might not be The One for Roan McAuley . . . but Shay was as certain as he'd ever been that if *he* were to ever have a One, she would be it.

Which was the problem entirely. Because Shay Callaghan didn't believe in The One. Not rationally, anyway. Certainly not forever and always.

And Kira MacLeod was absolutely a forever and always kind of woman. She deserved no less . . . and so very much more.

The abbey bells continued to peal, filling the brisk November afternoon air with their loud, raucous clanging, joyously announcing that another brand-new union had been formed within its ancient walls. Walls that, if they could speak, would give testimony to the hundreds of forever and always vows to which they had borne witness.

The entirety of the island's small population crowded around and behind the bridal party as they pushed forth out into the grassy field that lay between the crumbling abbey and the single track road that led back to the village proper. It was full-on cacophony, with the bells ringing and the noisy, happy shouts reverberating through the late afternoon air.

For Shay, all of the unleashed energy and din served to create a bubble of sorts, one that encapsulated him, in that exact moment in time, blocking out the rest of the universe, and the reality of the world outside that bubble. It was, perhaps, the only moment when he could step aside from all that he knew to be true, all that he'd witnessed firsthand . . . and allow himself to believe, for the tiniest and purest of moments . . . that it actually made any sense for a man to consider cleaving himself to a woman in any way beyond the physical.

And, while still safely cushioned inside his fairytale bubble, he couldn't help thinking that any length of time the gods saw fit to allow him to be cleaved, in any way, to the sweetness of soul that was Kira MacLeod, was worth the ripping heartache and devastation that was almost certain to follow taking such an insane leap of faith.

"Do you want a lift into the village? You could ride along with us." Graham stepped beside him as the throng moved beyond them and toward the roadway, where long lines of cars and all manner of conveyances had been parked.

"Hmm?" Shay responded absently, unwilling as yet to have his tantalizing bubble burst. He hadn't even been aware that Graham had hung back as well, he'd been so caught up in his thoughts.

"Is something wrong?"

Pop. Shay felt a distinct deflation in the general area of his heart, but it had been, after all, just a momentary fantasy. He calmly shifted his gaze away from the crowd in general, and Kira in particular, thankful for Graham's furrowed brow. Nothing like the scrutiny of a close friend to help realign one's priorities. "No," he said, easily. "And thanks, but I'll meet you there in a wee bit."

Graham's look of concern didn't ease. If anything, it deepened. Which was annoying. Perhaps Shay wasn't hiding his uncustomary rioting emotions as well as he'd assumed. He needed to get a grip, and quickly. Retreat, and regroup, that was the best move.

Instead, a quick thump of anxiety beat sharply inside his chest when Graham's intent gaze—and no one was so intent as his science-minded friend— shifted with laserlike accuracy from Shay . . . to the retreating, beautifully gowned, and quite lovely form of one Kira MacLeod.

"Perhaps you were hopeful of a different kind of lift?"

Feeling a little rattled now—first Tessa, now Graham—and further annoyed with himself because of it, Shay jerked his attention from where it had once again strayed to Kira, back to Graham—only to find amusement crinkling the corners of his best friend's eyes.

His first instinct was to defend Kira, but he tamped that down. He'd apparently given enough away already. "I—have work to do," he said, intending to sound as if he were merely distracted by a case, which wasn't at all a rare thing. Only the look on Graham's face made it clear he knew the real distraction was presently carefully picking her way across the stone-filled field. "I need to drop by my offices."

"On a Sunday?"

"I'm trying to avoid a trip back to the city this coming week, and it would be helpful if I could get these briefs done and faxed so they're already waiting on the appropriate desktop start of business tomorrow."

"It's barely three in the afternoon," Graham said, steadily, the light of amusement not dimming in the least, but perhaps increasing, as the corners of his mouth quirked now as well. "Surely you have time to hoist a glass and say a few words before attending to the needs of those trying to undo what was so beautifully done here today."

Whatever was left of the bubble now lay empty and flat at his feet. Not a surprise. Bubbles were meant to pop. He just didn't know why the prick had carried such a particularly painful sting this go-around. His expression smoothed further. "You do know I truly wish you and Katie, as well as Roan and Tessa, all the happiness in the world," he said, never more sincere. "Nothing would make me happier than to watch you grow old together and bounce many a rosy cheeked grandbaby on your aging, knobby knee."

Graham merely cocked a brow. "But?"

"But I have work to do. I can't help that it happens to be what it is. It's what I do. Everyone deserves to have their needs well-represented, no matter the situation involved."

"And you do it quite well, solicitor."

Shay merely held his gaze evenly, said nothing.

"Is there some rule," Graham went on, his gaze still as intent as ever, "against enjoying oneself, simply for the moment? Not every quest for pleasure has to end in a lifelong commitment."

Shay stifled a sigh. This wasn't new territory. "In the city, I'd agree. Which is why, as you well know, I conduct that part of my life there. Here on Kinloch, however, we both know the truth of it," Shay said, and knew Graham understood his meaning. It was, in fact, the irony of all ironies, to his mind. While Shay spent at least half of his time in Edinburgh devoting himself to tearing asunder the unions made in holy matrimony . . . here on Kinloch, nary a single soul had ever divorced. Not ever. Not once. For all of the four hundred recorded years in the history of the isle. "I'll meet you all later, and raise my glass then. Several in fact, to be sure."

He moved past Graham, expecting his friend to shrug off the exchange and let him go. Graham and Roan both ribbed him on many an occasion about his mysterious paramours in the city, waxing ridiculously rhapsodic about the life of debauchery and decadence they were certain he must live there, to counterbalance the life of a monk he lived on Kinloch. He let them have their ribald fun, knowing he'd have his own opportunities for giving back as good as he got. Which he did, in his own dryly acerbic way. It was the way of old friends, and he normally didn't mind it in the least. But he was thankful, on this day, to have it over with.

So, it surprised him when Graham spoke again, earnestly this time, without a hint of humor in his tone. "Shay, I know you spend a goodly amount of time as an intimate witness to the worst of what a man and woman can do to one another. But you were raised, for most of your life, here, an equally intimate witness to the glorious best of it. And though I've not been long in their ranks, I can tell you, you cannot even imagine the true gloriousness—"

"Graham," Shay said, a surprising note of warning creeping into what was normally his smooth, some would say relentlessly even tone. "Please don't proselytize the sanctity of the glorious union to me of all people."

Now it was Shay's turn to be surprised, as a very rare, hard light came into his friend's eyes . . . and a warning note echoed in his words. "Oh, I'm no' preaching for you to join us, mate. That is a decision each man makes for himself. I'm merely reminding you there's a balance of good to evil. And, perhaps, a bit of cautioning as well. Kira might share your desire for a brief crossing of paths, I'm no' to say. But given her heart has already been trod heavily upon once, you wouldn't want to be the man to do that to her again."

"I beg your pardon?" Shay felt his fingers curl into his palms. "What kind of man do you take me for? Why do you think I don't start things here, with any woman?"

"Kira is no' 'any woman,' " Graham replied.

"My point exactly." Shay was stunned, actually, at the force of anger that rose inside him and he fought to control his tone. "I'm afraid, however, I've missed yours entirely."

"I've been observing the way you look at her, mate. And I'm well aware of that look and the feelings that accompany it. I daresay our friend Roan could weigh in on the topic as well. At great length." His tone eased along with the hard lines around his jaw. "And I know ye've no reason now, with Roan wedded, to satisfy yourself with looks alone."

"I—"

"What I'm sayin' to ye is that I'm the first one to applaud a man following his heart and going after what he wants. But you've made it more than clear that ye dinnae believe a lifetime spent with one woman is possible."

"I've made it clear that I see how it's more often impossible than not for two people to forge a life-long commitment to one another, no' that I personally disapprove of it. Big difference."

"And yet, the tie that binds those two ideas together is that ye dinnae personally believe it to be possible. For you. And, given her past, I'd say that she deserves a man who not only knows his intent, but fully believes he can back it up, with all that is in his heart."

"And I believe I told you that I've no plans to conduct myself otherwise. No' here."

"As I said, I've seen the way ye look at her. The fact that you've been at all obvious in your interest says a great deal."

"I have no' been obvious. I'm the least obvious man on this island."

"Not to those who know you best. And I'm only speaking from personal experience. I know what it is to try to deny that interest. You'll tell yourself you can walk away, keep a distance, no' act on it. But the last barrier you had to hide behind just walked out those abbey doors."

Shay didn't bother to argue that point, because he couldn't. "So what was all that about not all pleasures have to lead to lifelong commitments? One minute you're encouraging me to go after a quick roll, the next—"

"I was testing the waters. I wanted to see your response." His gaze took on even greater directness. "And now I have. I canno' speak for Kira. As I said, perhaps that's all she'll be wantin' from ye. But I'm no' just concerned for her welfare here . . . I'm concerned for yours."

"I can take care of myself, Laird MacLeod," he said, adding a pointed note to that last part.

Graham ignored it. "All I'm trying to say is, even if she's on for a simple roll, no matter what ye tell yerself you'd settle for, I think you'll end up wanting more. Perhaps more than ye bargained for. I know the look," he repeated, then smiled. "Intimately. I'm saying this because I know you to be an honorable man, Shay Callaghan. One of the finest I've ever had the privilege to know and it's with pride I call you my friend. And 'tis only because I've been where you stand right now that I felt duty bound to make sure ye were thinking with all you have up here"—he knocked Shay on the forehead with his knuckle—"before you act on what's pounding in here." He aimed his knuckle at Shay's chest, but backed up a step and let his hand drop to his side. "Because you're going to act on it, my friend. Today, a fortnight from today, I canno' say. But as long as the two of you are on this isle together, you will."

Shay said nothing.

Graham grinned then, and any remaining tension eased completely. "I know the look."

Shay watched his oldest and dearest friend walk away, then catch up to his wife, whom he promptly swept up into his arms, eliciting a delighted laugh from Katie and good natured whistles and hoots from the merry band around them.

Shay slowly crossed the field, well behind the ebbing throng, rubbing at the increasingly annoying twinge in his chest. He tried not to think too closely about Graham's words of wisdom, but it was a challenge. He knew Graham to be honorable and as dedicated to the islanders in his role as clan laird and island chief, as he was to those closest and dearest to him. Just as he knew Katie would benefit from that honest dedication, and that if any couple was going to go the distance, Shay believed they would.

Roan was an equally dedicated sort, who wore his heart on his sleeve and saw the best in everyone. And Shay hadn't seen anything to indicate he'd be any less of a devoted husband to Tessa, despite their short courtship, than Graham was to Katie.

He wished he had that same kind of faith. Graham had been right in saying that Shay had surely been exposed to a lot of what could be right between a man and a woman. The difference was, except for university, Graham and Roan had spent all their lives on Kinloch. So that was all they knew. It was easier to believe the best of people when you were never exposed to their worst.

And Shay had not only been exposed to it, he was a constant active participant in the dismantling of it.

He stopped beside his car and fished his keys out of the sporran that hung at his waist. A hint of a smile curved his lips, as it often did when he looked at the old jitney. He'd bought it at the age of seventeen, with money earned sheep tending and hauling in nets full of fish. He'd never been so proud as he had the day he'd towed the auld girl home behind Magnus MacLeod's tractor. His father had been far less than impressed with the idea of his son driving about in what amounted to a taxicab, but then that was his typical reaction to just about anything Shay did, and by seventeen, Shay had gotten very good at shrugging the disappointment aside.

Shay had spent a long, happy summer putting the jitney to rights, prouder still the first time he'd driven her into the village under her own power. That was almost as many years ago now as the tender age he'd been at the time, and yet, she was still by his side. He ran a palm over the bonnet, the paint gritty and pocked from a lifetime of residing in salty air and unpaved roads.

His smile grew rueful, as he realized that the longest relationship he'd ever sustained, outside of his friendship with Roan and Graham, was with his car. "Aye, but a leap of faith I took fifteen years back, and look where it's brought us," he said under his breath. Perhaps it wasn't the kind of faith most folks needed to commit their hearts to another person, but it was something.

He started to open the door when a clearing of a throat caused him to go utterly still. Just a clearing of a throat, but he knew . . .

"Would ye have a minute for me, Shay?"

He took the briefest of moments to gather himself, or at least find his breath, then turned his head . . . and looked straight into teasing hazel eyes and the sweetest of smiling faces. Kira MacLeod stood just behind him on the tiny strip of flat land between the rocky edge to the meadow, and the track road just beyond the cars. She stood so close that the light citrus fragrance she wore teased his senses. So close that all he had to do was shift the rest of his body fully around and she'd be half in his arms. The steady island breeze had caused wispy tendrils to come loose from her swept up hairstyle, and it took every ounce of strength he had not to reach out and smooth away a stray strand clinging to her lips.

His gaze lingered there. And his fingers curled more tightly into his palms.

And he knew, right then, his heart thudding loudly, while a thunderstorm of want pounded through his veins . . . that Graham was right.

As long as they were both on the same island . . . he was going to act.

Heaven help them both.

Chapter Two

For a moment, Kira thought he wasn't going to respond. He was simply staring at her. Well, there was nothing simple about it, actually. There was a certain light in his eyes, eyes that were a unique shade of ochre, like that of a finely aged whisky, which lent a singular intensity to his gaze, and made her feel quite as if she were the only woman left in the entire universe.

Which was saying something given all the noise and clamor of the wedding celebration, everyone shouting and hollering as they got into their cars and began to make their way, like a merry holiday caravan, into the village, horns tooting, song bursting forth from several who had piled into the back of Maddaug's open lorry. She'd just been thinking, smiling to herself as she walked down the row of vehicles, that a person would have thought it was middle of summer, and not nigh on winter, the way everyone was carrying on. The sun was rapidly setting and it would be full dark before it reached half past four.

The days were short in winter, aye, but oh, she'd loved every second of this one, from the preparation, to the ceremony, to . . . well, just every last bit of pomp and circumstance of it. The boisterous celebration was simply the proverbial icing on the cake. Everything was as it should be and she couldn't be happier.

For which she was eternally grateful on more levels than would be obvious to anyone else. As excited and thrilled as she'd been for her closest and dearest friend, Tessa, on this most special day of her life . . . Kira had privately wondered how she'd feel as she watched Tessa and Roan pledge their vows. Would it bring back hard memories? Would the day turn out to be a harsher test for her than she'd thought she was ready to endure?

"Aye, of course," Shay responded, at last, pulling her from her thoughts. His normally low voice sounded even deeper to her ears, more intimate, with a bit of grit making it even more gravelly than usual. "What is it ye need?" he asked.

You, she thought, feeling suddenly a little helpless. She'd been attracted, aye, but she hadn't expected to feel all shivery and goose-pimply and incredibly aware of his every breath and pore. It was only when he finally lifted a questioning brow that she realized she was standing there, essentially gawking.

"I—I, well . . . I . . ." She stammered, suddenly tongue-tied now that the moment was finally upon her. *For goodness' sake, you're behaving like an addled schoolgirl in the midst of her first crush. String a decent sentence together, why don't you?* Kira smiled, widely, hoping it made her seem more her normal self, but afraid from the way his eyes widened slightly that the effect was more that of a swanning loon. *Oh dear.*

"Yes?" he prompted.

She took a short, steadying breath. This wasn't supposed to be the hard part. "Would it be possible for me to, that is to say, for us—do ye think we could manage some time together—what I mean is . . . I need you." *Dear lord, a swanning loon would be sane compared to this babbling.* She'd known the man since she was a child. Granted, it had been only in recent months that she'd begun to look at him . . . well, the way she'd begun to look at him, but you'd think the way her tongue had tied itself into knots she was introducing herself to the King of England. Had England a king, of course.

It was just . . . he drew her. His quiet, easy confidence. The way he always seemed in command of any situation, without saying a single word. The way he carried himself, the alertness she saw in his eyes despite his otherwise inconspicuous demeanor. There was an aura of intense awareness with him . . . of tightly leashed power. It had been the stuff of many a fevered dream and fantasy, in fact.

She'd often wondered what it would feel like to have him direct all that focused intensity toward her and her only, but she hadn't thought it would render her a babbling idiot.

"You . . . need me?" he repeated, slowly, as if uncertain he'd heard her correctly.

And she heard a note of . . . alarm, was it? Which was when she realized how her blurted declaration might have sounded. "Oh! Not like that—I meant I need to *see* you, not that I need you as in like I *need* a man—" She broke off and could feel the flush of mortification steal up her neck and tinge her face. A face she well knew to be pale enough that, even in the growing dusk, the blush would appear as two rosy splotches, staining her cheeks in a way that wasn't remotely becoming, but made it look as if she'd just finished some arduous task. Such as plowing a field. Oh . . . dear. This *so* wasn't how she'd thought this would go. "I probably shouldn't be bothering you here, now."

"It's fine," he said, quite clearly even more concerned now. "Is something wrong, Kira?"

"Wrong?" Damn, the word had come out like a squeak. But he'd said her name, and it sounded so . . . good. Really good. And she'd so badly wanted to have her femme fatale moment, to be all alluring and enticing as she basked in his smoldering gaze. Instead, his only thought was probably that she might need immediate medical assistance. Lovely. "No," she said, quickly, wishing she could start this conversation over. "It's . . . business, actually."

Now he looked surprised again, and perhaps a little . . . disappointed? Surely that was her own imagination at work. Her quite overactive imagination.

"Regarding?" he asked, his demeanor all solicitor now, no smolder.

Any chance at a femme fatale moment was officially over. As was any chance she might have with him. Kira took a breath and fought down her disappointment in herself. She'd finally found her way back to wanting a man to notice her, and this was how she'd handled it? Truly, she was a disaster. The reality of which allowed her to finally get hold of her ridiculous self. "I've stopped in at your office once or twice over the past fortnight, but have managed to do so when you've been on the mainland. I kept meaning to call and schedule an appointment, but then I thought today—we're both here—so I'd have a chance to mention it directly. I realized after the ceremony that once we get to the pub it will be too loud, so I waylaid you. But I'm sure you'd like to get on to the pub so you can toast Roan. Tessa is likely wondering where I am as well."

"I'm sure Roan and Tessa will survive with only the rest of the entire village to toast them."

She smiled at that, well imagining the chaos that the pub had surely become by now. "Thank you, I appreciate that. I'm not normally one to accost folks as they go about their business."

"You didn't," he said. "I'm sorry I wasn't in when you stopped by."

He sounded so sincere. She could only imagine that grave earnestness was what made him such a successful lawyer. "Will you be in this week?"

"I may have to go to Edinburgh early on, though I'm trying to skirt around it. Regardless, I'll be back by Thursday. Would that be soon enough?"

"Aye, that would be fine." Perhaps by then she'd have found the dignity she'd somehow managed to lose completely during the past five minutes. "Sometime that morning, then?"

"I'm not certain of my schedule, but just drop 'round whenever it's convenient. I'll make the time."

Her smile came more naturally now. "Thank you," she added, then stuck her hand out. *What, like you need to shake on setting up a simple business appointment?* Honestly, what was wrong with her?

He looked down at her hand with a moment's confusion, or at least it seemed so, from the way he frowned at it. But just when she was about to snatch it back, he took her hand in his.

And that femme fatale moment came roaring back in full force. At least, on her end, it did. His palm was warm and surprisingly a bit rough for a man who earned his keep inside an office and various courts of law. It took a moment longer for her to realize that he was neither shaking her hand . . . nor letting it go.

Her gaze lifted to his and that focused intensity was back, but with an additional edge that made tiny hairs of awareness lift all along her arms, up to the back of her neck. The sensation was disconcerting in its intensity . . . and entirely, wonderfully pleasurable in its exclusivity.

"Thursday, then," he said, at length, that very grit and gravel causing yet another skittery cascade of tingling awareness.

"Thursday," she echoed. He was still holding her hand, so she forgave herself the breathless note even she could hear.

And then his hold tightened, and for the briefest of moments, she could have sworn he was going to pull her closer still. His gaze dropped from her eyes to her mouth, and she felt a distinct wobble in her knees. Was he—could he be actively contemplating . . . *kissing* her? Had she gone off into some kind of dream state at some point? Because surely it was a moment out of her own private fantasies. Though none of them had done this reality one whit of justice.

Her lips parted and the most delicious shiver of anticipation raced through her. It had been a very long time since she'd felt a man's lips on hers . . . and yet it felt as though she'd waited a lifetime for his.

A split second later, just when, perhaps, her eyes might have been fluttering shut, his hand was sliding away from hers and reality came thunking back in as his expression returned to one of active concern.

"The sun is setting. You're cold. Had I more than this short jacket—" He broke off and began to quickly undo the silver filigree buttons that adorned the front of his formal jacket, matching those on the cuffs of the sleeves.

"No, that's—dinnae worry," she hurried to say, a bit mortified now. How silly she was. How very, very silly. To think, for one second even, that he . . . "I'm fine," she said, more calmly.

"You're shivering."

How to tell him that the very last thing she was at the moment was cold? Much less that he was the cause of all the shivering . . . none of which required his jacket as a cure. Still, as the reality of her surroundings crept back in, she did pull her shawl more tightly around her, noticing as she did so that all the other cars had now departed and that the sun, indeed, was dipping low on the horizon. "I should be getting into town—we both should, I suppose, before the toasts are all made and the ale gone. Wouldn't be right for the rest of the wedding party not to show."

"Let me see you to your car," was all he said, in his typical man-of-few-words way. In fact, she had no idea at all what he was thinking. Which was possibly just as well. No need to add insult to injury.

"It's right there," she said, nodding across the single track to where her tiny red Fiat sat parked just opposite his. Not a coincidence, but he never need know that. "I'll see you in town." She'd already been backing up, but stumbled a bit as her low heel caught on the rough edge where the grass met the road.

Shay sprang forward, hand out to steady her, but she managed to steady herself on the flat of the road before he could round the back of his old jitney. She'd always thought it a whimsical choice of vehicle for a man who seemed anything but, and who could certainly afford far better now. She knew he'd had it forever, and it was likely a sentimental thing, but she'd been away back when they'd come of driving age. In fact, he'd come to Kinloch at age seven, and she'd gone off to boarding school shortly after, returning only after her divorce, so she didn't know much more about it. Or that much about him, really. She'd never asked him about the car. Maybe now she would.

"I'm fine," she assured him as she started to cross the road, then quickly made her way to her car, feeling his gaze on her back, which set off another round of sparks she was going to have to start getting over. "No time like the present," she said, crossing around to open the driver's side door. She did her best to slide her voluminous frock into the tiny, aging two-seater with as much grace as possible, and waved as she rattled off down the track toward the village. Hopefully the pub would be so crowded she could lose herself in the mob for a bit, gather herself, then slide out after the bride and groom made their departure.

"So you can go back to your cottage. And your weaving room. And hide," she muttered. She had work to do, yes. And she had to go over the plans she intended to show Shay on Thursday as well. Plans for the basket weaving school she wanted to open, on the island. Weaving artisan basketry was an ancestral Kinloch tradition, as well as the sole foundation of the island's economy, so there were likely to be some complicated, centuries-old laws to untangle and work around to bring her vision to life. "But, at least you have a vision now," she said, as she pulled around past the pub and began the search for a place to park. "You have a purpose."

The only real question was—or had been—would Shay just play a legal role in that vision? Or the more intimate one she'd hoped he would. She'd thought that perhaps the time spent together, hammering out the legal details for launching the school, would give her a chance to figure that out.

"Och, well, now you'll simply be able to devote all your time and energy to getting the school up and running." It was just the recent weddings and people running around falling in love that had gotten her thinking about romance again, which wasn't a bad thing. It was good to want to feel something again, wasn't it? It was a sign of healing and growth, having optimism about her future. So what if it wasn't going to be with Shay Callaghan? She'd get his help with the school, and . . . eventually she'd expand her horizons where other men were concerned. Somehow.

The idea didn't invigorate her spirits as she'd hoped it would.

And it wasn't thoughts of building on auld Conal McAuley's croft, which Roan and Tessa had already singled out when they'd proposed the school idea to her in the first place, that dominated her thoughts as she drove into town.

No, it was the memory of those whisky-gold eyes staring intently into hers, the feel of his warm palm . . . and how he'd tightened his hold on her hand . . . just as he'd dropped his gaze to her mouth . . .

She shifted in her seat, gripping the steering wheel more tightly . . . and pressed her thighs together against the ache that built there as she replayed that moment through her mind again. And again.

She hadn't really imagined that part . . . had she?

Chapter Three

The following morning Kira was in her weaving studio bright and early. Well, it was early. She wouldn't vouch for how bright it was. Inside or out. But it was get to work or thrash about in her bed another hour or two, pretending to sleep. She was tired, more than a wee bit cranky, and not feeling particularly creative, but she needed to occupy her mind with something other than Shay.

"And wouldn't that be a nice change?" she muttered as she picked up her current work in progress from the basin of water where she'd been soaking the spokes. It was a small basket, or would eventually become one, that incorporated both the colorful waxed linen strands that the Kinloch clans were known for in their artisan basketry, as well as thicker and tougher lengths of willow, and a few other natural odds and ends she'd gathered on the island. The idea of pushing the boundaries of their ancient traditions to create work that didn't exclusively use waxed linen was seen by some on Kinloch as innovative and just the thing their island industry needed to remain vibrant and relevant in the global market. Others, namely the clan elders, saw it as a sacreligious breach of their cherished and much celebrated heritage and weren't shy about making their displeasure known.

Kira respected the elders' sentiments. She'd trained at her grandmother's knee and held the old ways in deep regard. But she had to stay true to her own vision and creative calling, something her grandmother would have championed. To that end, Kira had made it clear when she'd first introduced her new design ideas to Roan, who controlled the marketing and sales of their baskets, that if there ended up being no market for them, that would decide the matter. She'd continue to make them for her own creative outlet, but would find a way to celebrate old traditions in a more pure form for the baskets she wove for market.

However, Kira's baskets had gained immediate notice. In fact, she'd recently completed an exclusive order for a famous Italian shoe designer to use in his Milan showroom. She smiled privately as she remembered his recent, brief but colorful visit to Kinloch. Next to the wedding plans, Maradona—just the one name—had been the focus of conversation island-wide. Still was. He'd been quite a flamboyant and colorful figure on their otherwise quiet little isle. The fact that he'd brought some of his amazing shoes and handbags as well, and made gifts of the former to the younger weavers and the latter to the island's oldest clan elders, had gone a

long way toward creating a grudging détente between Kira and the traditionalists.

Kira smiled, thinking that the road to winning
approval would be long, but all roads could be
traveled. She just had to take it one step at a time.
That was how she'd gotten this far. She let out a little sigh, forcing her thoughts away from Shay, away
from the painful divorce that had sent her back to
Kinloch, away from all of it. The only thing she
had to think about was how to make the new pattern work. She'd already worked the slenderest of
willow spokes into the base and had woven the ini-
tial rows with slender willow weavers interspersed
with other organic material. Now she began to
weave the thickest ply waxed strands in an intricate
braided pattern in and around the unwieldy willow spokes, tucking them in and through the
other material as well as she went.

The result was a rustic, uneven weave, with irregular gaps and an unwieldy, wild shaping to the
basket itself, but the very earthiness of it called to
her artistic soul. She probably wouldn't rim it, but
band it with a few rows of hand-dyed round reed at
the top, then leave the spokes bending and twisting up and outward. Not a functional basket, but
an art piece, a talking point. It was both harsh and
beautiful, wild and barely tamed into shape, much
like the island they lived on, which grew both the
rugged willow, and the flax that was spun into such
gorgeous, beautiful, and pliant waxed threads. She
still wasn't sure this particular idea was going to
work because the elements involved were so dra-

matically different, and willow was a beast to work with, but so far, she was liking the results well enough.

Besides, the multicolored stranded braiding took some serious concentration, which was an added bonus this morning. She studied the open weave and considered adding an assortment of baked clay and blown glass beading to the pattern and made a mental note to rework her diagram, see how it might fit in a midpoint band.

Less than three rows later, however, she put the unfinished basket back on her worktable and swore under her breath. "Never weave when you're upset," she murmured. "It comes out in the work." Those were her grandmother's words. Kira had found weaving to be immensely therapeutic. Normally, within minutes, whatever mood she'd been in when sitting down would smooth out. The combination of the repetitive motion and seeing a pattern come alive under her own fingers would take her out of her head and whatever stresses . . . or pain lurked there.

"Not today."

Today, the tension showed in the work. She liked the idea of taming these unruly elements and forcing them to work together, but it was, in the end, to be a harmonious blend . . . not a tortured union.

"And you know all about those." She shoved her stool back and stood, rolling her shoulders as she trudged out of the studio that her grandmother had had built onto the side of the tiny cottage a full generation ago, and into her small kitchen. Memories of the wedding reception at the pub the night before immediately filtered, unwanted, back through Kira's mind as she set the teakettle on to boil. Like viewing some of Tessa's professional photographs, Kira could picture the night in a series of mental stills. She rummaged in the cupboard for a tin of biscuits, but her thoughts stayed on the previous night.

To be sure, the pub had been packed, but rather than mingling and losing herself in the crush as she'd planned, she and Shay had been pulled to the front of the bar where Roan and Tessa, along with Katie, Graham, and Katie's friend Blaine, were stationed. Kira was pushed, literally, up against Shay, time and time again, throughout the evening. Her plans to head home early had been for naught as the bride and groom hadn't left themselves until the wee, wee hours.

And as much as Kira had loved seeing Tessa come into her own, both as a woman overcoming a difficult and challenging past, and now, as an island resident and jubilant bride to one of the most beloved clansmen on Kinloch, Kira had very selfishly wished she could have absented herself from the reception almost as soon as she'd arrived. Worse was the fact that she was well aware of why she was moping about. It wasn't because of the less-than-desirable impression she'd made on Shay. And it wasn't because the event brought back painful memories of her own wedding day. It hadn't.

It was because, despite giving herself a stern talking to on the way into the village, she hadn't been able to get past the notion that she and Shay had, indeed, shared some kind of . . . moment, however brief, back by that roadside. In fact, by the time she'd made it to the pub and jockeyed her little car into a narrow alley behind the village, she'd managed to convince herself that if the day was a celebration of hope and faith, then maybe that was the sign she'd needed to take a little leap herself. So what if she hadn't started on this new path with exactly the right first step? She'd still taken one.

She shouldn't just turn tail and run because the path wasn't perfectly smooth. Right? She'd taken one step. All she had to do next was to take another. Simple, really.

She'd even entered the pub with the half-formed idea that if the moment presented itself, and she could get past the embarrassment of acting like an addled schoolgirl, she was going to talk Shay into a dance, as surely there would be plenty of music played that night. It was to be a rousing ceilidh, with any number of villagers contributing on their own fiddles and flutes, tin whistles and bodhrans. In fact, it was more likely she'd have a harder time avoiding a dance with him, since they were both in the wedding party and would surely be pushed onto the floor numerous times.

"Right," she muttered, and bit off half a biscuit as she waited impatiently for the water to come to boil.

It had been a night filled with singing and dancing, along with heartfelt recitations of ale-inspired poetry and ballads sung with the poignant earnestness only a Scot can deliver, which made hearts soar and even men weep. Every man and woman in the pub had likely pressed hands or more together at some point during the long, boisterous night. Except, of course, for Shay and Kira.

But then, it was hard to get the attention of a

man who refused to so much as look at her. And she wasn't mistaken about that, given their proximity to one another all evening. In fact, a man would have to work quite hard to completely and utterly ignore a woman who'd been half plastered against him for an entire evening. And yet, Shay had managed the task. Heroically, even.

Kira had swiftly gone from mildly embarrassed, to feeling enormously stupid, to just wanting to get the hell out of there and go right back to hiding in her cottage. She and Tessa had pledged to stop hiding from life. To become "bad-ass non-hiders" to use Tessa's phraseology. Tessa had pulled it off, and in quite brilliant fashion, with the wedding and celebration as proof. Which was ironic, since Kira was the one who'd fancied herself ready to start living again.

Now she cringed. Imagine, thinking she was some kind of Cinderella, coming out of her self-imposed life of weaving servitude to the island economy, ready to go to the ball and reclaim her role as a vibrant and desirable woman.

"Not so bloody likely after all," she snorted, and finished off the rest of the biscuit. Half the tin was empty before she'd realized it.

But all the sweet biscuits in the world couldn't erase the flash-parade of images. How Shay had all but gone out of his way to position himself on the far side of Graham or Katie whenever possible so as to keep from being pushed against her, or crowded into her personal space in any way. And when he had been, repeatedly so, he somehow managed to keep his gaze fixed anywhere but on her. Other than the occasional "excuse me" when he'd been roughly jostled against her, he hadn't spoken so much as a single word to her. Granted, aside from his short toast to the bride and groom, he hadn't said much otherwise, either. Nor had he danced.

She had, almost defiantly so, and she certainly hadn't lacked for partners. But when she would return to their group and inevitably get nudged to his side, still heated and flushed from the music, hoping for even the briefest flash of awareness . . . Nothing.

She'd imagined the smolder then, standing by the roadside with him. She must have. That's all there was to it. She'd been so smitten and overwhelmed by her reaction to his stoic, chiseled face and gravelly voice that she'd lost her foolish head. She'd gone for so long without even considering a man's touch, much less allowing herself to want one again, so perhaps it wasn't so surprising that his had simply swamped her senses and made her imagine ridiculous things.

She honestly hadn't thought it would be so challenging a chore as all that. In fact, she'd expected she'd end up laughing at herself for taking so long to do it, for making such a big deal of it.

Only that's exactly what it felt like now, in the dawn of a new morning. A challenge. And a chore. Neither of which felt fair to her.

She did laugh at herself then, just as the kettle let out its shrill whistle. "Fair," she all but snorted as she poured herself a cup. "As if life has ever been that."

She was digging into the bottom of the tin for the last biscuit when there was a rap on the front door of the cottage. She glanced at the wall clock. It was barely eight. "Who'd be out here at this hour?" Though it was a Monday morning and working life began early on the island, she was fairly certain there wasn't a man or woman on Kinloch who wasn't nursing a wee bit of a hangover this morning. More likely a romping one, given the duration of the celebration. At the very least, she couldn't imagine anyone wanting to pay a social call so soon into the new day.

She supposed she should at least be thankful she'd chosen to steer clear of the ale. And the whisky. In her state of mind, she hadn't imagined getting sozzled would do much to improve the evening. She shuddered to think what kind of false courage that would have given her . . . and, armed with it, what ill-advised action she might have taken.

The knock came again.

She dropped the empty biscuit tin in the dustbin and set her empty teacup in the sink. She'd shuffled halfway to the door when she realized she was in little more than a nightshirt and a robe. Neither particularly flattering. Nor, most likely, was her bed head or complete lack of makeup.

She paused for a moment, undecided on whether she should make a mad dash to the loo and at least run a comb through her hair, but then came yet another knock. No time. And honestly, it wasn't as if there was anyone on the island who was going to care what she looked like. As far as she was concerned, if a person chose to stop by so early without advance warning, they got what they got.

Feeling both righteous and a bit put out—after all, she *could* have still been sleeping—she crossed to the door and yanked it open. "Aye, ye dinnae have to keep knockin'. Give a girl a chance to . . ." Her burst of words drizzled to a stop as she saw who was on her stoop.

"Hullo, Kira."

She spent the briefest of moments wondering, a bit wildly, if perhaps she was still asleep, and dreaming this. Because there he stood, every ridiculously handsome inch of him, looking directly at her now, eye to eye, as if the endless hours of avoidance hadn't even occurred.

And, unlike herself, he looked like a fresh breath of cool November air.

Of course he did. Kira wanted to glance heavenward and demand to know what she'd done to deserve further embarrassment in front of this man, but railing against the gods would have to wait until later. *Indeed,* she thought, *life wasn't fair a'tall.*

"Mr. Callaghan," she said, hearing the frost in her tone and not working overly hard to correct it. Or at all, really. She found she wasn't in a forgive-and-forget mood this morning. "What is it I can do for ye at this early hour?"

Shay glanced at the watch on his wrist and she noted a flash of surprise before he glanced back at her. "I've been up and working for hours and . . . I finished. I was on my way home, and I pass directly by, so I thought perhaps you'd prefer no' to wait till later in the week to discuss . . . whatever it was you wanted to discuss. I hadn't realized the time. My apologies."

"You've been at work? And already finished for the day?"

"Aye," he said, without additional explanation.

It was one thing for the farmers and crofters and fishermen, but he worked in an office—his own office—and surely no one would have minded if he'd come in at a more normal hour, especially given the celebration the night before.

He nodded toward the side of her cottage. "I saw the lights on in your studio and assumed you were already at work as well."

"Oh. Well, I was . . . but then—never mind. I'm—really no' prepared for a meeting at the moment." She made a lame gesture to her hair and clothes.

Only then did Shay seem to take in the rest of her. And it was only then she realized his gaze had been exclusively focused on her face. Quite the shift from the night before. Now, when she looked as if the angel of death had paid her a lengthy visit . . . *now* he looked at her?

"I'm—I'm sorry," he said, with an uncustomary stammer. "I should have called ahead. It was just . . . a spontaneous thought. I'll leave you to your morning then." With a brief nod, he turned to leave.

Kira had every intention of stepping back inside her cottage and closing the door on his retreating back, possibly slamming it. Instead she heard herself say, "You left the celebration when I did. That was nigh on three in the morning. How is it you've been at work already?" *And what business is that of yours anyway?* she asked herself.

But he had already paused, was already turning around. Maybe it had been that uncustomary stutter in his response. But there was something . . . different about Shay Callaghan this morning. Though she couldn't quite put her finger on it. He was as controlled as ever . . . and yet . . .

"Actually, I had intended to go directly by my office after the ceremony, then on to the pub from there, but ended up following you in, so . . ."

"So, you're saying you went from pub to office, then? At three in the morning? You haven't slept?"

"I wasn't going to anyway."

She was too busy glancing over him to consider why that was. He was freshly shaved, his thick thatch of brown hair looked as if it had seen a comb or brush recently, and he most certainly was no longer wearing his formal clan colors. He wasn't in a suit, but his trousers were crisply pressed as was the starched collar of his buttoned blue and white striped shirt. Ever the natty solicitor, even in somewhat casual togs.

He met her gaze squarely. "I keep a change of clothes at the office," he explained, before she could ask.

Kira happened to know, as did everyone, that Shay's offices on Kinloch were on the floor above Roan's, in a small three-story stone building perched at the north edge of Aiobhneas, the only established village on the small island. She imagined his offices in Edinburgh were far more posh—they would almost have to be—but it wouldn't surprise her to think that he had amenities such as a shower in his office here. He wasn't a prig by any stretch, but Kira couldn't exactly imagine him in worn dungarees, muddy Wellies, and disheveled hair, either, which was fairly standard for most hardy souls who made their living in the Outer Hebrides.

"Well then," she said, feeling even more the ratty wretch now that she'd taken in all of his glory.

Shay stood for another moment, then nodded again. "I'll be on my way. I'll see you Thursday."

Again, he was almost at the end of the stone walkway, leaving her clear to close the door . . . but no. An apparent glutton for punishment, she blurted, "Can I ask you something?"

He paused again, waited a beat, then turned to look at her once more. Again, eye contact was direct, as it had been during their roadside interlude. And if he found anything about her appearance offputting, it certainly wasn't conveyed in the way he kept his focus utterly riveted on her. "Aye," he said, at length. "Anything."

Kira felt somehow . . . pinned, by his direct gaze. Right there, in her own doorway. "I made something of a fool of myself yesterday. After the ceremony, I mean, by the roadside."

"It was a day of celebration," he said. "You were happy for your best mate. It was normal to be excited."

"That's very gentlemanly of you," she said, a surprising smile working its way to the corners of her mouth. "You're being quite gentlemanly now, too."

"Other than the early hour of my unannounced visit, you mean," he said. His expression remained smooth, but there was something else there now . . . hovering about the corners of his mouth.

Her smile became more of an actual curve of the lips. "Was that dry humor, coming from you, Mr. Callaghan?"

"I believe it might have been, Miss MacLeod," he said, and she spied the smallest hint of a quirk at the corner of his mouth.

Her heart might have stuttered a bit at that, but what made it skip a full beat entirely was when she spied the hint of a dimple the slight twitch etched into his cheek. She knew his every expression— not that she'd been studying him while in town, not at all, she just . . . knew them—and couldn't say as she'd ever once seen that before. It wasn't as if Shay Callaghan was a dour man, not by any means. But he wasn't one for loud laughter or back-slapping good humor. In fact, come to think of it, he didn't seem to smile much, but neither did he ever frown. He was always just . . . smooth, steady-as-you-go. Solid. Sturdy. Someone who could always be counted on to be the calm head, the pillar of strength.

Maybe that was why she was so drawn to him. He was loyal and steadfast and true. The very things she'd thought she'd had in a husband. All of which, in the end, turned out to be fiction.

But now there was this glimmer of humor, and a dimple, for God's sake . . . and it did crazy things to her insides. Like he didn't already do that just by, well, by being him.

"What was it you wished to ask me?"

He'd taken her off her guard now, making it easier to go forward with her question. After all, she hardly had anything to lose at this point. "Nothing important, just . . . you seem like a very direct man, as you were with me after the ceremony yesterday. As you are right now."

"Aye, I believe I am."

"So . . . how do you explain why you went so far out of your way during the reception celebration to avoid so much as looking in my direction? Was it something I said or did? Or is it that you can only hold my gaze out of the public eye?"

She thought he might find some polite way of sidestepping her question, or pretending not to understand her meaning.

He did neither of those things. Instead, he walked back toward her, which made her heart skip again, then start beating in double time. He stopped just in front of the porch step. And he had no trouble holding her gaze now. "It was something you said, aye, but no' in the way ye mean. It wasna a bad thing. It was . . . the opposite of that."

Her brows knitted together. "What do you mean, then? If what I said was a good thing, then why avoid me? I had—I had hoped we'd have the chance to dance together." There. She'd said it. Put it right out there. Bad-ass non-hider, that's what she was. Tessa would be ever so proud.

She thought she might throw up. Her stomach was in complete riot as she waited what felt like an eternity for his response.

"And that is precisely why I avoided ye."

She pressed a palm over the stab to her heart. "I see."

"No," he said. "I dinnae believe ye do." He stepped up on the porch then, and came quite close. So very close, in fact, that she had to grip the edge of the door to keep from stepping backward.

If her heart had been beating quickly before, it was in full gallop now.

His gaze searched hers and she felt . . . absorbed into the brilliant depths of it. If she'd thought they'd shared a moment yesterday, it didn't come close to competing with the moment they were having right now.

"You were the brightest light yesterday," he said, as serious as if he were standing in front of a judge. "Your eyes shining, your smile so merry. I confess I was blinded by it. By you. And I have been for quite some time now."

Her mouth dropped open, then snapped shut. Had he truly just said that? Or was she dreaming again? "What are ye say—?"

He placed a finger to her lips, and the merest brush of that warm skin to such a sensitive part of her about sent her straight to the floor in a pool of want.

"When you followed me to my car . . . I . . . wasn't prepared for that. Then you looked me straight in the eye and declared that you needed me, and my thoughts being where they were, regarding you—"

"I—"

He pressed his finger more firmly, and her heart wobbled along with her knees. There was such intensity in his gaze, as if he were willing her to understand him, to truly hear what he was saying. As if he wasn't doing a fine job already of finding the words.

"I wasn't prepared for my reaction to that. To you. Now that you're . . . free."

She covered his hand and pulled his finger

away, but didn't let go. "I've been free since I came back to this island nigh on two years ago."

"You were the subject of interest of my closest and dearest friend."

"What? Oh, you mean Roan? Aye, but he was ne'er going to do anything about it. We're simply friends. That's all we were ever meant to be."

"Aye, but that's no' something he realized until he met Tessa. And friends—"

"Don't poach," she finished. She started to let go of his hand, but he curled his fingers around hers and kept them, joined, just below her chin. "So," she said, shaky now, "why not follow up at the reception? What better place to make your wishes known than by asking me to dance?"

"At a wedding reception, with the entire village watching, romance and happily ever after brimming in the air? No. I wouldn't have done that."

She frowned. "I'm afraid I don't understand. Why?"

"It's no' happily ever after I'm searching for. It doesna exist. No' for me."

"Do you really belie—"

"Kira," he said, and the wobble was now accompanied by the most delicious shiver at the sound of her name on his lips. "It doesna exist for me. And seeing you after the ceremony, so flushed with happiness, I realized that it will exist for you. Just no' with me. And so . . ."

"You avoided me."

"I did. It seemed the right thing to do. The only thing. As it turned out, you weren't at a loss for partners, which isn't surprising in the least, and I do apologize if I seemed rude, but it seemed enough that I was leaving you to your entertainment, I didn't need to watch you enjoying it."

So, he was saying he'd been . . . jealous? Really? It shouldn't have made her feel that good. But, after the night she'd put in and how utterly rejected he'd made her feel . . . she might have reveled a wee bit at his confession. "But you're no' avoiding me this morning. Or have you regrouped now and we're back to strictly business?" She honestly had no idea how she was conducting such a civil, rational conversation when her hormones were rioting and her entire body felt as if it were about to explode from overstimulation. It was simply too much to take in, all at once.

"That's what I told myself when I turned in to your cottage, aye."

She held his gaze, his confession giving her the strength and confidence to do it. "And now? Because this doesn't feel like business. Strictly."

"And now the desire to kiss ye is stronger than I ever believed possible."

She trembled at that. "But?"

"But nothing. It's the truth."

She held his gaze for what felt like the longest time . . . then took the next step. "So, then, why are ye still standing there, Shay Callaghan?"

Chapter Four

Shay thought his heart might drum clear through the wall of his chest. How had this moment come to pass? It had not been his plan. He always had a plan. He could barely hear, much less think, with all that thrumming reverberating in his ears. And his body surging to full, rigid attention wasn't helping rational thought, either.

"Because I've nothing else to offer ye," he managed, throat tight, body even tighter.

"I don't believe I asked for anything else."

"No," he agreed. "Ye didn't. But surely, ye want—"

"What I want," she said, surprising him then by leaning still closer, "is to feel your mouth on mine. It's what I've wanted for quite some time now," she added, echoing his own words.

He swallowed. Hard. "Have ye now?" Contradicting bolts of bone-jarring terror and raw, swamping lust blasted clear through him, making it impossible to determine what was the right path to take, the right step. He knew what he wanted, but what a man wanted in the moment, especially one as heated as this, was often not what he needed in the long run. Or what was good for either of them.

"Aye," she said, her voice dropping to barely more than a whisper.

Then, any hope he might have had of reclaiming his place as a gentleman, putting what was best before what was desired, fled when her gaze dropped to his mouth.

" 'Tis," she breathed.

Damn Graham and his bloody predictions, but Shay was well lost to it now. He slid his free hand to the back of her neck and had the sweet taste of her on his lips, invading his every cell and pore, a mere breath later. Och, but she was like the finest of champagnes, sipped in front of the coziest of fires. Bubbly and sweet, yet warm and inviting. She was the embodiment of his wildest fantasy come true . . . yet somehow all grounded in the warmth and comfort of home and hearth. She drove him to want to take her, right there, up against the wall, like a rutting, wild beast . . . while simultaneously wanting to cradle her in softness, sip from her, and take her as slowly and thoroughly as it was possible for a man to take a woman, to show her everything that was or could be inside him.

And he thought he could stand right there and kiss her lush, sweet mouth until the end of time . . . then die a happy man. It was a single moment of pure contentment the likes of which he'd never once experienced before, and would have sworn, in court, under oath, was beyond him to ever feel.

Only now . . . he had. Now, he knew.

He felt her gasp, heard her little moan as her lips softened beneath his. She released his hand and slid both of hers to his shoulders, then up the back of his neck and into his hair. Her touch made him feel as if he'd suddenly been plugged into an outlet that sent surges of electric sensation charging over and through him. He'd certainly been touched by a woman before, far more intimately, and quite pleasurably, in fact. So what was it about this simple act, drawing her short nails across his scalp as she urged his mouth more tightly onto hers, that was so overwhelmingly intoxicating . . . he couldn't rightly have said.

Lost entirely now, he let himself sink into the moment, allowed himself a release of control—well, he hadn't allowed it so much as he hadn't seemed to have much choice in the matter. That alone should have him staggering back, pushing her away, until he could figure out what, exactly, was going on here. He'd never once been the sort to knock on a woman's door and an instant later have her in his arms, her mouth under siege by his own, consumed with such ardent passion that he couldn't stop himself. He didn't like not being in control, or shouldn't have. But there was not a single damn thing not to like about how he felt in that moment, nor any clear argument that could be made for not having himself more of it.

She made the most delectable whimper when he wove his fingers through the thick fall of her hair and tugged her mouth more tightly against his, and he felt himself tremble in response. Never had he been so in tune with a woman's every breath and gasp. She dug her short nails into his scalp now even as her whimpers turned to soft moans. He groaned himself, and took the kiss deeper still. Then she teased his tongue with her own and what fragile hold he did have left on his crumbling control shattered completely.

With a sound more growl than groan, he pulled her tightly against him, taking her tongue, dueling, as he backed them both through her front door, catching it with his foot and slamming it behind them, stopping only when her back came up against the nearest wall. The jarring, abrupt stop did nothing to abate their connection.

"We shouldn't, Kira," he managed, in a desperate last attempt, as he slid away from the sweet, intoxicating depths of her mouth and laid a trail of hungry kisses along her jaw instead, incapable, in that moment, of ending contact entirely. He continued his heated journey, pausing at the soft spot below her ear. "I'm no' the man for you. I know this, even if you do no'."

"I believe that's for me to decide," she said, tipping her head forward against his shoulder, allowing him to nudge her hair aside and continue his sweet assault along the silky smooth trail to the nape of her neck. "Who says I'm looking for anything more than this?" she managed, between ragged breaths.

"You should. It's what you deserve."

"I might think I deserve a lot of things. We all

do," she said, groaning as he nipped at the soft skin at her nape. "Doesn't mean we get them."

He forced himself to lift his head, break free of the taste of her, only long enough to nudge her head back so he could look into her now glittering eyes. "Maybe you should hold out for that."

"Maybe holding out only means you get nothing. Maybe this is better than nothing."

Her words weren't intended to hurt, to pinch at his heart, he knew that. She was talking about life, in general. And, after all, hadn't he just gotten done telling her he wasn't worth her wait? Yet, the pinch was there, all the same.

"This is better than anything I've had, and I've barely tasted you," he said, hearing the tremor in his voice, and helpless to do anything to smooth it out. In truth, it did terrify him, this utter loss of control, as well it should, and yet he was in the grip of her, and a certain degree of helplessness seemed to come with the territory. It was territory he wasn't willing—or able—to relinquish. Not quite yet. "If I thought I was a man who could promise you eternity, I'd pursue you to the ends of the earth, and do whatever it took to prove myself to you."

He couldn't believe the words spouting from his mouth, so overwrought, so insanely over the top. And yet no words had ever felt truer coming off his tongue, no closing speech in front of a judge more heartfelt. He couldn't rationalize them, but neither could he deny them.

And, hearing his enamored pledge, she wasn't twisting out of his arms, looking at him as one

should at a madman, professing himself like that
to a woman who, in truth, he barely knew.

And yet, he did know her. It felt, inexplicably, as
if he'd always known her. Now he knew the taste of
her, but it seemed like just another element in the
long list of what he already knew. And, having her
in his arms . . . well, it felt as if she were occupying
the exact right spot.

She steadied her breath then, or tried to, and
slid her hands from his hair, until her palms caressed his cheeks. He wanted to rub against them
like a cat soaking up the warmth of the sun. In
fact, he craved the feel of her skin against his, and
would gladly rip off every last stitch of their clothing if given the least bit of provocation. With his
teeth, if need be.

He'd never thought himself a particularly primal man. He had his needs, his wants, his desires,
but he'd never been less than fully in control, even
in the most tremulous moment of release. He realized then it was because he'd always only been ex-
periencing his own sensations, careful, of course,
to be considerate of his partner's needs. But the
connection had ended there, a fact he found entirely normal. What more could a man experience
than his own sensations, after all?

But this . . . the strength of all that he was feeling was intertwined with her in a way that couldn't
be separated into his experience here, and her experience there. He couldn't even find words to describe the way it all wove together. She made him
lust, she made him want, she made him feel . . . car-
nal. He craved. It shouldn't feel healthy, it shouldn't

feel . . . normal. And yet it made him want to shout, to howl . . . roar. And to claim.

Like an out of body—hell, out of mind—experience, it made no sense, and yet, this felt like the first time that everything made sense. An utter sort of clarity he'd never known before.

She was indeed The One. His heart knew it. His soul knew it. Every last cell that formed him knew it.

All he had to do . . . was accept it.

And that was where the obstacle loomed, enormous and all-imposing, beyond his powers to scale and conquer.

"I don't know that any of us gets eternity," she said, her voice a little rough, but her gaze steady on his.

He tried to calm his own ragged breath, pull his thoughts from their primal, chaotic swirl, and organize them into something rational, or at least sensible.

"And you have nothing to prove to me," she said. "I know who you are, Shay."

And he understood her meaning. That knowing had little to do with sharing thoughts and dreams, and revealing every quirk and foible that made them who they were, in the day-to-day realm.

She *knew* him.

"And that's all I need," she said.

"But is that all ye want?"

"Doesna matter. It cannot. No' really."

"It should."

"You could be struck by lightning the moment you leave this cottage. Should I not take what you're offering, because it might be the only thing we share? Life isn't fair, Shay. I know that better than anyone. As do you. So maybe we're better advised to take what we can get, and find a way to be satisfied with that, happy with that, revel in it, for God's sake. Because it sure as hell beats standing on the sidelines . . . or hiding out in a secluded cottage."

"Does it, then? What of the hurt to come, the disappointment, the . . . loss when you've allowed yourself such great wants, only to see them go unfulfilled? It's no' the end that comes at the hand of fate that concerns me. 'Tis sad, heartbreaking, but though life may have come to an end, that love endures. It's the end by choice I'm speaking of. The promises broken, the dreams and faith abandoned. There's such cruelty in it, even if no' intended, and it comes at the hand of choice, no' fate, which makes it that much harder to bear. I don't want anyone to make that choice against me . . . but more important, I never want to be in a place where I need to make that same cruel choice."

"Aye, that does happen, and aye, 'tis cruel, no doubt. But what of it? It's a terrible dark time, that's for certain . . . but it won't kill you, either. I'm testimony to that, aren't I?"

Now he framed her face with his palms. "And how is it you've been through it, to the hell and back of it . . . and yet you're willing to risk that journey again?"

"Because I've also been to the heaven of it. And it's worth it, Shay. Even if you only have it for a time. It's worth it. The pure and utter joy of loving and being loved . . . 'tis a thing to be cherished.

Squandering such a rare offering because ye're wary it might be snatched away seems a sad waste, doesn't it?"

"You've a rare strength, Kira, and you're surely braver than me. I dinnae think I could stand myself if I were the cause of inflicting pain on you."

She surprised him by smiling, and it was so direct, so surely given, she amazed him. "You'd never hurt with intent. And I believe I've been fairly warned. So I've only myself to blame, then, haven't I, if I'm no' to have the happy ending?" She drew her fingers along his cheek, and then feathered them across his lips.

He shook a bit harder under her delicate, yet sure touch, as if the ground was about to vibrate the floor right out from under them. "So that is what ye want, then, after all. The happy ending."

"Well, I'm not cut out, or able to close off parts of myself to enjoy dallying for the sake of dallying."

"What of the take-what-you-can-get philosophy, and be happy with it?"

"Oh, I meant that," she said, easily, "because I havena any other choice. It has to begin somewhere." She smiled into his eyes, so easily, so fully, but there was a trembling in her hands now, too. "That doesna mean I don't have my hopes that I'll end up with more. I wouldn't involve myself otherwise."

"And if yer hopes are dashed?"

"Then I hurt . . . and I heal. But 'tis no' only about me, this, is it? What of your pain, Shay, what of your disappointment? What if I'm the one who can't see it through? Why are you so certain I'm the one who'll be hurt?"

"That's just it, I dinnae think there is any way to escape unscathed, on either side. I see the ravages of it, every day. Even those who don't mean to hurt the one they loved, do it anyway. A person can't help feeling . . . and then losing that feeling, even if it breaks the heart of someone they otherwise cherish." He saw the flicker of knowing, of remembered pain, flash quickly over her face, and felt horrible for bringing her own past to mind.

But the expression went as swiftly as it came, and her voice was as sure as it had been before when she said, "It's a risk, aye, the hope that both parties will forever want the same things, want each other. But you're forgetting . . . not everyone wants to escape. You're surrounded by great evidence of that, an island full of them, in fact."

"Aye, I know, but—"

"I dinnae know how you do wha' ye do, Shay. I truly don't. And I clearly see how it would take a toll on you or any man, to be such an intimate part of other people's pain, day in and day out. I question, though, why inflict it on yourself? Why do it? It clearly takes a toll on you. So much so, it's informed your life choices, made you cut yourself off from what I think it is you might really want." She tightened her hold on his face, making him aware all over again of the intimacy their bodies shared. "I know it was your father's work, but it doesnae have to be yours, does it? And this isn't a judgment of your father, but I think maybe ye need a colder, or perhaps a more singularly practical heart for that kind of work."

"What makes you think I'm no' cold and practical?"

"This," she said, simply, and leaned in and kissed him.

He realized then that he honestly had no choice in the matter at all. She was here. So suddenly now in his arms, in his life. He'd taken the critical step . . . and there was no turning back. No pretending he hadn't done this, tasted her . . . and finally wanted what he'd never allowed himself to want.

She kissed him . . . and he took her. Laid claim. A full out siege, in fact. She teased him, just once, with the tip of her tongue, and he hungrily pulled it into his mouth, suckling on her, taking her inside him the way he wanted to be taken inside of her.

Her gasps quickly turned to moans and she writhed against him, arching away from the wall, thrusting her hips forward. He pressed her back to the wall, sliding his hands behind her thighs and urging her legs around his waist.

No more thinking, only acting. Only taking. Stepping farther down the path . . . whether to his salvation or his destruction, it no longer mattered. It was a journey already undertaken. Retreating now wouldn't change anything.

She dug her heels into his buttocks, finally able to press herself directly against the hard, rigid length of him, her thin nightgown only molding her more perfectly to him. His thighs shook under the restraint of not driving himself forward between her thighs. His hands shook as well as he slid them up her waist until he could cup her breasts.

She cried out against his mouth, her hips moving rhythmically against him now as he filled his palms with the soft weight of her breasts, rubbing, gently rolling her tightly budded nipples between his fingers. He was moving his hips, too, no longer able to control it, not entirely sure he was going to be able to stop, or contain himself, as his body was already begging for release.

She was pulling at his shirt, trying to tug it from the waistband of his belted trousers. And when she finally managed it and tugged open buttons, pulling up the white cotton undershirt he wore beneath it, and her hands finally touched his hot flesh . . . what restraint was left, snapped.

He slid her farther up the wall and broke free of her mouth, only so he could close lips wet from hers over first one rigid nipple, then another. She cried out again, twisting against him, her hands knotting in his hair, pressing him closer, urging him to take more.

Her thin nightgown tore easily under his teeth when he yanked. She didn't even flinch. Her thighs merely tightened against him and she groaned, from somewhere deep in her throat . . . a sound as primal as the way he felt.

Her nipples were perfect rosebuds of dark pink against pale, soft skin, and the taste of them, the feel as he drew the tip of his tongue over them, making her shudder and twitch, was the sweetest thing he'd ever known.

He wanted all that pale, creamy skin bared to him, wanted to run his tongue over every inch, every freckle, every dimple and curve. With only that goal in mind, he ordered, "Hold on," and slid his arms around her, holding her to him as he blindly moved into her cottage, thinking he only needed a surface big enough for them to lie on.

"The door, there," she panted.

The hot thrill of knowing they were of the same mind, without question or pretense, made his need for her that much fiercer.

He took in absolutely nothing of her surroundings, other than the shadow of a bed in the dim lighting of the curtained room.

"It's a bit lumpy, I'm afraid—" she began, but he cut her off with his mouth on hers, as he propped one knee on the mattress, then lowered them both down upon it.

He made quick work of her nightgown and robe as her hands moved frantically over him, pulling off his shirt, tugging the undershirt over his head. He shucked trousers and boots in short order. But, once naked, rather than the growling, animalistic coupling he'd imagined, she instead pushed him to his back, startling him into a moment of inaction.

Her cheeks were most beautifully flushed and her hair was mussed and wild, the way it would be when a man's hands had been in it. Her man's hands. His hands. Another primal thrill shot through him and he wondered what in the hell he'd become. But it was her smile that caught at him, as it always did.

"What is it?" he asked, when she didn't immediately speak. "Oh," he said, as it occurred to him why any woman would halt a man about to do . . . what he'd so clearly been about to do, "if it's about protection—"

She laughed then, a short little lilt, but rather than make him feel dundering for the awkward mention, he found himself smiling along with her.

"I've no doubt you're always well prepared, Mr. Solicitor. For anything," she teased, still breathing quite unevenly, hair wild about her flushed face.

I wasn't prepared for you, he thought.

"But, ye needn't worry on that score," she assured him. "I'm already protected."

"Are ye now?"

She lifted an eyebrow at that, but she didn't look insulted. In fact, she laughed again. "Why, Mr. Callaghan, could it be you're a wee bit put out at the notion that I might have felt the need for protection, when I haven't been with the likes of you as yet?"

"Well, no . . . of course no', you're a grown woman, free to do as ye like, I didnae mean—"

"It's okay," she interrupted him. "I rather like it that I stir up your possessive instincts."

"Ye've stirred me up, all right, but I've never—"

"Shay," she said, her voice softer, her gaze as steady as her smile. "Would it make ye feel any better to know that I'm no' happy to know you're carrying protection about when ye haven't been with the likes of me as yet, either?"

He might have smiled at that. A wee curve of the lips, anyway. "So, what is this all about then? Why did you stop me?"

She brushed at the hair on his forehead, then traced a finger over his lips again. "On the off chance this really is the most beautiful dream I've had of you yet, and I simply haven't woken up from it, or that you'll do as you threaten to do, and take off for the hills once we've . . . done what we can do, I thought I'd rather like to slow all this down. Savor all the . . . bits. And the pieces." She slid down a little lower then and pressed a kiss to the center of his chest, glancing up to meet his gaze with a particularly wicked twinkle to her eyes that he wouldn't have thought her capable of.

It was a discovery he didn't mind making in the least.

"And, what of my, erm, bits and pieces?" he asked, wanting to be playful for her, with her . . . but not entirely sure how. His hunger was still an almost savage, commanding thing. It was all he could do to lie still.

"I don't know," she said, then pressed another kiss, then yet another, until she was close enough to surprise him with a quick, soft nip of her lips over his nipple.

The little sizzle of pleasure that gave him was a distinct surprise, but before he could say, or do, anything about it, she began a trail of soft little kisses along the narrow line of hair that arrowed down the center of his abdomen, and murmured, "But I daresay I plan to find out."

"Kira, ye dinnae have to—oh . . . God . . . almighty . . ." The words trickled off to a long, strangled growl, right before he slammed his head back against the mattress, and closed his eyes. Her tongue, brushing the very tip of him . . . "Och, luv, but I dinnae think I—I canno'—"

And, oh, aye, though he was quite wanting to let her, he gritted his teeth and resisted the need to simply let go. "This is no' how I plan for things to go." He reached down for her, pulling her up, then rolling her under him. "No' this time."

"This time?" she queried, smiling merrily up at him.

"Aye," he said, certain, at least, of that much. "This time."

And, with that, he laid claim to her mouth again, glorying in teasing, tasting, dueling tongue to tongue. It was both urgent and languid. He kissed her with absolute intent . . . and yet felt he had all the time in the world to get there.

He splayed his fingers into her hair, raking through the silky strands as they continued to kiss, ardently, thoroughly, as if that mating alone was their only goal. And though their bodies were in full contact, and he wanted desperately to slide inside her . . . at the moment, he found the longer they took, just kissing, the more intimate he felt with her, the more he felt he began to know her, feel what made her arch against him, what made her gasp, what made her growl . . . what made her soften, and what made her turn aggressor.

And by the time she wrapped her legs around

his hips and lifted herself to him, it was as if a lifetime had passed, unspoken between them. He pushed into her, slowly, deeply, and she took him, oh so fully and completely, but it was her gaze on his that told him she was taking far more into her body than just his own. She wove her fingers into his hair, and turned his mouth back to hers . . . and never once, in his entire life, had he had such a pure sense of what it was to finally come home.

Chapter Five

This time, when he opened his eyes, it was to find the late afternoon sun spearing gold daggers of light through the slit in the bedroom curtains.

They'd dozed after that first time, partly he thought from their exertions, but mostly because both were sleep deprived. She'd fed him a late breakfast of bangers and mash, and it had felt remarkably normal and not even the least bit awkward, sitting in her tiny kitchen in nothing more than his trousers, watching her fuss at the stove wearing nothing more than his striped shirt. As if his entire life hadn't just taken a very abrupt, utterly fantastical turn. They'd talked of nothing important, more interested in feeding themselves and each other. Then he'd taken her to the shower . . . and taken her there, as well.

Damp and a bit giddy with such saturation of pleasure, they'd tumbled straight back into her bed, and taken a very long, languorous time exploring each other ... and he'd learned exactly how it would feel to let her finish what she'd begun that first time.

In fact, he was thinking now that it was certainly only fair that he return the favor, when he felt her stir next to him. He tipped his chin down to find her looking up at him, that same, steady smile on her face, and in her eyes. And that's when it struck him, what it was about her that made him feel so distinctly at ease, so ... at home. She looked at him with complete faith and trust, that he'd be exactly what she thought he would be. And rather than make him want to run for the hills, as she'd said earlier ... her trust made him very much want to be that man.

Because she had an ability to love that he absolutely did not question. A man would be the luckiest on earth to have all of that given to him, and so freely, without artifice or guile.

The only thing he questioned was being able to give her all of those things in return. Because it would be the worst kind of travesty if he took from her, and could not equally give.

Her smile grew, and he sincerely doubted it was because she could read his thoughts. "What's amusing?" he said, feeling as if he had sandpaper for a voice.

"I was just thinking that last night I fully believed you didnae want me. Wouldn't even dance with me. Wouldna even look at me."

He pulled her to his side and half under him again. He buried his face in her neck and nipped the lobe of her ear. He'd become someone en-

tirely different with her. There was nothing refined about any part of him now. Nothing held
back, nothing reserved. "I want nothing so much
as I want you," he said, his thoughts still lingering
where they'd been a moment ago.

She shivered then, and he reveled in her instinctive response. It made him want to pull her
closer still, into the protection of his body. The
feelings coursing through him grew more primal,
the more time he spent with her. In fact, in that
moment, he'd have taken down with his bare
hands anyone who dared to harm her or threaten
to take her from him.

It was complete insanity, the intensity of his feelings, this drive to want, to have, to possess.

And yet, he didn't wish to escape the asylum.

He lifted his head to look down into her eyes,
questioning everything he thought he wanted from
love . . . quite well aware that all that had changed.

"I want nothing more than I want you, Shay
Callaghan," she said, stroking his cheek.

He was sure that the depth of his rioting needs
was reflected in his eyes. And yet, she looked into
them, unflinching, baring those same needs and
desires to him.

"How have we come to this place?" he asked her,
quite sincerely. "I've only just made it known I fancied you. It's been less than a single day that I've
known your thoughts ran on similar lines. Had I
pursued it, I'd have thought of dinner, perhaps. A
drive. Maybe taking the ferry over to Castlebay. I'd
have courted you, and hoped for . . ."

"This?"

He shook his head.

She frowned, just briefly. "No?"

"I don't know that I could have ever hoped for anything like this. I didn't know this existed. No' for me."

She smiled then. "And now?" She pushed his hair from where it fell in heavy hanks across his forehead, the gesture an absent one, as if she'd been doing it out of long practice.

"And now it's like this."

"Like what?"

He propped his weight on one elbow and captured her hand as she was about to smooth the hair on his neck. "This."

"I don't get your meaning."

"You opened your door to me mere hours ago, knowing me, but no' truly knowing me. And for me, the same. Now, hours later, it's as if we've spent many days, months, years perhaps, in just this way. There's an ease and comfort with you, Kira, that . . ."

"Is that a bad thing?"

"No, it's a magical thing."

"But?"

He pulled her hand around and kissed her knuckles, then opened her hand and pressed a long kiss to her palm, before curling her fingers closed over it. "How long is it possible to believe in magic?"

"As long as you want to believe," she said, without hesitation.

When he said nothing, she added, "It's rather like my grandmamma used to tell me when I found, just before leaving for boarding school, that St. Nicholas didn't truly exist. I was crushed.

I'd always quite fancied the idea of him, the promise that someone was watching over me, caring that I behaved well, and would reward me with a twinkle in his sage, wise eyes. She told me that if I didn't believe in him, then he'd surely never pay me another visit. But as long as I believed, the possibilities were endless."

"And did St. Nick keep up his annual visits?"

She nudged at him. "That wasn't the point. She was just telling me that a closed mind is like a closed door. Good things can't enter through a door that's firmly shut. But an open door is a welcome portal."

"It's also an undefended one. Anything—or anyone—can stroll in, and not always with the best intentions."

"True. But a closed door is rather like creating a jail, with you the willing prisoner. No one can get at you, but the solitude makes for poor company after a time, I would think."

"There's always visitation," he said, in an effort to lighten the suddenly somber mood. For which he only had himself to blame.

He earned another nudge for that, but her smile broadened to a grin. "Aye, something else ye can control. Who ye let in. And how long they'll stay."

He rolled to his side then and carried her with him, so she was half sprawled across his chest, her face just above his. Now he toyed with her hair. "And how long would you wish to stay?"

"As long as you'd have me by your side," she said, just like that, without hesitation.

His heart bumped hard in his chest. He wanted, like mad, to believe it could be true. He had no doubt she meant it. In that moment. "Even after all I've revealed to ye?" he asked.

"Aye." She nodded.

"Why?"

"Because of this," she said, and he knew she was referencing the same thing he had a moment ago. She smiled again. "This may come as a shock to ye, but I've never once dragged a man into my cottage and had my way with him."

"No?" he said, and wished like hell his heart would slow down, just enough so that he could get it back under control. "Not even auld Dougal, then?" he said, who, at ninety-seven, was the oldest, and quite possibly the most toothless, of the McAuley clan.

She barked a laugh. "Well, only because he hasn't come 'round, of course."

"Of course."

She laughed at his deadpan delivery and it delighted him that she understood and appreciated his understated form of humor.

"In the meantime, I have you."

"A puir substitute to be sure."

She sighed, but smiled into his eyes as she leaned down to kiss him, lingeringly. "What is it I'll have to do," she said as she lifted her head, "to ease your worries?"

"I dinnae think it's about words being spoken, Kira. I dinnae doubt that you mean what you say, any more than I question the strength of the want I have for you. What's between us doesn't have to follow logic to exist. If we both believe it does, then it does." His lips quirked a little. "You see, I do have a wee bit of a crack in my door."

"So ye do at that." She smiled into his eyes again. "Where does that leave us then?"

"We give it time, do with each other what we both wish to do. There's no' much else to do, is there?"

"So, you're no' running then."

"I couldna, nor do I want to."

"And what of the pain and disappointment you're so sure is to come?"

"Well, there's no avoiding that now, is there?"

Her eyes widened and she pushed herself up on his chest. "Really, then? Well, perhaps we should just say our parting words now, Mr. Gloom and Doom."

He tugged her back down. "That's no' what I meant."

She settled on his chest, but for the first time he saw wariness in her eyes. And despite his knowing that a bit of wariness would be a wise thing for her to adopt if she was going to tangle herself up with him, that didn't set well at all with him, as it turned out. Not well at all.

"Go on," she said, "explain yourself."

"All I meant," he said, cupping the back of her head, "was that I'm already well and truly tangled. So if bad is going to happen, there's already no avoiding the hurt and disappointment. Stopping now won't change it."

"Then all we need to do is make sure we stay tangled," she said, trying to tease, despite the thread of wariness still there.

"Aye," he said. "'Tis simple as that."

She gave him a gauging look. "There's nothing simple about it. Though, to me, it's joyful work. However," she said, "if you're already convinced it canno' survive the tests that time will surely deliver, then you'll most certainly fulfill that prophecy."

"I know that, too."

She smiled now, but it was more rueful this time. "So, I should jump off the ship now, then, is what you're saying. While the waters are still relatively shallow and the shoreline close."

"In the end, it would likely be the easier course, aye."

"Do you want me to jump, make it easier for you to steer back to the deep waters alone?"

"I want you right where I have you."

"Even with no guarantee that I'll stay there? No life preservers, if you will?"

"Even then."

"Then I only ask one thing."

"Which is?"

"No more maudlin talk of how we're all doomed to fail in our commitments to one another. You might see it play out at court, over and over, but when you come to me, I want you to see me for who I am . . . not who you fear I might turn into. And, perhaps more challenging still, but equally important, I want you to be the man you want to be with me, the man you've been today. No' waste what time we give ourselves worrying about the man you fear you'll turn into."

He looked into her eyes, so steady. So true. "You're right," he said, at length. "No more maudlin talk." He rolled her under him and kissed her, and when she tried to talk, he kissed her some more. "I'm being the man I want to be with you," he murmured, trailing kisses along her jaw, then down to her collarbone, then, as he slid his body down, between her breasts, lingering on first one nipple, then the other. "And what this man wants, is to taste you." He slid down farther still, and was exactly that man.

And when she arched beneath his tongue and hands, when he felt her build toward yet another shuddering climax, fully reveling in the joy of knowing he was the one delivering her so much pleasure . . . he hoped she'd overlook the fact that he hadn't exactly agreed to her other demands.

He prayed like hell that by the time she brought it up again . . . he'd know if he could make her that promise.

Chapter Six

"I appreciate your meeting with me," Kira said as she stepped into the office that Graham kept in town. He mostly worked in the labs he'd crudely constructed in the crumbling clan castle, *Flaithbheartach,* though he could even more often be found in the flax fields. The office in town was for clan business, and located just a block or two down from the building that housed both Roan's and Shay's offices.

"Shay said you needed to discuss a business proposition that would impact the island economy?"

She nodded and took a seat across from the broad expanse of black slate that was the surface of his desk. Graham, himself, as brawny as he was tall, was even more imposing than the massive antique. Had she not already known he was more keen scientist than scowling patriarch, she might have felt nervous about her proposal. But she also knew him to be a fair leader who truly wanted what was best for the citizenry of Kinloch.

"How much has Shay told you? Did Roan speak to you of it before the wedding?"

Now Graham's eyebrows knitted in a mild frown. "No. Should he have? What is this that everyone is already in deep discussion about it? I didn't think it was possible to keep a secret on this island."

"Oh, it's no' a secret. Just an idea that Roan and Tessa had and brought to me, thinking I'd be the perfect one to champion it. And I only brought it to Shay to see if it was legally feasible before discussing it with you."

"I see." He sat back in his equally overlarge office chair. The leather was so worn it had cracked through around the edges. Kira knew that despite his lofty station on the island, no one had less pretension about him than Graham. In fact, she'd be surprised if he'd even noticed the deteriorating condition of the antiquities that surrounded him.

He didn't say anything further, but continued his steady regard for another minute.

"So . . . would you like to hear the proposal?"

He nodded. "I would. But, if I may, could I ask you something of an entirely personal nature first? And please know, you're more than welcome to tell me to bugger off and I assure you it won't impact my decision-making on your project, but—"

"Yes, Shay and I are involved. With each other. I hope we'll have your support. And Katie's."

His eyes widened in obvious surprise at her bluntness. But he didn't correct her assumption that that had been the question he'd been about to ask.

"Our involvement has nothing to do with the business at hand, though, if that's your concern."

"My concern isn't that, or Shay. Well, that is to say, my concern at the moment isn't Shay."

Meaning he was concerned about her. Now it was her turn to widen her eyes. She'd spent the first nine years of her childhood growing up with Graham on Kinloch and had certainly been sociable to him upon her return, so there was the comfort of a long, if general, association. But they'd never been the kind of acquaintances who shared personal details with each other. In fact, she was closer to having that kind of friendship with Graham's very outgoing wife, Katie. And she'd only been on the island a few months. "If your concern is for me, I can assure you, I'm fine." There was a bit of mortification in her response. Other than Tessa, she'd never openly talked about her reasons for coming back to Kinloch with anyone, but she was absolutely certain every last soul knew the circumstances behind the move, if not the more intimate details.

She'd spent a goodly part of the time since her return, holed up in her grandmother's cottage. Weaving mostly, or at least that's what it had become when brooding and feeling sorry for herself had ceased to provide any actual comfort. She'd interacted professionally with Roan while marketing her baskets, as that was his job, and she'd made certain to smile and nod at everyone when she had to come into the village to buy food or supplies. But, otherwise, she'd kept to herself. And she realized, on an island this small, people had their opinions about why a thirty-one-year-old woman would, for all intents and purposes, become a hermit. It couldn't have been seen as healthy.

And now Graham seemed concerned that his friend had hooked himself up with a woman of questionable mental stability. She'd have laughed, if she hadn't been so embarrassed. Of the two of them, she felt her outlook on things was far healthier than Shay's.

"Good," Graham said, and seemed to be content with her answer. Then he went on to say, "Has Shay told you about himself? His family?"

"I was born here, so he didn't have to," she said, not in a patronizing way, but wanting to get things back on a more comfortable footing. "I know his mother left him here as a boy, to live with his father, and I know Mr. Callaghan was anything but an easy man, especially with Shay."

"Have you thought any about what he does for a living . . . and perhaps why he does it?"

"He runs his late father's divorce practice in Edinburgh. I imagine he does so either for the income, or to honor his father's wishes, or both."

"You can't imagine, then, that he does so because he enjoys it."

"No," she said, instantly. "Definitely no' that."

Graham nodded, and a bit of the tension in his posture seemed to ease up. "You'd be right then. He doesn't."

Kira dipped her chin for a moment, and stared unseeing at the accordion binder she held in her lap. "I don't want you to think I'm prying. Anything I want to know, I'd ask Shay directly." She lifted her gaze to Graham's. "But your insight, as a friend, would be appreciated."

"Because others see us more clearly than we see ourselves?"

"Yes."

He nodded and settled back in his chair. "I started the subject, so 'tis a fair request. What is it you want to know?"

"You bring up his family, his mother, leaving him. As far as I know, they never had contact past that time. And we know his father was less than supportive of his only child and son. So, are you saying you believe his commitment to remaining a bachelor extends back beyond being a practicing divorce attorney?"

"Possibly."

"But he's had the deep bonds of friendship with you and Roan for a lifetime. And nothing but support from the islanders—"

"Islanders who are all descended from two clans, neither his own."

"Right, but we're more than our heritage, are we no'? You're saying he's an outsider, a man apart, but surely he feels as if Kinloch is his rightful home?"

Graham's expression gave away nothing. "I can't speak for him. You'll have to ask him how he feels about that."

"Has he said as much to you? Not asking you to break a confidence, but—"

Graham shook his head. "Shay has never once spoken on any of it. He's no' exactly the chatty type when it comes to revealing his thoughts. That would be more Roan's niche."

Kira smiled, briefly, thinking perhaps she'd gotten Shay to open up far more than he had to anyone else. But she didn't speak of it; that was between them. "Aye, that would be the truth of it."

There was a beat of silence, then Graham said, "Ye truly care for him, don't you?"

She met his gaze squarely then. "I truly do, aye. I know it's a recent thing, our involvement, but it's no' a recent thing, my . . . well, my feelings for him."

"I don't believe his are, either."

Kira swallowed at that, hard. Shay had said as much, but Graham's confirmation . . . somehow strengthened the importance of it. "He . . . mentioned me? Before . . . before the wedding?" Seemed the safest way to characterize the start date of their relationship.

"No, but he wasna too good about hiding his interest. Not from where I stood, anyway. But I know him as well as anyone could."

"Oh. I see. But you've . . . spoken on it?"

"The day of the wedding, aye. But no' since then. He hasn't been 'round much. In Edinburgh, and . . . out of his office more." The corners of Graham's eyes crinkled a bit. "And ye do have Katie's blessing, by the way. I'll warn ye not to give her an opening unless you're prepared to divulge every last moment of your time spent together."

Kira smiled a little at that. "Thank you. And for the warning as well."

Graham leaned forward, and caught her gaze squarely once again. "And how are you faring?"

Her shoulders softened a little, which was when she realized how rigid and stiff they'd become. Not so much in defense of herself, but for Shay. "Are you asking as my clan laird?"

"I'm asking as a friend. At least, I'd like to think we're friendly. Especially as it looks like you'll be wanting to continue your involvement with Shay for some amount of time."

"Some amount of time," she echoed more softly. "Aye. Aye I would." She took a steadying breath and smiled. "I'm faring quite well. We've only just embarked down this new path, but it's one I'm excited to be on." Her smile grew. "And, truth be told, ye only have yerself and Roan to blame, really."

He lifted one eyebrow. "And how is that?"

"You go carting home a delightful woman from the States and make her your bride-to-be, then Roan goes and becomes lover and protector to my closest and dearest friend, and weddings are happening all over the place . . . it's hard not to have a renewed sense of faith and optimism in the face of all of that happiness and hope. I was already well on my way, but you lads make it hard for a lass to procrastinate."

Graham smiled truly then, and Kira was reminded of how transforming such a small thing could be. Graham was more the distracted type, where Shay was mostly serious or thoughtful, but it took only a single smile to reveal the depth of either man's true warmth.

"If we can be an inspiration, I'll no' shy away from it," he said. "I've never been happier, nor has Roan. And we'd be very happy, of course, if that were to spread to Shay. Just . . . have a care with him. And with your own heart. I canno' think of a woman better suited to him, but I'm no' so sure he'll ever allow himself to be well suited in return. No matter how deserving he is, or how much he wants it."

Kira's cheeks grew warm, but in a good way. Graham's heart was truly in the right place. "Thank you. For your concern for me, and even more, for him. He has good friends. I don't know how we'll fare, but we've been open about that from the start. And . . ." She lifted her shoulders. "We'll see what we see. Rest assured both of us have our eyes wide open."

"I appreciate your letting me speak so freely."

"That's what friends do," she said, happy with the idea that she'd made a new one that day.

"Indeed. So . . . tell me about this weaving school you want to open."

Her eyes widened. "I thought you didn't know about this supposed 'secret project.' "

He smiled again, and this time there was a knowing gleam there that made her pulse jump a little, as it would any living, breathing woman. Kira began to see why Katie was always glowing.

"Tell me about the parts I don't know. The parts I can help you with. Years back, Roan had tossed the idea around when he began converting the stables and hunting lodge into the home he now lives in, but when his own work became more demanding, the idea was lost along the way. I'm glad he thought of it again, and thought of you to run it. Because I think it's a fine idea. A fine idea, indeed."

Kira opened her accordion folder and took out the heavy sheaf of papers, very excited to hear that . . .

but even as she enthusiastically went over all of the plans, and learned what kinds of clan laws she'd have to contend with, their earlier conversation was never far from her mind.

She had a lot to think about. And more questions. Questions she feared had no immediate or easy answers.

Chapter Seven

"We'd take this section here, clear the stone, and renovate and remodel the croft house first, then what used to be the stables and barn." Kira scrambled around the rocks and stood where they could see the far corners of the property, each boundary marked by low, stacked stone walls. She pointed to the shambling building in the northwest corner. "The stables will house the offices, the barn the actual classrooms, and the croft house will be expanded to provide living quarters for the students during their stay. Those who don't find accommodations in the village."

"What of the instructors?" Shay asked, though, in truth, he really didn't, in that moment, give a flying fig about schoolteachers. Other than the one standing next to him. He'd been gone three days and he was like a man dying of thirst who'd just found his only well.

"They will all be McAuley or MacLeod weavers,"

she chattered on. "I already have quite a list compiled of those interested in taking a session on. Some of the names might surprise you," she added, with that devilish smile. "They did me."

Och, but he was this close to putting her over his shoulder and carting her straight to her cottage. But when his stay in Edinburgh had been extended, he'd promised to meet her here, straight from the ferry.

With more control than he thought he'd ever need, Shay stepped up on the rocks beside her and scanned the property. "I've gone over all the paperwork and it seems in order. With Graham's help and support, I dinnae think you'll come up against any real opposition at the council meeting tomorrow. Has anyone approached you directly with concerns?"

"Just a few queries about making sure our lessons focus on the traditional weaving, and no' my own designs. I've assured them that while I eventually hope to offer advanced classes to help students find their own creative and artistic voices, in general, the idea of the school is to spread Kinloch weaving traditions beyond our isle, in hopes of increasing the interest in what we do. There's also the added benefit that the more people who know of our work, the better the chance that it will never completely die out. Not to mention it's great for tourist trade."

Shay stepped down and held a hand up to assist her down as well. "Sounds like you've thought it all through quite thoroughly. I don't think ye'll be needing much counsel from me."

"Oh, I need counsel," she said, tugging him closer.

It was the end of the first week of December. They'd been involved now for a little more than a fortnight. When he was at work, and she was in her studio, their lives continuing around them as before, he wondered and worried about the choice he'd made, and all he was risking.

But when he was with her, it seemed the most natural, right thing in the world. The ease with which their lives had begun to mesh would seem to make a mockery of his fears. In fact, he didn't want to imagine getting up in the morning and not having her be part of his day.

He'd done his best to do as she'd asked, to focus on the good and leave the worrying to fate. With her, it was easier than he'd thought it would be. But on his own . . . or worse, when standing in a courtroom, or sitting at a deposition table, he'd be lying if he said all the doubts and fears didn't creep in and grab his gut in a cold fist.

But he wasn't in Edinburgh today. "Good," he said, "because there is perhaps some of my more . . . personal counsel you might benefit from."

"Oh?" She tried to maintain a serious expression, and failed spectacularly. "And on what topic would you like me to receive your . . . counseling, counselor?"

He made her squeal a happy, joyous sound when he abruptly pulled her hard against him and cupped the back of her head with his hand, slightly knocking askew the cap she'd tucked her hair beneath to keep the wind from whipping it about.

"First," he said, as he settled her snugly in his arms, "this must go." He flicked off the knitted wool cap and her hair came cascading down.

She lunged for it with a free hand, but the wind caught it and danced it over the rocks. "The wind will snatch my hair into a nest of knots before we make it back to the jitney."

"Oh, you won't have the wind to blame that on." He wove his hands into her hair, and tightened his fist just enough to bend her head back, and push her mouth up toward his. "I'll gladly sort out every knot. Later," he breathed across her lips.

"Promise?"

"Oh, aye. I've many things I can promise you this night."

Her eyes sparkled as she immediately slid her arms over his shoulders and around his neck. "Do tell."

"I'm much better at demonstrating."

"I thought solicitors prided themselves on their . . . oral skills."

He smiled then, and was dazzled anew by the way desire widened her pupils whenever he did. In fact, it was likely the reason he found himself doing that far more often these days. "Oh and aye, that we do. Allow me to show you, milady." He dipped his head so his lips brushed hers. Her eyes fluttered shut and she sighed, instantly softening under his repeated brushed kisses.

"More," she whispered with a whimper, when he lifted his head. She urged his mouth back to hers with pressure on the nape of his neck. "I've missed you."

Och, but he'd missed her as well. Like the very devil he had. And they'd spoken every night, and sent notes via e-mail each day. It should have been pathetic, their complete inability to be truly apart from one another. And if it hadn't made him feel so bloody fantastic every time that little white envelope had popped up in his inbox, he'd have worried about that, too. "If I start in here, we're going to be uncomfortably naked on some very hard ground. And quite chilled by the time I'm through."

"Will we now? My, my, solicitor, sir. I don't know that I've ever been counseled so . . . ardently." She batted her eyelashes at him, making him laugh. She joined him. "Oh, I should confess it's my mission in life to make you do that more often, ye know."

"If anyone could, 'tis you," he said, quite honestly, not as surprised by it as he once was. He started to carefully pick his way across the field.

"You could put me down rather than risk life and limb on these rocks."

"I could," he said simply, and kept walking.

She said nothing more, but rather tightened her hold on his neck . . . and began to do rather delectable things to the side of his neck, just above the starched collar of his shirt. "Mmm. I miss the smell of you," she said. "Oh, while I remember, I had your shirts cleaned and pressed."

He paused before skirting a particularly large outcropping and glanced down at her. "Did you now?"

She smiled up at him, a wholly unrepentant gleam in her eye. "Aye. Raised quite a few eyebrows in the village, both when I dropped them off, and again when I picked them up for you."

"I can well imagine," was all he said. Mostly because rather than providing an opening for his fears and concerns to come creeping in . . . he found he rather liked the idea of her public claiming of him. He angled his head so he could catch her gaze. "No one said anything . . . untoward to you, did they?"

"Untoward?" she repeated, the teasing twinkle in her eye, even as she quite seriously pretended to give it some thought. "No, no I can't say anyone did. At least not to my face. In fact, I'm no' so certain we're going to find any opposition to our burgeoning relationship. If anything, I should warn you before you head back to the village, or to your office."

"Warn me?" He'd reached the road and let her slide her feet to the ground. "What of?"

"Well, I met with Katie yesterday, to go over the marketing and separate site ideas, to tie the school in to our official marketing Web site, and she warned me that there was quite a buzz about us, perhaps even a bet or two being made over pints of ale."

"Bets?" he asked, truly flummoxed by the idea. "Whatever on?"

Kira rolled her eyes. "What do you think? Christmas is coming, everyone is in a festive mood what with all the lights being strung and the decorations and gifties starting to fill up all the shop windows."

"And?"

She cupped his cheek and bussed his mouth. "And we've had two weddings in three months, with your best mates as the grooms. What do you think they're betting on?"

And that's when the door not only creaked open, but flung itself wide. "Ah," he managed, though he couldn't have rightly said how. His throat had closed over and his heart had clutched.

Kira was, as always, intimately tuned into him, but rather than pull back herself, or take offense, she smiled and kissed him, noisily, instead. "I'm no' the one placing any bets, okay? And I'm the only one ye have to worry about. They'll rib you and give you a hard time, aye. I say we torment them with ardent displays of public affection and keep them guessing." She wiggled her eyebrows. "It will be a burden, of course, but I'll bear up under the scrutiny somehow."

And, just like that, his heart clicked right back into gear . . . though he couldn't have said the door made much progress in closing again. "You're a wonder, you do know that?" he asked, amazed by how resilient she was, and had been, throughout their time together. It was true that, after their first almost overwrought day spent in bed, they hadn't spoken of the future . . . or potential lack thereof. They'd talked of his work on the island, and, to a lesser extent, in Edinburgh, about the school, about the positive reports Tessa and Roan had been sending back from their working honeymoon in Malaysia, where she was working on a new story and he was setting up another outlet for their basket sales.

Kira made it so easy to be with her, to be in a relationship with her. It was more than he could have hoped for . . . and everything he'd never allowed himself to want for himself. As long as he kept his thoughts on the moment, he was quite content. Happier than he'd ever been or knew he could be.

When he could keep his thoughts in the moment.

But an adulthood spent dissolving marriages wasn't something he could overcome in a fortnight, especially since he was still doing it. No matter how delightful a companion Kira had already become to him, there was still this unavoidable sense, in the back of his mind, that he was being drawn inexorably closer to the edge of a cliff. And the ledge was becoming higher and higher every day.

Then her palms were on his cheeks and she was drawing his mouth down to hers. She kissed him, this time there wasn't anything teasing about it. And when he lifted his head, she looked quite serious.

"What is it?" he asked.

"You're a wonder, too, Shay Callaghan. Don't forget that part."

"I—"

But she'd already slid from his arms. "We can come back for my car later on," she said, and walked to the other side of the jitney and climbed in. There was nothing to do but get in himself.

Once settled in the driver's seat, but before he could say anything, she said, "I thought if it was okay with you, we'd stop in town and pick a few things up at market . . . before going to your place."

"Aye, I'd planned to feed you before I ravish you. We'll need our stamina—wait, at my place did you say?"

She leveled an easy look at him, but that seriousness lingered in her eyes. "Aye. We're always at my place and I thought it was maybe time for you to have to launder the sheets and clean up the dishes."

She'd said it that way to keep it light, and he knew he should strive to do the same. After all, even if he knew she didn't mind in the least having him at her cottage, as she had said on more than one occasion, she had every right to think she'd be invited into his home with equal enthusiasm.

"I—I've been gone for days, and was with you for the two before that, so I canno' vouch for—"

She placed a hand on his thigh as he maneuvered the stick shift and changed gears. "You know I dinnae care about the state of your place. Any more than you cared about the state of mine."

"I know," he said, quite well aware how badly he was mucking this up. She'd caught him off guard.

They drove on as a full minute passed; then she said, "If you'd rather no', just tell me so. We can plan it for another time, then."

He pulled the car over and let it idle.

"Shay," she said, after another moment passed in silence, " 'tis okay. Truly. I shouldn't have been so clumsy in inviting myself over. We've just gotten in a bit of a routine about you coming to see me and I—"

"You wanted to feel equally welcome in my home," he finished. "And of course you are."

"But?"

"But nothing. I'm no' ashamed of where I live, it's quite a nice little cottage."

"Except that's no' the actual issue, is it?"

He swallowed a sigh then, knowing she wasn't going to just let this pass, nor, in truth, should she, when he'd made such an awkward moment out of it. "I've made too much of it, and I'm sorry. You've nothing to apologize for and I should have invited you myself. Long since."

"But you haven't." And she said it in such a way as to make it clear she knew it wasn't just an oversight or thoughtlessness on his part.

"No," he agreed. "I haven't." He turned to look at her then. The least he owed her was to be direct, as she'd been with him. "I've done well with this change in my life. I've embraced it as fully as I know how to. And I've enjoyed it, more even than I thought myself capable."

"But if you let me into your personal world, then I'll make a permanent impression on it. And you're no' willing to risk that, if I'm suddenly no longer a part of your personal world." Her expression softened a little. "I do understand that. It's why I sold my flat in London even before my divorce papers were signed. In fact, it's why I left London altogether. I shouldn't have pushed. You'd have invited me when you were ready."

"And what if that time was . . . distant from now?"

"There's no deadline, Shay. When and if it truly bothered me, I'd say something."

"Isn't that what you're doing now?"

She opened her mouth to speak, then closed it again. After a beat, she said, "Maybe you're right. I didn't mean it as a test, not consciously, but clearly it was. I am sorry. I'm usually more direct when something is bothering me. That wasn't fair. I know your doubts are still there," she said, "and I didn't mean to push you. Not now. And please know, I didn't bring up the village part as some underlying scheme to pressure you—"

"I know that. I do know you, and you wouldn't do that. It's simply part and parcel of the two of us forming a relationship. It doesn't happen in a cocoon."

"Much as you might like it to," she said, not unkindly.

He paused then, but he owed her the truth, if nothing else. "Perhaps. Yes. Would be simpler to navigate if the only concern I had were my own feelings, and yours."

"Nothing is ever that simple or uncomplicated."

He laughed then, but there was little humor in it. "That is the biggest twist of this. It is both the most uncomplicated, easiest thing I've ever done . . . and the very most complicated and tangled relationship I've ever allowed myself to have."

She nodded, but it was a moment longer before she said, "When you think on it, when you're alone, how do you feel?"

"Mostly I try not to." He flinched when he saw pain flicker across her face. He immediately reached for her, touching her cheek, then taking her hand. "I didnae say that to hurt you, and yet I did just that. I'm sorry, I am. What I meant was, if I don't think about the bigger picture, it's easier to just be. I do think of you. Endlessly. I can't imagine a time when I didn't. You're like part of my atmosphere now, critical to my every breath."

"Shay," she breathed, clearly awed by his blurted confession.

"And, I suppose I think that, the longer I'm in this relationship, the more normal it will become, to where it simply becomes the bigger picture.

Does that make any sense to ye? It's no' because I see no future with you."

"No, I understand, I do. It's because you still won't let yourself trust that there will be one."

"You asked me to be the man I want to be when I'm with you. I try to be that man all the time. And if it means not dwelling too closely on the parts I haven't come to terms with as yet, then that's what I'll do."

"Then maybe I was wrong to ask that of you."

"What?"

She lifted a shoulder, but squeezed his hand where he'd linked his fingers through hers. "Maybe we're just playing a giant game of Let's Pretend and it will blow up in both of our faces because we're not really dealing in reality."

"This is our reality."

She turned to face him more fully. "Reality is me mentioning coming by your place and you blanching at the mere thought of it. We shouldn't just pretend you didn't."

"I don't believe we are."

"Because I've gone and pushed it. And I worry that if I push, you'll walk. So I don't. Or didn't. But you seemed . . . when you crossed the field toward me earlier, I don't know . . . it felt like you really missed me. There was a different sense when you scooped me up out there and I guess I just . . . I just wanted to let go of all the worry and allow myself to believe this is real and good and whole and . . . okay."

"It is real and good."

"But it's not okay. We're not okay."

"So, it's only okay if things are smooth sailing then?"

She sighed. "I don't know what I'm saying anymore." She pulled his hand up to her mouth and kissed the backs of his knuckles. "I just know I want you. And I want to be able to want you openly, fearlessly, and with everything there is in my heart. And to not worry that will scare you away."

"Have you no' been doing that already?"

"In my actions? Aye, I have. But I don't want to be anything less than everything I am when I'm with you."

"Haven't you been?"

She answered that by saying, "There's a part of me I don't share."

He frowned. He hadn't thought she'd ever been anything but completely open with him. In fact, it was her absolute ease in being herself with him that so captivated him, and made it possible for him to be the same when he was with her. "And what part is that?"

"The part that means sharing thoughts. Putting thoughts and feelings into words. I show you, but—"

"But you don't tell me."

She shook her head.

"Because that would be pushing."

She nodded, then tipped her chin down, looking at their joined hands, watching as she traced her fingertips over the back of his hand.

Shay slid his hand from hers, but only so he could reach down and release the lever that allowed his seat to slide all the way back. Then he reached for her. "Come here."

"Shay—"

"Please."

She shifted so that he could pull her across the center stick and settle her in his lap, her back to the steering wheel, her lips inches from his own. He looked into her eyes. "I've already hurt you, and that was never my intent, you know that."

"You haven't hurt me, Shay."

"The fact that you feel you can't tell me every and anything that's on your mind means I'm no' being the man I want to be for you. I'm sorry for that."

"I know you're trying, I do. And I'm happy. Happier than I've ever been. You do understand that."

"If you're even a fraction as happy as I am, then aye, I understand that."

A little of the tension eased from her body then, but he knew they still had much ground to cover.

She cupped his cheek. "I know it's no' something that will change overnight. I dinnae have the barriers you do, the worries."

"I'm no' fragile, Kira. You're treating me as if I'm some mental case, too unstable to hear the truth. Aye, I have some issues with happily ever after. But you're the very best thing I could have ever hoped to have in my life, and I just want to make sure I can live up to your expectations."

"See, that's what I meant, when I said to remember that you're a wonder, too. You bring me just as much joy as you say I bring to you. Just by being you. It's no' like it's a burden to love—" She broke off then, and looked away, her cheeks blooming a hot pink almost instantly.

Shay's heart stuttered badly and there was no

stopping the tremor in his voice when he spoke, but speak he did. "Is that the part then that you're not saying?"

When she didn't reply, he propped a finger beneath her chin and nudged her gaze back to his. It was with great alarm that he saw giant tears swimming in her eyes. "Kira, no, don't, I didn't mean to—"

"I'm no' fragile, either, Shay. Sometimes I'll get my feelings hurt. And sometimes I'll hurt yours. We'll both get past it, for the very same reason that we were able to be hurt in the first place." Two tears formed at the corners of her eyes, but he gently knuckled them away before they could fall, his heart ripping at the mere sight of them.

"I hate it that I've made ye cry."

She smiled then, even as more tears formed. "But that's a good thing, don't you see?"

"No. I feel like a bully and a lout."

She leaned forward and kissed him. And kept kissing him until he kissed her back. In fact, it was her sheer will and determination that had a burning sensation forming in his own eyes.

Their kisses swiftly turned from gentle nudges to all-consuming heat. When she finally turned her mouth away from his, and buried her face in his neck, they were both panting hard, and the windows of the jitney had steamed over.

"I cried because it scares me, how much I care for you, and that you may never care the same in return," she said, the words muffled against the warm skin of his neck. "We both have our fears, Shay. The tears weren't calculated." She lifted her head then, and looked at him, her eyes still liquid and drenched with emotion. "But the look on your face when you saw them . . . went a long way toward . . ." She broke off then, and shook her head.

He tipped her chin back to his, and knew she'd find his moist now as well. He saw the surprise, and the way her pupils expanded as she took that in.

"Tell me," he said, the words a bit hoarse. "Say . . . anything. No censoring, no editing. If we're to figure this out, then maybe there can't be a moratorium on what can and can't be discussed. I don't know, Kira. I don't. I have no laws for this, no textbooks. I'm . . . winging it. And I don't wing."

She gave a watery little snicker at that, and a bit of his heart was restored.

"At least I don't wing well," he said, caressing her cheek now. "So, I'll be more honest with you. I'd like to talk about my work more, with you. I don't because it crosses the line, and because I'm afraid it will make you want to avoid talking to me. It's a tough subject, and sensitive to us particularly. But . . . you bring me such perspective. About so many things. The kind I've never had before. Maybe it will make me better at my job, more compassionate, at least. I don't know. But it's also a big part of who I am, of what I do, and it's . . . hard to keep myself from talking with you about it." He drew his thumb over her bottom lip, and reveled in the way it made her shudder. "There, those are my words, my thoughts, the ones I edit, the ones I censor out. Now, will you tell me yours?"

Her lips continued to tremble, even when he slid his finger away. "My thoughts," she repeated, then let out a soft, wavering sigh. She held onto his gaze for several long moments, then seemed to gather herself. "I'm . . ." She trailed off, then gave a short, half laugh.

"It's okay," he said. "You don't have to say anything. I just want you to know that if there's something you want to say, now or in the future . . . then say it."

"It's no' that. It's . . . well, it's silly really. In some ways I'm not at all traditional, but in some ways . . ." She let the sentence trail off, her thoughts trailing with it, then took another small breath, smoother this time, and returned her gaze to his, steadier now. "I will tell you why you're a wonder to me. You're strong, you're steadfast, resilient, loyal. I feel completely and utterly cared for when you're with me, as if no harm could ever come to me, because you simply wouldn't allow it. And I realize that might be fiction, but—"

"It's as true as I'd be able to humanly make it," he said.

Something in her expression melted, and she drew her hand along his cheek again. "That, right there. You're direct, you don't beat around the bush, and you don't mind saying whatever it is you feel. You have no idea how rare that is. I appreciate the way you take things in, figure them out, and how you always have everyone's best interests at heart. I'm certain that's what makes you such a sought-after solicitor. I'd have been a very lucky woman indeed to have been represented by the likes of you during my own divorce.

"And even though it tears you up to watch it, to

be a part of it, you continue to do what you can, to do the best you can. You think yourself cynical and cold because you've worked hard not to let your work cut you up completely, but that's just survival. If you were cold and unfeeling, you'd have had nothing to protect in the first place. And you'd have made a lousy lawyer. So, it's all part and parcel. But you show me the same utter dedication you show your clients. You're a passionate man, you are, and I feel . . . like I'm the only woman in the world when you look at me. You have no idea . . ." She broke off and her eyes grew moist again, only this time, her tears tugged on his heart in an entirely different way.

"I want to be the man you speak of."

"You are," she said. "That's just it. You are. Flaws and fears and all. I'm far from perfect. I've my own insecurities. As much as a person can heal from being cheated on and utterly rejected and humiliated . . . I have. But I'm human. Of course it terrifies me that after I allow myself to be completely vulnerable to you, you might choose to walk away. I say I'll heal, but it wouldn't be an easy task. In fact, it scares the living daylights out of me."

"So . . . why are you risking it?"

"Because," she said, softly, "I'm only so scared because wha' I have with you is so brilliant. I'd have to be daft to walk away from that, now wouldn't I?"

"Kira—"

"Shay, we've known each other less than a month . . . but I'm falling in love with you. There." She blew out a long breath. "I've gone and said it, haven't I? Maybe I should have said it as it was happening. After all, if it's going to spook you, then best to be spooked now, and well before I'm parading your laundry about town. But . . . I was afraid. It's ridiculously soon, and I wondered if it was just me, reaching for security, without having the basis of knowledge, the foundation, to truly back it up. But then you show up at my door, and well . . . my heart, it just swells at the sight. I know what it is to love. I've loved before. And maybe time is of no real consequence, because . . ." She trailed off, lifted a shoulder, then looked away again. "I'll stop babbling on now. I've said enough. More, I'm afraid, than you wanted to hear."

Shay sat, utterly still, and kept hearing those words again. And again. *I'm falling in love with you.*

With him. Kira MacLeod. In love. With him.

He couldn't have formed a single word if he'd wanted to, the lump in his throat was so large. So, instead he tipped her face to his, and lowered his lips to hers. And he poured everything he thought he knew, and all that he didn't have the words for, into that single, emotionally scorching kiss.

And that kiss led to another, then another still, as his hunger for her grew the more he let himself go, let his guard completely down.

Loved him, she did. Him. Shay Callaghan. A man who hadn't even earned the love of his own mother.

He tangled his fingers in her hair, and took the kiss deeper still, and she gave back with every bit as much fervor and passion. She squirmed in his lap until she straddled him, and he groped alongside the seat until he found the lever to release it completely, making her squeal in surprise, then laugh as she landed full on top of him.

Her laughter swiftly turned to gasps, then moans as his hands roamed down her spine and over every dip and curve, at her waist, then lower, until he cupped her and urged her more tightly against him.

No words now, only actions.

The windows had completely steamed over, and their skin had grown slick. She was peeling his shirt open, and reaching between them to un-buckle his belt and open his trousers even as he fumbled to pull her cardigan over her head and unclasp the hooks of her bra. They were in a pretty remote spot, and in the recesses of Shay's mind, he hoped, given the late hour of the day, no one would happen by. At least not for the next half hour or so.

Beyond that, the world could have come to an end, and it wouldn't have stopped him.

"Come here," he said, as she finished sliding her garments off and leaned back down to kiss his jaw. He nudged her mouth back to his, then bracketed her hips with his hands and shifted her so he could . . . "Oh," he said, the single word coming out as a long, satisfied groan.

"Aye," she agreed, on a trembling sigh, as he slowly, surely, filled her.

She began to move then, and he matched her rhythm easily, perfectly. It had always been like this between them. And it always would be. He knew that. Had utter faith in it, as he did in her. It shouldn't have been such a revelatory moment . . . but such moments happened when they did.

And this, as she fitted herself so perfectly to him, to all that he was . . . was his.

But it wasn't the time for words. So he took her mouth, and he took her body, and he told himself that the words would come.

Of course they would.

Chapter Eight

"I'm so glad it's turning out to be everything you'd hoped." Kira pressed the phone closer so she could hear Tessa clearly. The connection to Malaysia was terrible.

"Better," Tessa said, "amazing."

"I can't wait to hear all about it. Will you be home by the solstice celebrations on the twenty-first?"

"We have to go to Edinburgh to do some of the marketing for the calendar Roan posed for."

"During Christmas?"

"It's good for the island and this is when the thing comes out, so we have to take advantage while we can." Tessa paused for a moment, then said, "Maybe you and Shay can come stay in Edinburgh and we'll celebrate the holidays together. Roan just mentioned that Blaine will be in the city then, too," she said mentioning Katie's dear friend. "Apparently he's still digging into all that Iain

McAuley mess. Anyway, you should come. Shay has a place in the city, right?"

Kira had already told Tessa everything, or most everything, about the big change in her life. It had felt good just getting the chance to tell someone, and, at the same time, get Tessa's perspective on . . . things. Tessa had known of Kira's interest in Shay before her own big day, and hated that she was absent for her friend now, especially since Kira had been there for her during her tumultuous love affair with Roan.

"He does, and he's already told me he'd like me to see his offices there. Introduce me around."

"That's good then, right? He is involving you in his life, introducing you to people he works with. All good signs."

"Aye, he is, and they are."

Tessa knew Kira well enough to hear what her friend wasn't saying. "But you don't want to come?"

"No, no, it's not that, not at all. In fact, I think it sounds like a lovely holiday. It's just . . . he still hasn't invited me to his place here yet. And I don't know that I want to extend the boundaries of our relationship any more broadly, if you know what I mean, until he's feeling sure enough of us to include me fully in his life here. Introducing me in Edinburgh is good, but also . . . distant. His other life, as it were. I do want to be a part of that, but it's his life here—our life here—that's most important."

"Maybe this is just the path he needs to take to get there. It's been a week, you said, since you talked about all this?"

"Aye. As I told you, we didn't go to his place that day because . . . well, it was such a turning point, a good one, and . . . I wanted the invitation to come from him."

"And . . . it hasn't? Has he even mentioned it?"

"He ended up back in Edinburgh and has been swamped most of the week with a big case they're trying to wrap up through mediation so they can avoid a court trial over the holidays. So, no, but to be fair, I don't necessarily take it as an indication of anything other than bad timing."

"Okay," Tessa said, then paused. "Are you sure?"

"Aye, I'm sure," Kira said, and as she said the words, she knew they were true. Essentially, anyway. Life had sort of gotten in the way just when it seemed they had made a critical leap forward, but that was what life did. "Neither of us are big on the Christmas holiday. Apparently his father was generally too busy working to do much and Shay spent most of his Christmases with Graham's family, or with whatever family Roan was with. You and I know what it was like at school, and, well . . ."

"I know. I know it's hard for you. I remember you saying Thomas used to make a big deal out of Christmas."

"He was like a child in his excitement over it, aye," Kira said, referring to her ex. "I've . . . just kind of avoided all that since."

"Understandable. But maybe . . . I don't know, maybe it's because I'm a disgustingly-in-love new bride, but maybe this could be a new beginning for you and Shay, a time to forge new traditions, to put your own stamp on the holiday. You know? Or maybe Edinburgh would be perfect, and you could both escape the whole event. I know you said the island celebrations were a bit over the top."

"They are." Kira smiled, though, thinking about all the plans being made and how festive everything was. She'd completely hidden out through the past two, but this year, walking through the village . . . rather than thinking about her marriage and all the bittersweet and downright painful memories associated with it and this time of year, she'd instead found her thoughts going back much further in time. Remembering, instead, her holidays as a child in Kinloch, waiting for St. Nick. She'd loved the season when she was little, every last thing about it. And, yes, she'd thought about Shay, and what it would be like to have a brand-new holiday memory with him, to help dim some of the more painful recent ones.

"Have you two talked about it? What you'll do?"

Kira laughed. "We've talked about talking about it, but with this case he's working, we've barely had time to say hello and keep current on what's happening day-to-day. He's due home later today, so perhaps this evening." Though, if their brief phone call last evening had been any indication, it was doubtful either of them had talking as the foremost thing on their mind. Had Shay not been interrupted by yet another business intrusion, she might have had her first ever experience with phone sex.

"I've got to run," Tessa said. "Let me know what happens and we'll make plans. Otherwise, I'll see you in the new year!"

"Okay, that's good," Kira said. "You sound . . . happy, Tessa. Remind me to give that husband of yours a big hug when you get back. I owe him."

"I am," Tessa said, sounding like the young girl

Kira had gone to boarding school with again, which was a miracle in and of itself, given how broken Tessa had been when she'd first arrived on Kinloch. "And give your man a hug, too . . . and hold on, Kira. I saw the way he looked at you. He is your man. Just . . . hold on to him."

"I plan to," Kira said, and they disconnected just as a rap came on the cottage door.

Kira scrambled out of the kitchen chair and almost tripped over herself to get to the door. Shay wasn't due back until later and, by now, he usually just knocked once to let her know he was there, then entered on his own. Still, she scrambled.

She realized she was still in nightgown and robe, but didn't care. Having gotten an idea for the basket design she was weaving in the wee hours, she'd risen early and dived right in. Besides, she'd been too restless to sleep without Shay next to her.

She held her robe closed with her fist, and opened the door. Then clutched her robe more tightly at the sight of a liveried footman, standing on her doorstep. "I—I'm sorry, can I help you? Are you lost?"

"Kira MacLeod?"

"Aye, that's me. What's this—"

"I've been sent with an invitation. If you'll be so kind as to read it, miss, and give me your reply?"

"I—what is this all about?"

The man, in full powdered wig and gloves, no less, made quite the show of handing her a crisp, white envelope. She couldn't quite tell if he was merely staying in character . . . or if he simply was a character.

She broke the seal and opened the envelope,

then slid out an engraved invitation. She read it out loud. "The pleasure of your company is requested at No. 23 on the North Road, this evening. Half past six. Requested attire . . . Anything you don't mind being torn off your—" She stopped, suddenly realizing whom this was from . . . and that she was reciting things out loud to the footman that perhaps she'd ought not to. She cleared her throat and finished reading in silence, her heart already pounding, then looked back at the footman. "I'll be there. I—what I mean to say is . . . I accept the invitation."

"Quite good, miss," he said, and actually sketched a sharply delivered bow that the Queen would approve. "I shall be round to pick you up at quarter past the hour."

"You'll—you're picking me up?"

"Aye, miss."

Kira was grinning now. "Okay then. Oh, let me get you a tip, hold on."

The man looked as horrified as if she'd suggested she might be stripping naked right there in her doorway. "That won't be necessary, miss. I'll ring at quarter past six."

"Thank you," Kira said, and watched him bow again, then make his way down the walk. She craned her neck to look around to the side lot, to spy what he was driving, half expecting to see a carriage and team of horses, but a viciously cold wind chose that moment to whip past the open doorway, and she ducked back inside and shut the door.

She turned and leaned back against it, and read the note again, then held it against her chest.

Then she might have danced a little jig. Just a small one. Twice. She wanted to dash to grab her mobile and call Shay straight away to find out what was behind all this, but he'd clearly set a plan in motion, and she was willing—quite willing—to play along.

"I guess I'd better go see what outfit I won't mind never wearing again." She skipped to her bedroom.

When the footman rang again, precisely at quarter past six, Kira was already in her long, black wool coat and slim heeled boots. She grabbed the handles of the gift bag she'd put on the front table, and followed the footman outside. No carriage awaited, but there was a sleek black town car. She couldn't recall that there was anyone on Kinloch who drove a town car that Shay might have hired out for the evening, but that didn't really matter.

What mattered was that Shay had finally invited her to his home. And he was doing so in style.

Chapter Nine

Shay paced the length of the floor of his cottage, surprised he hadn't worn a groove in the rug by now. He'd checked the champagne at least a half dozen times, to make sure it was chilling properly, and the food he'd had ordered and delivered was all arranged perfectly in chafing dishes. Music played, candles were lit.

And it all felt so ridiculously over the top. It had seemed like a good idea when he'd planned the whole thing from Edinburgh. What must Kira have thought when she opened the door to a liveried footman? He'd fully expected to hear from her, asking a dozen or more questions, but all he'd received back was her formal acceptance. And he'd felt too big the fool to ask the footman what her mood had been after reading his note. Too much? Would she think he was making a mockery of what was very important to her? It was the last thing he'd intended.

"Och, and bloody hell." He and Kira had started things off in such a different manner from the norm. He'd never really had the chance to court her, to date her. They'd sort of moved straight onward into a full-on relationship that . . . well, that was blissful heaven, actually. But he'd wanted to do something special for her, and he'd wanted to reassure her, show her in a way that could not be mistaken, how much he wanted her here. Their discussion in his steam-filled jitney had truly been a turning point for him. In many ways. This week, while in Edinburgh, his mind had been, of course, on the case at hand, but it had also been on Kira. Relentlessly. In fact, the two had gone in tandem. He'd—

His musings were mercifully interrupted by a sharp rat-a-tat on the door.

He strode to the front door and swung it wide just as the footman was stepping back to allow Kira to step up.

"Hullo," she said, her eyes twinkling.

"Hullo," Shay said, and his heart clicked right into place. Just as it always did, every time he saw her. And he knew he'd been silly to worry about anything. In fact, he knew he could stop worrying—about everything.

"Come in," he said, realizing they were both staring at each other. "Please." He stepped back to let her pass, then quickly took care of the footman. "Thank you," he said. "For everything."

The man smiled and sketched a light bow. "My pleasure, sir. Milady is quite charming."

"Thank you. I think so, too."

"Have a good evening," the older gentleman said, then stepped back.

"I hope to," Shay said, then closed the door and turned to find Kira slipping out of her heavy coat. "Here, let me help you with that."

"Wait," she said, and handed him a small, handled bag. "Here, take this first." She laughed as he frowned at what looked like an unwieldy pile of sticks, protruding from the tops of the tissue paper stuffed inside the gift bag. "Some people bring wine, I bring baskets."

He took the bag and set it down. "Let me help you with your coat."

"Bag first," she said. "I want you to see it. I've been dying to show it to you; then I realized, when I finished, it was yours all along."

He pulled out the basket and disentangled it from the tissue paper. It was an unwieldy, unusually shaped form, combining hard willow twigs and richly dyed waxed linen; there were beads and other raw materials. It was earthy, wild. Barely tamed, was the phrase that came to mind. "It's stunning," he said, and meant it. "I dinnae know how you look at all these bits and pieces, and imagine something like this."

She ran her fingers over the patterning. "I wanted to work with really different materials that were almost completely at odds with each other, things you couldn't imagine in the same, woven pattern, that when bound together, would form something truly beautiful." She looked up at him. "Kind of like us."

He smiled then. "Thank you." His tone was

equally heartfelt. He was truly touched. "No one has ever . . . made me anything. It will mean a great deal to me, Kira, every time I look at it."

"Good," she said, her smile bright. "That was my hope."

He set it on the entryway table. "I'll need to think on where I want to put it." He helped her out of her coat and she turned around to face him. He took in her shiny hair, curled and pulled back from her face, specially for the occasion. And her dress was silky and sexy and form-fitting and . . . "You look so incredibly lovely, and I—come here," he said, and all pretense of a civilized little dinner flew straight out the door as he pulled her into his arms. "God, I've missed you."

Kira had slid her arms around his neck, but he felt the extra squeeze at his heartfelt proclamation. "It's so good to hear you say that. I did, too. I suppose it should get easier as we get used to it." She eased back in his arms so she could look up into his eyes. "But I don't sleep well at all anymore when you're not next to me. I keep reaching for you in my sleep. How silly is that?"

"No' so silly. I don't sleep well, either." He drank in her smile, her brilliant, sparkling eyes, and the love and trust and adoration he saw there. He'd spent a lot of time thinking on that, on whether he was worthy of such love, then realized he was an idiot for questioning any of it, risking it with his own foolish fears. He made her happy. Just being himself. Her smiling face was proof of that. What more of a guarantee did he need, for God's sake? "I wanted to woo ye," he said.

She giggled a little at that, and it was a delightful sound that warmed his already thoroughly smitten heart. "*Woo* me, now, did ye? Well, I must say, I don't typically need a liveried footman and town car." She tipped up on her toes and kissed him. "But it was rather exciting. You shouldn't have gone to the trouble."

"It wasn't trouble, it was my pleasure. I . . . I wanted to do something special for you, but mostly, I wanted to announce to you, the world, anyone who cares, that this evening, I'm entertaining a very special woman. In my home. And that it means everything to have you here. To see you here." He tugged her closer. "I want ye here, Kira. I want ye in every nook and corner of my life. I hated coming back to an empty space. You're right, about it being like a jail. Only I never knew it. Now I canno' imagine going back to it."

Her eyes had grown a bit moist, but her smile was so wide he didn't doubt her tears were born of happiness. "So," she said, trying for a teasing tone even as the waver in her voice betrayed the depth of emotion she was feeling, "are ye saying I have full visitation rights then?"

He laughed, scooped her up against him, and swung her around.

"I like your home," she said, as she took in the whirl of her surroundings. "It's no' remotely cell-like," she noted, as he settled her back on her feet. Then she caught the twinkle of lights, turned her head, and gasped. "Ye have a tree!" She swung her gaze back to his. "I thought ye weren't much for the Christmas holidays."

"I haven't been. Before," he added. "If it's too hard for you—maybe I should have asked, but I'd thought, hoped—"

They had talked of her marriage and her divorce during one of their phone calls from Edinburgh, but now he wondered if he'd gone overboard, getting a tree.

"No," she said, sliding from his arms, but grabbing his hand as she walked closer to the tree. "It's beautiful. I love all the colorful lights." She looked back to Shay. "But there are no ornaments."

"I don't have any, and it seemed . . . I don't know, wrong, I guess, to just buy them. At the celebrations with Roan and Graham growing up— mostly Graham in this case—there were always handmade ornaments and ones given or received as gifts. They all had meaning and I rather liked that. Not only the memories associated with them, but the foundation they built, so . . ." He bent down and slid out a small box from under the tree, then straightened and handed it to her. "I hope it's okay."

"Okay?" She jumped up into his arms, and wove her arms around his neck, kissing him firmly on the mouth. "It's . . . perfect."

Shay smiled and kissed her back, but didn't put her down quite yet. "Ye havena opened it yet."

"The fact that you thought to . . . that you . . ." A quizzical look crossed her smiling face. "What happened this time in Edinburgh anyway? You're like . . . a changed man."

"Aye, but that happened the day I met you. I've just finally come to fully understand it."

"What happened?"

"Open the box," he said.

She slid from his arms, then turned and leaned back against him. He circled his arms around her as she tore off the paper and opened the small box. Inside was a small, badly chipped, hand-painted china angel, hanging from a frayed gold string. She dangled it from her fingers. "She's lovely."

"Hardly," Shay said, amused, then turned Kira in his arms. "When I was back in Edinburgh, working on this divorce . . . there was nothing new or different about it, nothing I hadn't witnessed a hundred times over. But I kept thinking about our talk, and how much ye ground me, and how easy it would have been to ring you up and talk to you about it, about what a shame it was, and how ridiculous and sad it was that this couple felt they had to argue over belongings that were, otherwise, utterly meaningless. And so, I thought about the worst case scenario. With us. What if that was us, five years from now, ten, twenty? And I thought about my life, and how . . . and how I'd made sure that nothing in it had real meaning."

He gestured to the room, and turned her so she could take it all in.

"It's a nice place, Shay. Comfortable furnishings, beautiful antiques, lovely paintings and art. It's peaceful, and calm. Like a retreat. And that makes perfect sense, I guess."

"Thank you, and yes, it is all that. But there isn't one thing in this house that I'd miss if it were gone. That I'm attached to. I don't know that I even realized I'd done that. My car—" He broke off, and let out a short laugh. "That's it. The only thing I care about." He turned her back to face him. "How pathetic is that?"

"It's no', Shay. It's survival. For you."

"A hollow life, if you ask me. Or at least, that's how it felt to me, when I came back here, to pack, after . . . after our last night together. And when I was in the city, listening to all that bickering about stupid things . . . I thought, well, if I was going to fight for something, I'd at least like to fight about something I cared about."

Kira smiled, then lifted up and bussed him again, hard, on the mouth.

"What was that for?" he asked.

"I like that fighting spirit. All those years of fighting for other people. You're finally fighting for yourself."

He pulled her back into his arms. "I'm fighting for us. And I hope to God we never come to fight against one another, but I damn well want something worth fighting for." He lifted her hand, which still held the angel. "When my father died, I had all his things put in storage before selling his flat. I never looked through them. Here, either. He only kept a little place in the village, and . . ." He shrugged. "It was all left to me, but I wanted no part of any of it, so I sold it all off, along with most of the furnishings. But his papers and some of his personal things . . . I didn't know what to do with those, so I just locked them up. Anyway, while I was in Edinburgh, I went to storage, and . . . I went through his things."

"You did?" Kira's eyes were wide and that sheen of tears had returned. "Are you okay?"

"I'm fine, aye." He leaned down and kissed her temple, as much to soothe himself as to soothe her. "I don't know what I'd expected to find—something of my past, our past, his past, even, I suppose."

"And?"

He shook his head, laughed ruefully. "Like father, like son. And ye've no idea how much it pains me to say that. His papers were all business. In fact, there was nothing personal in them at all." He cradled her hand, holding the angel in his. "Except for this. I found a small box, either kept by my mother, or a nanny, I don't know. I found the certificate of my birth, a few photos of me as an infant, and the angel." He turned it over. The gold inscription on the back was badly chipped. "I believe it says First Christmas. I assume for a baby. I dinnae know why it's in such poor shape. As far as I know it's been in that box since I was an infant. So perhaps it was passed down. It could have been my father's or my mother's. I don't know. But it was the only thing they kept."

Kira looked up at him. "Why are you giving it to me? It's the only thing you have."

He turned her in his arms. "You're the only thing I have. The one I want to keep, to hold on to. This, the angel, is what I have of myself to give ye, Kira." He framed her face. "It's no' much, but it's wha' I have. And, so help me God, I'll do whatever it takes so that I'm never fighting against you, to get that back. Do ye understand?"

She nodded, tears gathering in her eyes. "I do."

Heart pounding in his ears so loudly he thought he might go deaf, Shay pressed the angel more tightly into her hands, then, with those exact words echoing in his ears, he slid his other hand down her arm to steady her . . . before lowering himself on one bent knee.

Kira gasped, clasping one hand over her mouth, and the other one, clutching the angel ornament, over her heart, as she realized what he was about to do.

But she didn't stop him.

He reached up and she lowered a badly shaking hand to his. He took it gently, but firmly, running his thumb over the back of her hand.

"I'd planned this whole evening out. I had so many things I wanted to say to you. But, like every other step we've taken . . ." He smiled up at her, stunned, at how utterly easy this was. "You're the one thing I'd fight for, Kira. The only thing I want to keep." He fumbled in his pocket, and drew out a small ring box. "I want you to know, every single day, that I mean to keep you. That I'll do whatever it takes, for us, to make this work. No matter the risk. I can't think of anything worse than losing you, so ye should know that I'll fight like hell to keep you. I am in love with ye, Kira MacLeod. Head over heels, with everything I have in me." He opened the ring box. "Please tell me you'll marry me. Be my wife, Kira. Take me as your husband."

Kira took the box with shaky hands, but she wasn't even looking at the diamond ring nestled inside. She was looking at him, lips trembling, tears forming at the corners of her eyes.

"If it's no' to your taste, we can—"

"Come here," she said, grabbing his wrist and tugging hard. "Come here."

He straightened and she launched herself into his arms. "I love you, Shay Callaghan. And I can't think of anything that would make me happier, or more proud, than to be your wife."

"So, you'll take me, then?" he asked, pushing her hair from her face, dashing the tears from her cheeks with his fingertips.

"Oh, aye, that I will. Just try and get rid of me."

He laughed, then he shouted, loud and long, and spun her around.

When they stopped laughing and kissing, and after he'd wiped a bit of moisture from the corners of his own eyes, he said, "I've dinner, all set up, but, right at the moment, I'd much rather feast on you."

"See? We're really very compatible."

"I'll show ye compatible," he all but growled, then made her squeal by swinging her up in his arms.

He spun them around, intent on heading to the second floor bedroom, but she said, "Wait!"

"What?" he asked, worried that he might have forgotten something important about the whole ritual. He'd wanted it to be a good memory. A perfect one. For them both to hold onto.

"The angel," she said, unfolding her hand, where she'd had it in a tight grip. "I want to put it on the tree."

He carried her over to the tree and she picked out a branch, then carefully slid the gold string over the needles, until he was safely anchored.

"First Christmas," she said, softly, then tipped her head up to look at him. "Ours. And I can't wait to fill our trees with more."

"You know," he said, looking from her to the ornament gently swaying from its perch, then shifting his gaze to the basket, proudly displayed on the entry table, then back to the woman in his arms. "Ye've only been here but a moment, and this place already feels more like home."

"It only took a moment to know it's a home with you that I want," she said, pulling his mouth down to hers. And they stood in front of the tree, kissing deeply, again and again, until both were out of breath.

But when he lifted his head, it was to find that rare devilish twinkle in her eyes. "Now," she said, "I believe there was some mention—a formal mention, no less—about wearing clothes that I didnae mind being torn from my body."

"Aye, I do believe I was in a rather heightened state of . . . missing you, when I wrote that part."

"I still can't believe you told the engraver to write that."

"Aye, we'll likely be hearing about it, in the village."

"You had the invitation done here? I thought maybe the city—"

"No. This is where we live, so this is where we love. I dinnae mind if the whole world knows I

plan to ravage the woman who will be my wife.
And often."

"Well, in that case, perhaps you should take me
to your bed. It's possible you're going to like what
you find underneath this entirely disposable dress."
She bit his chin. "A lot."

They only made it as far as the parlor wall.

Epilogue

"I've no idea what it's all about," Shay said, from the second office desk. "He only said that he'd like us all gathered at the main offices when he arrived back on the island."

Roan was seated on the edge of his desk, with Tessa leaning back between his legs. Graham was standing by the window, keeping a lookout for Blaine. Katie had her head bent over Kira's hand, studying her engagement ring.

"It's beautiful," she gushed, then glanced over at Shay. "You've marvelous taste," she said. "It suits her beautifully."

Shay nodded and Kira smiled. It was a week into the new year, but it felt as if a whole new life had begun. The plans for the school had been approved, with interior renovations already under way. They'd break ground on the additions in the spring, and hoped to have the entire operation running by the summer tourist season.

She and Shay had gone to Edinburgh over the holidays after all, and spent the week between Christmas and Hogmanay with Tessa and Roan, though they'd missed Blaine, who'd begged off at the last moment. It had been a magical time, seeing the city through his eyes, and a truly grounding time for the two of them as well. She'd loved getting to see the other part of his life, and him in his element there. She had been introduced to Shay's business associates and had a newfound respect for why he did what he did.

They'd initially talked about the idea of his cutting back his time in the city, or leaving the practice entirely. But the more they'd talked about his cases, the more she'd come to realize that he really did have a passion for what he did. It was never a happy time for his clients, but he did his very best to make sure they were able to move forward, claim their new lives as whole as possible. Divorce happened, and Shay knew he was helping those he represented. And Kira knew they were very lucky to have him on their side.

Shay had turned one of the bedrooms in his city flat into a studio for Kira, so rather than spend so much apart, she could accompany him to the city and work there. That would change when the school opened, but she was already enjoying the chance to get away from the island, and reclaim the things she loved about living in the city.

"I wish I knew what the big deal was," Tessa was saying. "Why couldn't Blaine have just told you whatever it was on the phone?"

"I couldn't get it out of him," Katie said. "And if I couldn't, you know it couldn't be done."

Blaine Sheffield was Katie's childhood friend, and, very briefly, her fiancé. It had been a pre-arranged marriage made in hell and Katie had been wise enough, at the last minute, to bail out . . . and run off to Kinloch with Graham, instead. Blaine had followed, but not to win Katie back. It was more a joint retreat to get as far away from the Sheffields and the Annapolis-based McAuleys as he could. At least until he figured out what to do with his newly disowned self for having the nerve to be outed on his wedding day, literally in front of God and everyone, and—Kira was fairly certain— for not manning up and going ahead and marrying Katie anyway.

From what Kira understood, Blaine had started working for Roan, doing some digging on Iain McAuley, who had presented an obstacle, a rather critical one, this time, in Katie's attempt to marry Graham. The wedding had gone off, but the mystery surrounding Iain McAuley had continued, and Kira knew Shay had wanted no loose ends, so he'd kept Blaine on it. He'd even done work in the city for Shay on some of his cases there. Turned out the man could ferret out anything. So . . . Blaine had found his niche. And he'd stayed.

Roan turned to Shay. "If this is still about the inheritance issue, you're going to need to officially call him off. I canno' see how Mr. McAuley has any claim here now or what possible harm—"

Eliza, Roan's secretary, took that moment to stick her perfectly pinned and coiffed gray head into the office. "Mr. Blaine has arrived."

Graham turned to look back out of the window,

having looked away while Roan was talking. "Sorry. I must have missed it."

"Well, have him come in already," Katie urged, smiling. "Why so formal?"

"Oh, I believe that will be made clear momentarily," Eliza said, eyes twinkling.

The door swung wider and Blaine strolled in, quite natty in a cutaway black jacket and silk striped trousers. A tartan cummerbund and bowtie finished off the look.

Kira thought, with his blond good looks, he pulled it off rather gorgeously, as if he'd been born wearing just that.

"Hullo, Blaine," Roan said, with zero reaction to Blaine's state of dress.

"Don't spoil it," Blaine said, pointing a finger at Roan, but there was clear affection in his tone.

And despite Roan's rolling of eyes, Kira knew he liked and respected Blaine, it was just their way. Kira winked at Shay, who gave her the smallest of smiles in return, but otherwise kept his own council, remaining behind the far desk.

"Thank you all for coming," Blaine announced to the room at large, clearly enjoying his dramatic entrance, but then, from what Kira knew, when didn't he?

Personally, she thought he was charming and rather adorable.

"As you all know, I've been putting my quite extensive and tirelessly dedicated skills to discovering what the real story was regarding one Mr. Iain McAuley."

"Have ye solved it then?" Graham asked.

"Yes, I have."

"Thank the Lord," Roan murmured. "We can all get back to work now. The fear and panic can finally be put to rest."

Blaine ignored him. "As it happens, there is a simple solution to the mystery of his arrival on Kinloch, and his attempt to usurp the clan lairdship and island chiefdom."

"Put us out of our misery already—"

"Roan," Graham gently chided. "Blaine, what is it you've found? Anything for us to be concerned about?"

"No, quite the opposite. That is, as long as you don't mind the fact that Iain will be returning to Kinloch. In fact, he'll be staying on here." Blaine pushed the office door completely open. "With me."

Kira remembered Iain from his brief but very memorable stay on Kinloch the previous fall. He'd have been memorable anyway, with his white smile and dashing good looks.

"Oh my, he's gone and borrowed from Blaine's closet," Roan said.

Kira might have kicked Roan's toes herself, but then Iain entered, decked out in full, formal clan regalia and she was too busy gawking to kick. He really was quite stunning, though the rows of lace on the front of the white shirt peeking out from the jacket front and at the cuffs wasn't something traditionally seen. At least on Kinloch.

Iain's smile was a bit abashed, but he kept his head up. "Hullo, everyone. I appreciate the welcome." His gaze strayed briefly to Roan, but settled on Graham, then Shay. "I'm sorry for any upset I caused during my last visit. Rest assured, I intend to remain a benign presence from this point forward."

"Benign?" Blaine said. "I hardly think so." Then he slid his arm through Iain's, and looked at the group. "I mean . . . look at him." The two smiled at each other . . . and the light finally dawned. On everyone.

Blaine faced the group again. "Turns out our stories are somewhat similar. We both come from rich, controlling families. And we both almost made very ill-advised marital choices rather than reaching for our own true happiness." The two shared another look.

And Kira knew that look.

Roan started to say something, but this time Tessa elbowed him in the stomach . . . and started clapping. "Has there been a wedding?" she asked over the din, as everyone else started clapping for the happy couple as well.

"Well," Blaine said, "we don't dress like this every day." He and Iain grinned again. "Though I think we totally should."

Everyone laughed and Eliza came in carrying a cake. There were two grooms on top.

"You knew?" Roan said. "How on earth did you know?"

"I always know," Eliza answered.

Shay came around his desk and tucked Kira by his side as a champagne bottle appeared and everyone started talking at once.

Kira leaned close and whispered, "You've been quiet. What do you think of all this?"

"That we should elope?"

Kira laughed and turned in his arms, and kissed him. "What? And deprive Blaine of planning our wedding?"

They were married in the abbey, on Valentine's Day. There were doves. A carriage drawn by six white horses. A gilded and pillared cake that was slightly larger than Kira's Fiat.

And a bride and groom who lived happily ever after.

If you enjoyed your time on Kinloch, pick up Graham's story in SOME LIKE IT SCOT, *and Roan's story in* OFF KILTER, *available at www.kensingtonbooks.com.*

Snow Angel

KATE
ANGELL

To the dedicated doctors, nursing staff, and receptionists at Mission Hills Veterinary Clinic in Naples, Florida. Dr. Angela Butts, Dr. Amelia Foster, Karen, Stacey, Chelsie, and Cincy—you have all my respect and admiration.

Prologue

Frost Peak Lodge, Aspen, Colorado
Three years ago

The steam rising from the cedar hot tub was pure foreplay. The vapors thickened then thinned on the cold night air. The condensation tickled exposed skin, while jets teased the buttocks.

Allie sat on the circular bench, her body liquid. Her head rested on the rim, her eyelids heavy, her lips parted. The water bubbled, ebbed, and bared her left breast, her nipple hard and peaked as she focused on the naked man across from her.

She knew him only as Aidan. They'd yet to exchange last names. He was a ski stud and hot tub god. A man so cut he could have been a sculpture. Broad chest, buff abs. She licked her lips, imagined tracing the faded tan line on his groin with her tongue.

His gaze was hooded as he stretched his arms

along the edges of the hot tub and smiled lazily at her. Could he read her mind? It appeared he had.

"Any regrets?" he asked.

"Not a one," she said. Aidan was pure female arousal. He touched her with his eyes and made her skin tingle.

"I'm glad you're here."

"So am I." Steam licked her lips as she released a soft sigh. She closed her eyes and let her thoughts drift back to the moment they'd met. This holiday would stay with her forever . . .

The mountain. The man. Aidan had courted her on the slopes for three days. He'd given chase, racing her down the advanced trails, pushing her performance. She'd taken their competition seriously. She skied with the speed and purpose of outrunning an avalanche. She had won.

At the end of the first and second day, he smiled, nothing more. He left her at the base of the mountain. Alone.

He'd spiked her interest. She wanted to meet him. On Christmas Eve, he introduced himself as Aidan. He had her at "*nice huck.*"

She'd shown off for him that afternoon. Halfway down Widow Maker's Run, she threw herself off the cliff's edge and caught big air, a thrilling stunt by an advanced skier.

She'd impressed him.

He made her heart pound.

Late afternoon shadows had nudged them to the valet ski check where they handed off their gear. They then entered the lodge bar, The Thirsty Squirrel. She'd ordered hot buttered rum and he sipped two fingers of scotch. Her drink had been served in a green mug rimmed with holly berries. A scripted *Merry Christmas* wrapped Aidan's tumbler. Happy Hour drew snow bunnies, ski bums, and serious skiers ready to party.

A DJ Santa spun tunes. "Jingle Bells" had made Allie smile. "I've worked ski resorts since I was sixteen," she told Aidan as they settled on their bar stools and shed their ski jackets. "I was once assigned sleigh rides during Christmas week. I harnessed big Belgium draft horses to a Santa-style sleigh with a curly dash. The route crossed a covered bridge then ran alongside a brook on a winding, wooded trail.

"Families were fun. I handed out warm blankets, a thermos of hot chocolate, and gingerbread cookies." She scrunched her nose. "Couples were another matter. They'd slide beneath the tartan plaids and once we got deep into the forest, the sleigh would start to rock. My job description didn't include listening to all that giggling and panting. I learned to wear ear muffs."

Aidan chuckled, deep, vibrant, and richly male. "That gives a whole new meaning to *dashing through the snow.*"

She agreed. "I refused to take out the sleigh until it was sanitized. The guys in the barn laughed their butts off the first time I showed up with my unusual request. By the tenth cleanup, it was no longer funny."

"We never know what life has in store for us."

"My sister would disagree. Beth's a chirologist."

He raised a brow. "She reads palms?"

"Beth believes your life is printed on your palm. She taught me the basics."

She'd waited for him to roll his eyes. He surprised her by turning over his right hand. "Read me, sweetheart."

She'd traced the line that curved above his thumb, leading downward toward his wrist. "You have a long life line," she said, liking the warm feel of his skin against her fingertips. He had a man's hand, strong and lightly callused. "You're a bit of a daredevil, but you could live to be one hundred. You work hard, but play harder."

He nodded, and she continued. She ran her fingertip across the top of his palm, just below his fingers, a sensual slide. His palm grew slightly damp. She was making him sweat. "A curved heart line indicates you're romantic."

"I do candy, flowers, and prolonged foreplay."

Her stomach fluttered over foreplay. She could imagine his hands sliding down her body, dipping between her thighs, then inching their way upward. Her breath stuck in her throat. She shifted on the bar stool, aroused by this man.

"The fate line runs from the bottom of your palm near the wrist up through the center toward the middle finger," she continued. "You have a star at the top of your fate line which means good fortune and great success."

She stroked the side of his hand. "The short, single marriage line beneath your little finger shows one walk down the aisle. No divorce."

He linked his fingers with hers, and sent her heart racing. "My parents have been married for thirty-five years. They still act like newlyweds."

Allie smiled, but said nothing. She seldom discussed her single mom. Margo, as her mother preferred to be called, didn't do mother-daughter. Margo liked to be *one of the girls*. She refused to grow up or grow old.

A sip of her buttered rum, and Allie turned the conversation to skiing; to the hazards of off-piste and the adrenaline rush of conquering the slopes.

"Your winter playground of choice?" she asked.

"Stowe," he answered. "I like Vermont. I stay at the Red Fox Country Inn and cross-country ski from the back door to the base of Mt. Mainsfield. The Stoweked Grille makes the best seafood stew in New England. How about you?"

"Solitude near Salt Lake City," she said. "No lift lines, crowded runs, or overtracked snow. The best chicken and chorizo chili in Utah is served at Wiley Coyote, a local mountain pub."

The bar crowd had begun singing Christmas carols at the top of their lungs. Allie leaned closer to be heard. She breathed in the scent of his cologne, spice and citrus. Subtle, yet masculine. "Are you pure powderhound?" she asked.

Aidan shook his head. "Winter's my favorite season, but year-round, I enjoy adventure racing."

She was familiar with the sport. It required a combination of skills, depending on the competition. Athletes often ran, mountain biked, ripped down rapids in a canoe, then rappelled off a one-hundred-foot rock face. The race could last a day or a week.

"Dangerous and disciplined," she admired. "You push yourself physically."

He finished off his scotch. "What makes your heart race?"

The sexy look in his eye challenged her to answer him. The intensity of his stare made her curl her toes in her snow boots.

"The savage beauty and intimacy of the slopes," she said honestly. In that moment she realized the closest relationship she'd had in four years was with her skis. A flutter of anticipation made her shiver. That would all change tonight.

They'd talked further, gotten to know each other over the next hour. He liked science fiction and action movies. She leaned toward mysteries and crime-solving dramas on TV.

Aidan owned a Blackberry Torch. Allie had a disposable cell phone.

He only bought black cars. Her sunglasses were always red.

He had two golden retrievers. She'd never had a pet.

He confessed to working high-end retail. She shopped blue-light specials, the bigger the bargain the better.

She admitted to being a ski instructor on holiday.

All around them, the crowd thickened, pressed, and Allie soon took an elbow to the ribs as several women sought space at the bar. Definitely snow bunnies, with their big hair, perfect makeup, fitted snow pants, and designer jackets with furry hoods. They cruised the lobby and the bar, never leaving the comfort of the lodge.

The ladies winked at Aidan; wedged themselves closer. They nearly knocked Allie off her bar stool.

Aidan had come to her rescue. He interlocked the wooden legs of their stools so no one could slip between them. His intimate closeness toyed with her body and sex played on her thoughts. They sat as privately as any two people could sit in a packed bar.

They'd swiveled slowly on their stools, brushing hands, bumping hips. He slid his knee between her legs. The rub of their ski pants was raw and sexual. A stirring inside her begged to be satisfied and she found it hard to sit still. Her fingers itched to touch him. Their chemistry was off the charts.

She'd taken a sip of her cocktail and let the caramelized brown sugar and dusting of cinnamon seduce her tongue. If Christmas had a taste, it would be hot buttered rum.

Their gazes had locked when the bartender asked if they wanted another round. They both passed. Aidan paid for the drinks and left a big tip.

They'd slid off their stools, grabbed their jackets, and cut a path through the boisterous crowd. He pressed his hand to her back as they crossed the lobby. The man had big hands. His palm fit at the base of her spine and the tips of his fingers brushed her side. A delicious shiver caressed her every nerve.

Only one clerk along with the concierge manned Reception. Red garlands draped the rustic beams near the main counter. Silver bells hung above the mantel on the fireplace in holiday celebration. Two evergreens decorated with gold pine cones flanked the bank of elevators.

They rode in silence to the twelfth floor. The doors opened to a set of suites. Aidan pointed Allie to the far end of the hallway.

His suite was far larger than her room. She took it all in. Two bedrooms branched off the living area. A kitchen and computer alcove framed the back. Sliding glass doors showcased night skiing, the mountain a black spike against the full moon. Electric high-intensity lamps lit the trails. The snow sparkled like diamonds.

Tall privacy walls encased a short wooden deck, the hot tub at its center, all bubbly and steamy and awaiting naked bodies. Allie lowered her eyes, but not out of shyness. She didn't want him to guess how turned on she was; she'd rather show him.

They had hastily lowered zippers, flicked snaps, and unhooked buckles. He moved with surety. She was all thumbs.

Aidan had taken her hand and lightly kissed her palm. He'd gone on to study her palm as she had studied his at the bar. "Your sex line indicates you're a good lover."

Her lips twitched. There was no sex line.

"Your fantasy line has spikes," he continued. "It shows you're kinky, sweetheart."

That made her smile. He'd lightened the mood, put her at ease, and made her want him even more.

They finished undressing. Fabrics rasped over their skin, fell where they might. Across her toes, the arms of her powder-blue fleece hugged Aidan's black wool sweater.

Against his ankles, her navy ski pants straddled his own gray pair. Between them, his boxer briefs humped her blue cotton bikinis.

Kicked to the side, the heels of his Nordicas rubbed the toes of her snow boots. Their clothes were getting it on.

She stared openly at him, this man of muscular

physique and hotter-than-hell face. Ink-dark hair mussed his brow, and his pale gray eyes were nearly opaque. His cheekbones slashed to a lean jaw. His mouth was sexy, his lower lip suckable.

He, in turn, admired her breasts and abdomen. He ran his finger over the tiny skier tattoo near her navel. His eyes dilated at her v-zone.

Allie took in his erection and inhaled her approval. She sucked in her stomach nearly to her spine. Her skull prickled and her skin itched. She was so turned on she could barely stand still.

He hadn't even kissed her.

She'd debated jumping his bones, right there on the plush brown carpet. They'd suffer rug burn, but she was wired, wanting, and tired of waiting.

She wasn't into ski lodge affairs, yet it was Christmas Eve. She had no idea where her mother was spending the holidays or if Margo was still alive. Years had separated them. All contact had been lost.

Her sisters had surprised her with a ski vacation. They'd wanted her to play, not work. Beth had booked Allie's room. Laura had prepaid all lift fees. Allie had saved for a year and sent them on a Caribbean cruise.

Her sisters loved the sun.

Allie lived for snow.

Her holiday stocking was presently empty.

She'd chosen Aidan as her gift and unwrapped him.

He stood before her, six feet of testosterone and male arousal. She wished he had a red bow around his neck, or silver bells jingling at his groin.

One corner of his mouth lifted, as if he'd read her mind. He believed in foreplay and prolonged the inevitable.

He'd taken her hand and led her across the living room. His backside was chiseled, his butt muscular. She could've followed him for miles.

The glass sliders hissed on their tracks as the inside warmth escaped, meeting air so sharp and crisp her nipples puckered. Goose bumps skittered down her spine and up her inner thighs. Her breath blew frosty. A fat snowflake tipped her nose. It had started to snow.

She closed the doors behind her, hoped she wouldn't turn into an ice sculpture. Amazingly, the cold hadn't affected his erection. He pointed toward the North Pole.

Aidan had stepped into the hot tub and drawn her in behind him. The water lapped her calves as the steam shot to her crotch. He lowered himself onto the bench then gave her room to pick her spot. She chose to sit across from him. Awareness closed all space between them.

Her heartbeat quickened. He'd teased her on the slopes for three days then aroused her further in the bar. She was on edge, same as Aidan. They'd soon find release . . .

"Are you still with me, babe?"

His question drew her back to the moment. She blinked, focused, then said, "I didn't go far." She'd already taken the memories of this man into her heart.

Allie leaned back against the cedar and looked at the sky. Snow drifted down, yet each flake melted within the rising steam of the hot tub. Only the farthest corner of the deck collected snow, a small white drift against the wooden siding.

Anticipation played between them, a sexual tease. She flexed her leg and made the first move. She skimmed the tips of her toes over his knee. The ball of her foot grazed the inside of his thigh then worked up and over his hip. She flicked her toes over his abdomen and he inhaled sharply. Her heel gently pressed lower, and his sex brushed the side of her foot, thick and tickling, and making her smile.

She teased lightly.

He groaned deeply.

His opaque eyes were hooded by his ink-dark lashes. Desire flared his nostrils. His release of breath was rough, rushed. His hips now rocked.

"My turn, sweetheart." He slid along the bench, closed the distance between them. He lifted her slightly, until she straddled his groin. Moist and trembling, she waited for him to fill her.

They were now breast to chest.

Thigh to thigh.

Sex to sex.

He could have entered her with the slightest shift of his hips. But he didn't. Instead he stroked her, long, lazy strokes that left her liquid. He massaged her scalp, her neck and shoulders. Making a fan of his fingers, he palmed her breast. She arched her spine, squeezed his hips with her thighs. He felt so good wedged against her wet heat, all solid and hard.

The warm whirl of the water seduced their bellies. The steam rolled off his shoulders and collected between her breasts. They grew hotter together.

He flattened his hands on her thighs, then went on to trace the crease of her sex with his thumbs. She was so ready for him, she nearly mounted his fingers.

Allie moved closer and he eased back. The man gave new meaning to prolonged foreplay. She squirmed, and he continued to tease her.

The play of his fingers wound her tight. So tight, the craving for the feel of him penetrating her made her pubic muscles clench. She leaned in and bit his lower lip. "I want you," she breathed against his mouth.

He slipped the tip of his tongue between her lips. "Want me more."

His control nearly killed her. Two could play this game. She would *make* him beg. She stroked his erection, squeezed him from base to tip until he threw back his head and hissed through his teeth.

Hunger glittered in his eyes.

His skin pulled taut across his cheekbones.

His lips flattened in both pain and pleasure.

She increased the pressure and he rocked his hips. His sex thrust between her palms. He panted, groaned, his body pumped with lust.

"I want you." He repeated her words.

She exhaled, a slow, sexy smile curving her lips. "It's about time."

He cupped her bottom, lifted her easily. He rose like a god from the sea. Water streamed and steamed between them as he stepped from the hot tub.

A slide of the glass door and they reentered his suite. He shoved the door closed with his foot. He headed straight for the bedroom. He walked damn fast.

Aidan was hot for this woman. She'd attracted him the first day of his vacation. He'd stood back and taken his time to meet her. She'd been pursued by numerous male skiers, yet she declined each invitation. Lady was selective.

He courted her on the mountain, a woman in tune with the slopes. She reminded him of a snow angel with her pale blond hair, sky-blue eyes, and winter-pink cheeks.

Yet her smile was far from angelic. Her lips were lush, the flick of her tongue sexy. He'd wanted her mouth on him for the holidays. Her kisses all over his body.

He'd made his move on Christmas Eve, hopeful she'd join him for a cocktail. Her acceptance had pleased him. He'd been hard from the moment they entered the bar.

A drink had led to the hot tub, now to his bed. He kicked open the door. The room had a rustic décor: a dark wood armoire and two overstuffed chairs in an evergreen print. A king-size bed welcomed sleep and sex.

Aidan didn't care if he slept a wink that night.

Their bodies were still damp, but he didn't take the time to towel either of them off. Instead he tossed back the dark brown comforter and laid Allie on the ivory cotton sheet.

He stared at her, this woman he craved. Her hair was wild; her gaze passionate. Her breasts were high and firm, her ribs symmetrical. Her stomach was bounce-a-quarter flat.

He was a leg man. Her skier legs were slender, toned, and ready to wrap his hips.

As he eased over her, the blend of cool sheets and hot-bodied woman nearly undid him. She rose up to meet him, and they kissed deeply. Their tongues mated with need and expectancy.

His heart was pounding so fast, he could feel the pulsing in his dick. He snagged a condom from the drawer of the nightstand, ripped the foil with his teeth, and slipped it on. She lifted her hips and he slid in to her. They were one.

Their first time was swift and fierce. She clawed his back and he clutched her bottom. He left bruises on her butt cheeks. He wanted her to take what he was feeling and make it her own. She did.

She arched against him, her body clenching.

His body strained against hers.

She let go, melting against him.

He came a moment later.

Afterward he tucked her so tightly against his body she became an imprint on his skin. A sexual tattoo, invisible, yet memorable. The best sex of his life.

They spooned for hours, making small talk. Her spine curved nicely against his chest. The firm roundness of her bottom pressed his groin, teasing him erect.

He would have taken her again, yet he felt the

need to talk, to deepen their connection. "I was born and raised in the Midwest. I'm an only child," Aidan whispered against her ear. "This year my father came down with bronchitis right before our family ski trip. My mother refused to let him travel."

Allie stirred and her shoulders stiffened. Her sigh sifted into him, her voice soft and hesitant. "I've lived in nearly every city in California, mostly in apartments, twice in a trailer, and once in a tent on Hermosa Beach."

He nuzzled her neck, her scent one of sun-touched snow and clean mountain air. "Your mother liked to travel?"

She shook her head and strands of her blond hair settled on his cheek. "My mom was always looking for a good time. I think she was lonely. Some women need a man. My mother never found the right one. She bar-hopped and we took our meals at truck stops. She refused to put down roots. I've two sisters. None of us has the same father."

"Tell me about your sisters."

"Both are older; both remain single. Both own homes, have cats, and are nicely settled."

"What about you?"

"I'm a ski bum at heart. I play wherever there's fresh powder."

He nipped her earlobe. "Play with me now, Allie."

She did. They played three more times that night.

When their hunger turned to food, they showered, donned hotel bathrobes, and she cooked for him. The refrigerator was fully stocked, and she made Monte Cristo sandwiches. They lingered in the living room, turned on TV, and watched the weather channel. An ice storm was forecast, which would close down the slopes. Traffic would be limited to emergency vehicles. They'd soon be snowbound.

His decision to extend his vacation came easily. He was drawn to Allie and hoped she'd commit to a few more days at the lodge. He wanted to know her better.

Once back in bed, he tucked into her softness. He liked holding her. Liked watching her sleep. Liked hearing her breathe.

He drifted off, a man content.

He wakened early, wanting to make plans for more skiing, more loving . . . only to find himself alone in a very big bed.

The quiet unnerved him. He lay on his back, fully naked, the bedroom air chilly. He ran his tongue over his lower lip, still numb from a long night of kissing. He cocked his head, noticed the scratches on his shoulder. A love bite centered over his heart. His morning erection craved attention.

The bedroom door stood ajar. "Allie?" he called.

No response. The silence scared him.

He intuitively knew she was gone.

He pushed up on his elbows, looked around. The sheets were untucked, the comforter sprawled on the floor. They'd shared a king-size pillow. The imprint of her cheek and chin remained on the cotton case. Her sexual heat lingered, along with her woman's scent.

Confusion and loss hit him hard. What the hell had happened? She'd wanted him as bad as he wanted her. Yet she hadn't stuck around, hadn't given them a chance. She'd left without breakfast or a good-bye.

He knew so little about her. He had no idea where she lived. Where she would next ski. Where she spent the summer.

They hadn't exchanged last names.

Chances were good he'd never see her again.

His holiday went to hell.

Chapter One

Chicago, Illinois
December 24th, three years later

The worst blizzard in twenty years was forecast for Christmas Eve. The winter snowstorm had struck much of the Midwest, and Chicago would be hit the hardest. Meteorologists had tracked the system for the past week. They predicted four feet of snow.

Law enforcement warned people to stay home. Schools and airports had closed. Rail service was halted. Interstate travel was seriously disrupted and traffic would soon be paralyzed. Snow removal couldn't begin until the storm passed.

Two-fifteen, and a few downtown businesses remained open for last minute holiday shopping. Only die-hard customers fought the biting wind and blowing snow.

Allie Smith had arrived in Chicago on the last outgoing flight from Denver. An invitation to spend

Christmas with her sisters brought her to Dutton's
Department Store. A bottle of Snow Angel cologne
was at the top of their gift lists. Dutton's was the
only store to sell the signature scent. Allie felt a tug
at her heart. She wanted to make them happy and
neither snow nor sleet would stop her from fulfill-
ing their Christmas wish. Beth and Laura meant
everything to her.

A ponytailed taxi driver named Jeremy Bott was
still taking fares from O'Hare. The heater barely
worked in his yellow cab. The defroster whistled
noisily. He kept wiping his jacket sleeve across the
front windshield. There was little visibility.

An hour's drive and Jeremy parked at the snow-
banked curb on State Street. He offered to wait
while Allie did her shopping. She exited the cab,
promised to be as quick as she could, which in ac-
tuality was quite slow. She had a sprained ankle.
She winced. It hurt like hell.

Earlier that week she'd been struck by a snowmobile while giving ski lessons at the base of a
bunny hill. A male college student had ridden out-
of-zone to show off and flirt with her. He'd spun
the machine in a circle, lost control, and knocked
Allie down. He'd apologized all over himself. Neither his regret nor ice packs had taken down the
swelling. She continued to limp.

The lodge physician had suggested X-rays. She
planned to see an orthopedist after Christmas.
Until then, she'd live with the pain.

On the icy sidewalk now, she braced herself
against a wind that threatened to blow her down.
Her sheepskin UGGS had little traction and she
slid toward the front entrance. The electric doors

swooshed open and an elderly doorman blocked her path.

He looked down his nose at her, as if she was a homeless person blown in off the street. Determined not to be dissuaded by his disapproving frown, she smiled at him, though she had to admit her white knit cap, worn ski jacket, and faded jeans had seen better days. Her khaki backpack had traveled many miles.

"Welcome to Dutton's, the ultimate shopping experience," the man said stiffly. "You've got thirty minutes until we close."

She nodded, and stepped deeper into the store. What she saw took her breath away. Her mouth went dry. The media promoted Dutton's as the American Harrods. The opulence reminded her of a palace. She admired the black Italian marble floor, gold columns, and wine silk brocade wallpaper. A crystal chandelier hung from the domed ceiling. Four uniformed operators stood at attention before the bank of elevators. The store offered seven floors of designer luxuries.

The grandeur was intimidating. The scent of old money and snobbery surrounded her. Classical music played softly in the background. Dutton's was far more than she'd ever imagined.

She exhaled slowly, trying to take it all in. Sales associates scurried to close up their departments. Security guarded the jewelry counter as personnel stored diamond rings and Rolex watches in satin boxes then locked them in a safe.

Allie passed Santa's Grotto to reach the octagonal glass counter where beauty products and fragrances were sold. Snow Angel was prominently displayed. The hand-blown bottles with twenty-four carat gold halos were arranged on silver wings.

She sprayed the test atomizer and perfumed the air. The scent was as ethereal as it was sensual, and captured the magic of a winter wonderland. A second spritz, and memories of downhill skiing, a hot tub, and Christmas Eve sex shook her. She nearly dropped the tester.

Aidan. She'd never forgotten the man. His image was as clear to her now as it had been three years prior. She could still picture his amazing body, naked and on top, thrusting into her. She'd arched her back beneath him as one sensual tremor after another possessed her whole body. They'd mated with an intensity that came full circle. He'd drawn her out of herself and into him, and she'd felt his pulse touch her soul. They'd experienced oneness and comfort. She'd fallen hard and fast for him. She'd never experienced anyone like Aidan.

Their short time together had terrified her. She'd never done serious, had never trusted forever. He appeared solid and stable while she was gone with the wind.

She was her mother's daughter. The memories of Margo's poor relationships crippled Allie. She'd been an emotional mess, so she'd done what she did best—left Aidan before he could hurt her.

She often wished she'd gotten his last name. She'd have made an attempt to see him again. Maybe she'd have worked up the courage to speak to him. She'd never know. Three years to the day separated them now.

She set down the tester cologne. Time was of

the essence. She glanced at her watch. She had seven minutes to locate a sales associate and pay for her gifts. She'd never forgive herself if two bottles of Snow Angel didn't sit under her sisters' tree on Christmas morning. The cologne was a fragrant reminder of her affection for them that would last long after the holiday.

A sign near the cash register sent her to stationery, photo albums, and frames. She hobbled to the back of the store, only to be directed to art and antiques. Once there, a hand-printed note taped to an oil painting of an old-fashioned Santa Claus pointed her to the bootery.

She kept walking, dragging her foot and breathing hard. *She was running a freakin' maze.*

The overhead lights flickered and an ominous silence took hold. Allie prayed she could check out and be on her way before the store lost electricity.

She moved to the main aisle, looked toward the front door. No doorman. She cut her gaze toward the elevators. No operators. She stood on tiptoe and scanned the first floor. No sales personnel. No customers.

Being alone in Dutton's Department Store on Christmas Eve gave her the creeps. She had to get out now.

She pulled her wallet from her jacket pocket, found a grand total of six dollars in cash, one personal check, and two credit cards. She panicked. How the hell was she going to pay for her gifts? There was no one around to ring up her sale.

Frantic now, she returned to beauty and fragrance. She located an ink pen on the counter and quickly wrote out a check to Dutton's for the price of the cologne. She slipped the payment beneath the register drawer, making sure a corner of the check would be visible to the salesclerk.

She cradled the Snow Angels in the crook of her arm and pushed for the door, only to be brought up short when a man shouted, "Shoplifters will be prosecuted."

Holy crap, security.

"I'm armed and won't hesitate to—" His words were swallowed in a blackout as the blizzard abruptly cut all power. She froze as red emergency lights flashed, followed by the buzz and click as the automatic doors locked. Snow beat against the main door and thick frost closed off the front display windows to the outside world.

Darkness shrank her visibility to ten feet in front of her.

What now? She was trapped.

"Hands in the air," the guard ordered right before he beamed his Maglite flashlight in her face, blinding her.

Allie squinted, raised her arms. She held a Snow Angel in each hand over her head. "I'm not a thief. I paid for the cologne."

"Where's the sales receipt?"

She didn't have one.

"Don't move," he said gruffly.

How could she? She had nowhere to go.

It took a minute, maybe two, before the store generators kicked on. The machines whirred, chugged, and struggled against the storm. Wall sconces soon cast a smattering of light near the elevators and along the far aisles. Shadows played against the darkness.

The guard lowered his flashlight, and the beam bounced off her chin. She blinked, focused on the man before her. He was short, wiry, and wore a black uniform. His legs were widespread. His fingers twitched over his duty utility belt, a belt so loaded with gadgets it rode low on his hips. He bounced on the balls of his feet, all antsy and edgy and itching to fight crime.

He considered Allie a criminal.

Before she could explain, heavy footsteps sounded down the center aisle and a second person walked out of the darkness. A much taller man, she noted, broader in the shoulders and thicker in the chest than the guard who held the Maglite on her. She was unable to see his face, but she sensed his authority. Perhaps he was head of security or the store manager.

"What's going on, Sam?" The growling whir of the generators distorted the newcomer's voice.

Sam puffed out his chest. "A shoplifter, boss. I caught her leaving the store with two bottles of Snow Angel. There may be more items in her jacket pockets."

"I'm not a thief," Allie ground out. "The store was about to close and I couldn't find a cashier. Go to beauty and fragrance, and you'll find my check under the register drawer."

"Verify her story while I pat her down," the boss said to the watchman.

Allie stepped backward. "Why don't you check my story first before you frisk me?"

"Sorry, miss, but I have to follow store procedure," the boss said without apology.

"Handcuffs, baton, Taser?" Sam offered.

Taser? She swallowed hard. The gangly guard was an alarmist. He'd blown the situation out of proportion. He was having a Barney Fife moment and taking his job way too seriously.

Allie swore she heard the man in charge sigh. "I thought we agreed you wouldn't carry a Taser, Sam," he said with great patience.

"It's the holidays, sir," Sam said. "Dutton's has been swarming with shoppers. Many customers aren't our usual clientele." He looked pointedly at Allie. "I wanted to be prepared."

She wanted to say something back to the guard, but kept quiet. She was already in enough trouble. She didn't want to be zapped for being a smart mouth.

The boss held out his hand. "I'll take the Taser in case the woman tries to run."

Allie shifted her weight. Her ankle hurt like hell. She wanted to tell these two to show a little respect for a paying customer. She'd sell her soul to sit down, to get her weight off her foot, even for a minute. The pain was making her light-headed.

She watched as Sam unclipped the weapon from his utility belt. He pulled the trigger and electricity arced. His scare tactic forced Allie back. Not so much for her own safety but for the guard's. The man's hand shook so badly, he nearly zapped himself. She didn't want him falling at her feet unconscious.

A few more sparks and Sam handed his supervisor the weapon, along with a smaller flashlight.

"I'll hurry back." He shuffled off, the beam from his Maglite sweeping the floor.

Silence stood like a third person between Allie and the boss. "Turn around and drop your backpack," he instructed. "Take off your ski cap, jacket, and boots, then put your hands on the jewelry counter."

Allie froze. This man with the deep voice and dominant presence was going to frisk her. He might even arrest her. She was at his mercy. She hoped to get through the ordeal with her dignity intact.

Allie. Aidan Dutton had a desperate need *to touch* this woman. To see her naked. To breathe in her scent and revel in its intoxicating effect. He would now feel her up and stroke her down. Slowly. He planned to take his sweet time and enjoy her discomfort. She'd yet to see his face, which was to his advantage.

He couldn't believe Allie of Frost Peak Lodge stood before him now, his snow angel in the flesh. She'd inspired the store's signature scent. The fragrance took him back to their Aspen holiday, to the chase, to unforgettable sex, to a bond that made a connection, but never fully formed. She'd snuck out of his suite without a trace.

He'd tried desperately to find her. The hotel had been cooperative. The manager had searched their database for a guest named Allie, yet there'd been no listing for the woman. It was as if she'd never existed.

She'd been at the top of his Christmas list for three long years. He let out a long, slow breath. Santa had finally filled his stocking.

Before they could move forward, he needed to know why she'd abandoned him, without a good-bye. She owed him an explanation and he intended to get it. He hadn't gotten over her leaving him like that. He could still feel the hurt.

Fate had placed him in Security when she entered the store. Sam had put through a call to the corporate offices and requested his presence. They'd then monitored the worsening weather and the immediate need to close. Six guards had hastily escorted the last few customers to the door. People needed to reach their homes before the brunt of the blizzard hit.

"Crazy-ass woman," Sam had grumbled, jabbing a finger at one of the monitors. "She looks half frozen."

Curious, Aidan had shifted his gaze from the televised weather report to the security screen. The doorman had tried to block the shopper blown in off the street, but she'd hobbled past him. By the intense look on her face, he could see she was on a holiday mission. He smiled. He had to admire her tenacity. Dutton's needed more shoppers like her.

She'd clapped her mittens and stomped one foot, then taken in the décor. Her eyes had gone wide and her lips had parted. She seemed out of her element, but that didn't deter her. She set her jaw and headed down the center aisle. Snow flaked from her boots, melting on the black marble tiles. She left a trail of slush.

Aidan had studied her, studied her hard. His skin prickled and something inside him stirred. A sexual stirring he hadn't felt in a very long time. Not since Aspen.

"A close-up, Sam," he requested. A zoom lens had brought her fully in focus. He'd stared at her until his eyes burned. Until familiarity gripped him, and awareness shook him out of his trance. His heart had kicked so hard, he swore he'd broken a rib.

He'd watched as the cameras tracked her to beauty and fragrance. It was slow going on her part. She had a significant limp. He wondered if she'd hurt herself skiing.

He found it ironic that her gifts included Snow Angel cologne. Fear sliced through him that she would pay and slide out the door before he could reach her.

He'd hurried from Security, jogged down the hallway. The elevators had been locked down, so he'd taken the stairs, two at a time. The moment he'd hit the first floor, the lights had gone out. He waited and let his eyes adjust to the darkness. He knew the maze of departments like the back of his hand. He was heir to the store.

He stretched his hands, feeling his way. He didn't want to knock over a display. He immediately headed for the fragrance counter. No sign of Allie. Had he found her, only to lose her again? His stomach sank.

Sam's shout drew Aidan to a cornered shoplifter.

The thief had been Allie.

She was his to frisk.

He grew hard. For the first time since he was a little boy, he believed in Santa Claus.

Her back was to him now as she set the cologne on the jewelry counter and lowered her backpack. She then removed her ski cap and jammed it in her jacket pocket. Her blond hair tumbled to her shoulders, thick and shiny and longer than he remembered.

She shrugged off her jacket, tossed it next to the Snow Angels. She toed off her right suede boot then flinched while removing her left. Her thick wool sock had rolled down and he noticed her ankle was bandaged. She stood before him now in a navy waffle pullover and worn jeans.

Her shoulders were set, her jaw tight, as she flattened her hands on the glass countertop. Her weight slumped on her right hip. She was ready for him to pat her down.

"Make it fast," she said. "I've nothing to hide."

Somehow he didn't doubt she was telling the truth. But this was too good an opportunity to pass up.

Aidan laid the flashlight on the counter so the beam flashed back on Allie. A halo surrounded her, making her look like an angel. *His* snow angel. He was determined she wasn't going to walk out on him again.

He rolled the Taser between his palms, debated sticking it in his back pocket, only to decide against it. Should the weapon accidentally spark, he'd receive fifty thousands volts to his ass. That would prove painful, debilitating, and embarrassing as hell. The last thing he needed was being put out of commission with Allie in town.

He slid the Taser down the counter beyond her reach, then moved up behind her. "This will only take a minute," he said. Or it could take an hour, depending on the intimate thoroughness of his search.

He went on to grip her shoulders, inhaled the scent of her hair. The crispness of the outdoors clung to her. She was pure snow angel. He wanted to pull her back against him, but now wasn't the time.

She'd rejected him in Aspen. But even though she'd left him, he had yet to let her go. He'd thought about her every day for three long years.

He went on to stroke down her arms, then circle her wrists with his fingers. He squeezed as if handcuffing her. She flinched and he released her.

He ran his hands down her back, slowly, yet firmly. Her body was toned, sleek, and athletic. He spanned her waist, patted down her abdomen. Flat belly, narrow hips. He slid his hands over her bottom then moved down her legs. She was all soft worn denim and warm woman.

Working his way back up, he skimmed the inside of her thighs, eased passed her hip bones. It took all his effort not to let out a low groan. He ran his knuckles over her ribs. He stretched the tips of his fingers toward her breasts . . .

"You copped a feel!" Allie swung around so quickly, he was forced to step back. "You-you——"

The dim lighting couldn't hide her shock at seeing him. She blinked, paled, looked at him as if he were a ghost from Christmas past. She hesitantly touched his chest. Her palm flattened over his heart. The beat told her that he was very much alive.

Fortunately her gaze didn't lower below his belt.

His attraction had become obvious. His sex now tented his gray slacks, a major bulge in his boxer briefs.

"Aidan?" His name was spoken as softly as a sigh. She curled her fingers into the fine cotton of his white long-sleeve shirt and clung to him.

He ached for her, so much so, he physically hurt. His first impulse was to draw her near, to let the years fade away and to recapture Aspen.

Yet a part of him pulled back. He fisted his hands, forced them to his sides. He had no idea why she was in Chicago or how long she planned to stay. The blizzard would benefit him. They were snowed in for at least one day, possibly two.

"It's Christmas Eve, Allie," he began. "Shouldn't you be at a ski resort?" The words came out more sarcastic than he'd planned.

The shadows couldn't hide her blush. She released his shirt. "I'm spending the holiday with my sisters this year," she said. "What are you doing here?"

"I work retail."

Her face softened. "So you once said."

They'd been naked when he'd told her. Her back had curved into his chest; his erection primed against her lower spine. The anticipation of taking her had tormented him until he couldn't wait any longer. But he had. For her. They'd talked, had sex, and slept. He'd awoken alone.

Their gazes held, yet their conversation lagged. They soon grew as quiet as the store. They stared at each other, so deep and intent, he felt her under his skin. As smooth as satin.

In that moment, she warmed him from the inside out.

His heat left her flushed.

She fanned her face.

He started to sweat.

"I've a cab waiting," she finally managed.

He looked toward the front door. "No taxi driver would wait for a fare in this weather. The wind's picked up and the snow's drifted. The cab would be buried."

"I didn't pay him." He could see she felt awful. She regretted stiffing her driver.

"You can always call the cab company and settle up after the storm," he suggested.

Realization hit her then. "*After* the storm? I'm stuck here?"

"I'm afraid so. We're snowbound."

Chapter Two

Allie Smith hated confinement. She needed the freedom of the outdoors. Clean air filling her lungs. The crisp bite of the morning chill turning her cheeks pink. She thrived on mountaintops with fresh powder and frosty air. She was at home there.

Here she faced a night in a department store with Aidan, and nowhere to run.

Did she really want to escape this man? She knew the answer, even if she wouldn't admit it. She was convinced that a conniving elf had put her in Dutton's with the man of her dreams just to tease her. This time there was no hot tub or warm bed. She was standing in the main aisle of a dark department store. The temperature was dropping by the second.

She openly observed him. He looked the same, only different. Tall and handsome, with five o'clock shadow that had arrived two hours early. His dark hair was cut short. His features were strong and his shoulders broad. She'd known him as a ski stud, but looking at him now, she saw a sophisticated businessman in a white shirt, burgundy and gray paisley tie, a braided leather belt, and sharply creased charcoal slacks. He looked preppie in his black tassel loafers and argyle socks. His style confused the hell out of her.

Would the real Aidan please stand up?

She found this new man sexy in a most disturbing way. Aristocratic came to mind. Polished and urbane. And to think he'd once been hers. She had unwrapped him on a Christmas Eve. He'd been the perfect present.

She let out a deep sigh. What a fool she'd been to run away, to lose him as both friend and lover. Now he thought she was a thief. His look was unwelcoming. He wasn't overjoyed to see her.

She reached for her ski jacket, retrieved her cell phone from the inside pocket. "I need to call my sisters. They'll be worried," she said.

She dialed, but no one picked up. She left a quick message. "It's Allie, I'm in Chicago at Dutton's—" and the connection failed.

Aidan pulled his BlackBerry from his pants pocket. He flipped it open, only to shake his head. "No bars."

Her shoulders sank. She tried sending a text. No go.

Seconds later, Sam from Security approached them. He shuffled down the aisle, herding a small group of stranded shoppers.

He looked at Allie first. "I located your check. My apology, Allie Smith, you're cleared of any crime."

She let go of the breath she'd been holding. *Score one for the Snow Angels,* her look told Aidan. He nodded in her direction, his opaque gray eyes holding steady with hers, though he didn't apologize for the pat down. The hint of a smile told her that he'd enjoyed touching her.

Sam next turned to Aidan. "I also found four stragglers. No one's happy."

The arrivals clustered at the jewelry counter. A tall man with spiky brown hair and a hot temper turned on Aidan. "Are you the store manager?" he demanded.

"He's the—" said Sam.

"First floor supervisor," Aidan cut Sam off. "I'm Aidan."

Sam's brow creased, but he didn't contradict his boss.

Allie caught their exchange. Both men appeared guarded. Almost secretive. They shared a workbond that didn't extend to the shoppers.

"I'm Chris Johnson," the newcomer said. "I was caught on the sixth floor in sporting apparel when the lights went out. I'm headed to Atlanta for a charity golf tournament. My flight leaves in two hours."

Sam flashed the Maglite in the golfer's face. "You're aware there's a blizzard?"

"I hate snow," Chris said. "I need to get to the airport."

Sam eyed Chris with suspicion. "Chris Johnson,

you say? I follow golf and you look different than you do on TV."

Chris stared down Sam. "Television adds ten pounds."

"It's not your weight," Sam said. "Johnson is shorter and blond."

"Check the color on your set," the man growled. "Damn storm. I can't miss my flight."

"Sorry, but Chicago's at a standstill," Aidan told the golf pro, his tone friendly but firm. "This could be the worst snowstorm in history. All transportation including air travel has shut down."

"Not good enough." Chris got in Aidan's face. The golfer shoved him back a step. "I'm a celebrity athlete. You're in charge. Do something, retail man."

Aidan went stiff, his jaw tight.

Allie was surprised he kept his cool.

Sam snagged the Taser off the jewelry counter and pressed the trigger. The guard's hand shook as electricity sparked, crackled. "Touch Aidan again and I'll jolt you into tomorrow," he warned the golf pro.

Allie bit down on her bottom lip, smiled to herself. She liked the way the guard stood up for his boss, even though Aidan was six inches taller and thirty pounds heavier than Sam.

"No harm done." Chris moved to the front door and pressed his palms against the frosted glass. "There has to be an emergency release."

Sam curled his lip. "If there was, trust me, you'd be the first to leave."

"The generator's old and runs minimal electricity," Aidan said. "We're lucky to have the light we do now."

That light suddenly dimmed. The entire building shuddered as the backup machinery strained against the storm. The Maglite flickered, the batteries running low.

Sam shone the shaft of light on all those gathered. Allie saw an elderly couple, their eyes wide, frightened, along with a younger woman with heavily lined eyes and a long sleek auburn ponytail. The redhead's face was pinched, her lips a glossed fuchsia line.

Allie crossed her arms, leaned against the jewelry counter, and watched as the woman approached Aidan. This could prove interesting.

"I'm Pamela Parker." She looked left, then right, making sure she had everyone's attention. "I'm a close friend of the Dutton family."

Aidan's brows pulled together, and uncertainty etched his brow. He seemed to doubt Pamela's familiarity with the store owners, Allie thought. That intrigued her. As the floor supervisor, he couldn't possibly know the Duttons' every acquaintance. He didn't travel in their social circle.

"The Duttons won't be pleased to hear good customers were stuck in their store on Christmas Eve," Pamela added. "Their son will be furious when I tell him. He's such a sweetheart."

"Is he?" Aidan asked, curious.

"Yes," Pamela stated with assurance. She spoke rather loudly, as if projecting her voice from a stage. "Alden and I have dated in the past."

"*Alden?*" Allie heard Sam cough into his hand.

She swore Aidan forced back a smile.

Allie wondered why he was so amused.

Sam shot the faint beam directly in Pamela's face. "Security attempted to get everyone out. You had plenty of warning, yet you kept trying on clothes. I found you in the fifth floor dressing room. Discarded garments were stacked to the ceiling."

The redhead had dressed in the dark, Allie noted. The front pearl buttons on her blue satin blouse were crooked and the collar was turned under. Yet the woman appeared confident, clutching two designer dresses with the price tags visible. Allie's eyes widened. She could pay her rent for a month on what those gowns cost.

Pamela lifted her chin. "I needed the perfect dress for Christmas Eve dinner and couldn't make a decision."

Sam had the solution. "You could wear one for the main course and one during dessert."

Allie grinned. Sam spoke his mind. A person would know where they stood with the guard. She liked that, a lot.

"We're the Murphys," the older man said, edging forward. "I'm Warren and this is my wife Marian. We both use canes. We were on the fourth floor in crystal and fine china when the elevators stopped. We took the stairs, but it was slow going. It's Marian's eightieth birthday." He turned to his wife and smiled. "I'd promised her a Waterford vase followed by afternoon tea."

Warren turned to Aidan. "I'm a retired postal worker. I've delivered mail in rain, sleet, and heavy snow, but I've never seen a storm this bad. I looked out the window on the upper floor and couldn't make out the building next door. The power company will be pulling its crew off the street so I don't think there will be any emergency responders. Are we safe?"

"Very much so," Aidan assured him. "Should the generators fail, we have departments with candles and camping equipment. We've battery-operated blankets to keep you warm. There's plenty of food, from tea room sandwiches to Swiss chocolates. We even have display beds with fresh linen should we be forced to spend the night. Sam and I will see to your every comfort."

Aidan glanced over at Allie. Her skin prickled. She had memories of just how comforting Aidan could be.

Marian Murphy touched Aidan's arm, a woman with a cloud of white hair and wire-rim glasses. She'd have made a perfect Mrs. Claus. "Thank you, son."

Allie couldn't help admiring Aidan. He was in charge, and as accommodating as he was kind. He'd put the Murphys at ease. The older couple huddled together and held hands.

They looked content, their hearts entwined. Allie envied them. She'd never known that special feeling with a man. She always took off before things got too serious. It was safer that way. Or so she'd always imagined.

The group glanced her way. "I'm Allie," she said by way of an introduction. When everyone looked at her foot, she added, "Sprained ankle."

Aidan met her gaze and she felt her cheeks heat. Those around them blurred, and it seemed as if they were the only two people in the vast department store. His expression was open, honest, and searching. He was too damn handsome for his own good. He made her mouth go dry. She wasn't one for stomach flutters, but he quickened her pulse and buckled her knees. She pulled herself up straight.

She owed him an explanation as to why she'd left Aspen. If she could roll back time, she would have stayed. She'd have fought her fear of commitment. Even though the idea scared the hell out of her.

Hindsight was twenty-twenty. It was too late now. There were few do-overs in life.

Overhead the generators quaked. The machinery must be ancient indeed. The wind howled, and severe gusts rattled the doors and display windows. It was unnerving.

"No telling how bad this storm is going to get," Aidan said. "I suggest we locate lanterns and flashlights in case we lose electricity."

"We need to set up a command post," came from Sam.

"This isn't the military," the golfer said, grumbling.

"Fend for yourself then," said Sam.

Chris's jaw shifted, and Aidan interceded. "Let's all move to the third floor, to camping and furniture. We can sit and be comfortable there."

Sam led the way to the stairs, and Pamela and Chris scooted in behind him. The Murphys assured Aidan they could make the climb. Allie shouldered on her jacket then worked on her right winter boot. She had difficulty fitting her left one.

She struggled for several seconds until Aidan hunkered down beside her. He ran his hands over the woolen sock. She winced, her ankle tender to his touch. "Your boot won't fit. Your foot's too swollen."

She held out her hand. "I'll carry it then."

He rose, passed her the sheepskin UGG. Their fingers brushed. His skin was warm and she wanted to hold his hand. She held back, barely. Instead, she carefully slipped the Snow Angels into separate jacket pockets. She then hefted her backpack and followed the snowbound group to the emergency stairs. Aidan brought up the rear with his flashlight.

The going was slow. She toe-tapped around the jewelry counter. Her ankle hurt like a son of a bitch. She locked her jaw and fought the pain. She was determined not to break down before Aidan.

The stairs were especially daunting. The Murphys rounded the curve in the stairwell long before Allie attempted the climb.

She counted the stairs, a total of thirty before the landing, a place where she could rest. She decided hopping was her best bet.

She bit the inside of her cheek and made fifteen steps before she was out of breath. She was halfway there.

She mentally psyched herself to continue. She was a skier in great shape. She could do this . . .

"You're hurting," she heard Aidan say over her shoulder.

"Just a little." She grimaced, keeping her face turned away from him.

"Don't be stubborn, Allie. You don't have to go it alone."

"I'm fine, really," she insisted. Why did she have to keep proving she was so tough? So she wouldn't get hurt?

"Sorry, lady, we at Dutton's aim to please," Aidan said with a seriousness that surprised her. He handed her the flashlight. "We take care of our customers."

He swept her up before she could respond, one muscled arm beneath her legs, the other across her back. He held her tightly.

Her whole body went limp. She welcomed his rescue. She wrapped her arms about his neck, breathed in his scent, and absorbed his strength. He was all male.

They ascended slowly, and found the Murphys on the second floor landing. A red emergency light had dimmed to a faint pink. Darkness crowded the corners near the door. It was cold and eerie.

"Only one more flight," Warren said, short of breath.

"Are the two of you okay?" Aidan asked, concerned. Allie noticed he wasn't even breathing hard.

"Sure," Warren said with a wink, as if remembering earlier days when he carried his wife in his arms. "We're catching our second wind."

"Let me get Allie to the third floor and I'll come back and help you," Aidan offered.

"We'll be fine," Marian reassured him. "Warren was a fine athlete in his day. He ran track."

Warren tapped his cane on the marble floor.

"That was sixty years ago, my dear. Back then I was six feet tall and muscled. Age has a way of bending a man. Nowadays I'm lucky to make it from the kitchen to the front door for the newspaper."

"You're still the strongest man I know," his wife praised.

Allie Smith caught the older couple's smile; a smile as loving as an actual embrace. It was a sweet moment, but a difficult one for her to comprehend. The Murphys' love stretched decades, whereas her own mother's relationships were short-lived and unsatisfying. Margo had taught her daughters that men left without notice and women should always leave first. That way the heartbreak hurt less.

Allie had never trusted a man.

Aidan, however, gave her reason to try.

She knew deep in her soul that the blizzard would decide her future with this man.

Beside them now, Warren straightened his shoulders as his wife took his arm. They tackled the steps together. "See you on the third floor," Warren called over his shoulder.

Aidan Dutton watched the older couple move out ahead of them. He clutched Allie closer. He'd noted her struggle on the stairs and that she was in pain. Her swollen ankle gave him an excuse to touch her again. He'd been relieved she hadn't fought him. Her cheek now pressed his shoulder and he heard her sigh.

He felt suddenly anchored. He didn't move, just held her close. Years ago, he'd carried Allie from the outdoor cedar tub to his bedroom at the

Aspen lodge. They'd both been naked and ready for sex. They'd been incredibly hot for each other. So hot, they steamed the sheets.

He could still picture her, lushly nude, her skin moist, lying on his bed. His body stirred with the memory. He set his back teeth. Arousal was not his friend. Yet he grew hard. He feared he wouldn't be able to take the stairs. He'd be stuck on the second floor landing for Christmas Eve, craving this woman and stiff as a crowbar.

He drew Allie higher against his chest. He didn't want her to witness her effect on him. He exhaled slowly. "How'd you hurt your ankle?" he finally asked.

She scrunched her nose. "A college guy's harmless flirting turned into a snowmobile disaster."

Aidan would've liked to wring the neck of the careless son of a bitch who'd done this to her. He knew men were taken with Allie. He'd witnessed her countless pursuers in Aspen. She looked like an angel, but had an independent streak that would frustrate the Almighty.

The fact that he was the one holding her now was all that mattered. He would have liked to kiss her pain away, but they had unfinished business. Until they cleared the air he needed to concentrate on their present situation. They were in the middle of a blizzard. He had six people under his care.

He cautiously continued up the stairs. His arousal was almost as painful as Allie's ankle. She was a lightweight, even in her winter wear. She shot the beam up the stairwell, lighting their way.

Up ahead, Warren and Marian patiently waited

for Aidan on the third floor landing. Warren held the door wide for them.

Aidan immediately located Sam's command post. The guard had accomplished a great deal in a very short time. He'd rearranged the leather furniture. A cluster of chairs and a short couch now surrounded an antique rococo coffee table. Battery-operated camping lanterns supplied sufficient light.

The Taser remained visible on the guard's utility belt. Sam was all huff and puff and built on bravado. Aidan knew the weapon gave him confidence. He wouldn't blow the man's cover.

Allie shifted in his arms, her gaze riveted to the amazing view from the tall multi-paned window reminiscent of another time. The fury of the storm fascinated her. Flurries of snow and a wailing wind beat against the glass. Frost so thick it resembled white velvet curtains framed the window. She'd never seen anything like it. The wintry blast held them hostage.

Aidan maneuvered between a black walnut billiard table and a filigree lattice bird cage to reach the group. Two chairs remained. "Pick one," he said to Allie.

She chose the club chair in Peruvian basket brown. His arms felt oddly empty once he'd set her down. He looked around for an ottoman. She needed to elevate her foot.

He soon found the perfect piece. Allie's gaze went wide when he set the vintage steamer trunk before her. The top was cushioned with preserved navy fabric from a 1920s seaman's peacoat. The epaulets and gold buttons bordered each end.

"My sock is dirty from the stairs," she was quick

to say. "I can't put my foot on something so beautiful."

"It's just an ottoman."

She pointed to the designer label and blinked at the price tag. "It's one-of-a-kind and very expensive."

He knelt beside her and lifted her leg so her foot rested comfortably on the peacoat. "Your foot's more important than a trunk."

"What will your boss say?" she worried. "I wouldn't want you to lose your job because of a dirty sock."

He grinned. Her concern set off pleasant warmth in his chest. "We won't tell him," he said, making her roll her eyes. Beautiful eyes, big and filled with a sparkle that reminded him of a Christmas tree ornament brushed a soft blue.

Her gaze went soft and his sex stayed hard. It took him a full minute to pull his body together and stand. He shifted his stance. Twice.

"Now that we're settled, I'm hungry," Chris said from the couch. "I missed lunch to do my last-minute Christmas shopping."

"There should still be a few refrigerated sandwiches at Tealuxe," Aidan said.

"What kind of sandwiches?" asked Chris.

"Finger sandwiches," Sam said. "It's a tea room, golf ball."

"I do love fancy sandwiches," said Marian Murphy. "I'd also enjoy a nice cup of peppermint tea."

"We can do tea," Aidan assured the older woman. "We can boil water on a portable Coleman stove. There's an InstaStart among the camping equipment."

"China cups?" Marian looked hopeful. "We could have a formal tea party."

Sam grunted. "Tea by lantern light in the middle of a blizzard, why not?"

"There should be a few holiday desserts left over as well," Aidan told the group. He looked at Allie's foot. "I'll bring back a bag of ice to take down the swelling."

Sam went to retrieve the small stove and a pot which he set on a Tuscan end table. He looked directly at Chris. "Propane's hooked up. Don't turn it on until we return if you want to keep your eyebrows."

Chris shot him a dirty look, but said nothing.

Aidan handed Sam a lantern. Both men then took the stairs to the seventh floor. They'd reached the sixth floor landing when Sam cleared his throat and said, "Allie's your snow angel."

Aidan went very still. He should have known he couldn't keep anything from Sam. He was a wise-ass sometimes, but with an acute sixth sense. The security guard had worked at Dutton's for twenty-five years. He was loyal and observant. He was also protective of Aidan.

"Why would you say that?" he asked.

"Body language, boss," Sam said. "The way you carried her upstairs, the way you look at her. Hell, you set her dirty sock on a five thousand dollar steamer trunk. You like her." Nothing got past Sam.

Aidan crossed his arms over his chest and clutched the lantern tightly. "I met Allie in Aspen three years ago," he admitted. "Our time together was short." Too damn short.

Sam narrowed his gaze. "I remember your ski

vacation. You dragged your ass for months afterward. You haven't dated anyone seriously since."

"The store's kept me busy."

"Not that busy," Sam disagreed. "You took off for Grasse, France, the next spring and spent six months at the House of Molinard during the production of Snow Angel, capturing a woman's scent. Allie's scent."

Aidan's secret was out. "Keep it man-to-man?" He wasn't comfortable admitting even to Sam that he'd had Allie on the brain for three long years. She was more than a secret crush. She was his future. Convincing Allie she belonged with him would take some fast talking and a single kiss. In that one kiss he'd know if she still cared for him.

"I've never betrayed a trust." Sam rubbed his knuckles over his jaw. "Your parents confide in me often. Arthur bought Judith a cashmere coat for Christmas. She sponsored a Hebridean whale in his name. There's an Orca named Arthur Maynard Dutton swimming off the west coast of Scotland."

Aidan smiled. "Last year, she set up a trust for a Key West dolphin. The year before, she was an advocate for a water buffalo in the Philippines. Dad's name is spread throughout the world."

"I know what Santa got you for Christmas," Sam said, grinning.

"Give me a hint."

"A blonde with a sprained ankle."

Aidan damn sure hoped he could keep her. "I'm taking it slow. With any luck, this blizzard will last for several days." He didn't trust Allie not to slip out after the storm. He refused to let her disappear again.

"Does she know you're a Dutton?" Sam asked.

Aidan shook his head. "No, and I'd like to keep it that way. She knows I work retail. A floor supervisor works best. I want her to like me for me. Not for my heritage."

He rolled his shoulders. "I'm damn glad my parents went to Phoenix for the holidays. I need time alone with Allie before I introduce her to them."

Sam smiled. "Pamela Parker knows you as Alden."

"She's a name dropper."

"She said the two of you dated."

"I've never met the woman."

"You're old news anyway," Sam said. "She's already started flirting with putter head."

Aidan blew out a breath. "It's going to be a long night."

The men proceeded up the stairs. "Let's hope there's food for seven," Aidan said. "I told the staff to take home all leftovers. We're implementing a new menu after the holidays."

They entered Tealuxe through the heavy leaded glass doors. Aidan paused at the entrance and looked around. The tea room looked lonely. Darkness hung low off the ceiling. He swung his lantern in a wide arc. Antique mirrors reflected the richly polished tables, the red velvet chairs, and settees covered in rich rose satin. Pristine linen was stacked on the tea carts.

An artist had painted a Victorian tea party on two walls. Those of the past and present sipped tea and savored iced scones. It was a blending of eras. A timeless tradition. His mother loved Earl Grey.

Sam crossed the room ahead of Aidan. The plush navy carpeting absorbed his steps. He pushed against the double doors that led to the kitchen, and listened. "The cooler is running, but the freezer's shut down."

Aidan came up behind him. "Let's eat before the food spoils. You collect the dishes—"

Sam frowned. "Paper products are my specialty. I know nothing about china patterns."

Aidan's mother favored the Royal Albert Botanical set. "Locate cups, saucers, and dessert plates with red tulips and lavender lilacs."

Sam grunted. "Isn't there a pattern with deer and bear?"

"The tea party is for Marian Murphy," Aidan said. "Let her enjoy it. Don't forget the tea infusers."

Sam looked confused and Aidan explained, "The mesh tea balls to steep the loose tea leaves."

Sam made a few indistinguishable comments under his breath as he packed sets of china in a corrugated box, then located the sterling flatware. "Plastic forks would work just as well," he muttered, this time loud enough for Aidan to hear.

Aidan raided the commercial refrigerator and walk-in cooler. There was more food than he'd expected. He loaded up on finger sandwiches and desserts, then chose a variety of tea tins. He went on to grab a bag of ice and several Ziplocs while Sam collected the china, a linen tablecloth, napkins, and a box of bottled water. Armed with the necessities, they took the stairs slowly.

"Tea party time," Sam announced on their return.

Marian Murphy was so excited she clapped her hands.

Her husband Warren smiled at her enthusiasm.

Allie leaned forward in an attempt to help the men unload the boxes. Aidan pressed a hand to her shoulder and eased her back, then gently squeezed her arm. "We've got it covered," he assured her.

"It's hard for me to sit still and do nothing."

She was an active woman. He'd witnessed her skiing, and her endurance was phenomenal. In bed, she'd been an Energizer snow bunny. She sat immobile now. Her ankle prohibited activity. She drummed her fingers on the leather armrest. The lady was restless.

"Does Dutton's sell canes?" she asked.

"This isn't a medical supply store," Chris said from the couch.

Aidan ignored him.

Though he would have liked Allie to lean on him, she'd rather manage on her own. "We have opera canes."

"They sound very formal."

"You can select one after we've eaten."

He packed a Ziploc with ice and gently placed it over her ankle, swollen to the size of a grapefruit. Not uncommon, he knew, but very painful. She winced, and he wished he could take her pain away. "Tea?" he offered. "Earl Grey, Darjeeling, or peppermint?"

"Darjeeling would be nice."

Aidan oversaw Sam as he poured water into a pot, then started the portable stove. The water came to a quick boil.

"That's all you had to do, push a damn button?" Chris was incredulous that Sam hadn't let him work the stove.

"I also adjusted the flame," Sam said.

"Chris could've done that," said Pamela Parker, taking the golfer's side.

Sam's jaw shifted. "Maybe, maybe not."

"Let's not argue." Marian took charge. She spread the linen tablecloth and set out the place settings. "Look at all these lovely sandwiches."

A flash of lightning lit up the room, causing everyone to jump and gasp. Seconds later, thunder boomed. The northern windows rattled violently.

"Don't worry," Aidan was quick to assure them. "We don't get thundersnows very often, but for your own safety, stay on the south side of the building."

Chris didn't care about the weather; he was more interested in the food. He pulled a face. "These sandwiches are bite size, crustless, and cut into diamonds."

"It's a formal tea," Marian said.

"I can't fill up on dainty and small," Chris argued.

"Drink a lot of tea," suggested Sam.

Tea infusers were distributed and types of tea chosen. Sam added hot water to the china cups. The group selected their sandwiches while their tea steeped.

Aidan filled Allie's plate. "Cucumber and mint cream cheese, ginger-carrot, and lemon-crab salad." He added two shortbread cookies and a slice of raspberry sponge cake to the dessert plate before passing it to her.

He settled in beside her, on a black leather wingback to her left. He sipped his Earl Grey and watched her savor each bite. She licked mint cream cheese from the corner of her mouth. The slow sweep of her tongue turned Aidan on.

He remembered her kisses. He could still recall the moist heat of her mouth as she licked her way down his chest. She'd tasted every inch of his skin, then gotten creative with her hands. There was passion in her touch, a need to rouse him fully. He'd remained erect for hours at a time.

His body stirred even now. He set the saucer over his zipper. The china didn't fully disguise the tent in his pants. He discreetly reached into his side pocket and made an adjustment. He didn't want Allie to notice her effect on him. Attraction was a bitch.

"These sandwiches are delicious," she said seconds later. "This is my first afternoon tea."

"My first and last," said Chris as he cleared his plate of the finger sandwiches and started on a gingerbread scone. "I'll never shop Dutton's again."

"It's not the store's fault you got caught in the blizzard," Sam said between bites of pineapple and smoked salmon on a pumpernickel wedge. "You must live under a rock. The storm's been forecast for days. Most people took its arrival seriously. You should have left for Atlanta earlier in the week."

"I'm not a weather watcher," Chris said, going on the defensive. "I had no idea the storm would get so bad I'd end up starving and freezing in a department store."

"Hardly starving." Sam glared at the golfer. "You've eaten ten tea sandwiches, but who's counting?"

"I, for one, am enjoying myself." Marian Murphy reached for a second tiny cream puff. "We're not leaving anytime soon. Let's get to know each other better."

"Better how?" Chris looked suddenly wary.

"Tell us something about you," Pamela encouraged. "We know you're a professional golfer."

"That's all you need to know," Chris said.

"That's all I want to know," said Sam.

"You're a security guard." Chris looked down his nose at Sam. "You work at Dutton's—"

"—and he runs the tightest security on State Street." Allie straightened on her chair. "Nothing gets by Sam. He's a major crime fighter."

"So you say," said Chris.

"So I know," Allie said. "Right before the store closed, Sam thought I was a thief. He stopped me in my tracks."

Aidan watched Sam watch Allie. Sam's chest swelled as he patted his utility belt. "It's the Taser. My weapon puts the fear of God in shoplifters. I'm the only guard on the block packing."

"Sam's taken good care of us," Marian said. "Aidan, too."

"Great care," Chris snorted. "How difficult was it to go to the tea room and bring back food?"

"You can fix dinner," Sam said.

"I love to eat," said Pamela. "I wish we were in New York. Post-theater Sardi's has the best sirloin and cheesecake in the city."

"Are you on Broadway?" Marian asked.

Pamela preened. "I'll soon be performing at the Colbert Theater. *Peaches* is a romantic comedy."

Aidan watched her flirt with the golfer. Her gaze was fixed on Chris as she leaned against him with her big breasts. Her body language said it all. No doubt the redhead hoped to snag a trophy boyfriend to get some publicity for herself. Pamela appeared very press friendly.

He knew Allie would never act in such a manner. That was another thing he liked about her. She didn't play those games.

"Interesting title for your play," Warren Murphy commented. "Is it about fruit?"

"I flash my boobs."

Warren's jaw dropped.

Marian's gaze went wide.

"I bet you're good in your role," Chris said.

Aidan saw the appreciative look in the golfer's eyes. Chris was imagining himself sitting in the first row when Pamela took the stage.

"The orange body paint clashes with my red hair," Pamela complained, "but I have the best D-cups in the theater district."

"Care to rehearse the play now?" asked Chris.

"Not in the store." Aidan put a stop to the theatrics. "Save it for the performance."

Pamela was stacked, and Chris apparently liked big-breasted women. The golfer leaned back on the couch and slipped his arm around the actress. Pamela smiled, equally taken by his company. Aidan would need a crowbar or fire hose to separate them later.

Marian looked at Allie. "How about you, dear? Any showbiz in your blood?"

Allie shook her head. "I'm a ski instructor."

"Not a very good one, given your ankle," Chris said.

"I wasn't skiing when I got hurt," Allie said, and left it at that.

"Where do you teach?" Warren next asked.

"Wherever there's fresh powder," Allie said. "I have contracts with several ski resorts. I shift around."

"Here today, gone tomorrow." Aidan spoke the words without thinking. He could feel Allie's gaze bore into him. He felt like a jerk for letting that slip out. He and Allie deserved privacy when they discussed their past.

To his relief, no one but Allie heard him. The group had switched topics and was now discussing the Christmas events each would surely miss.

Allie leaned forward, fiddled with the bag of ice on her ankle. "I'm prone to disappear," she softly admitted.

"I'm familiar with that fact," he whispered back. "You left me, remember?"

Her breathing deepened. "I had my reasons."

"Give me one." He needed the truth.

"You scare the hell out of me, Aidan."

Chapter Three

Aidan's expression froze. Allie Smith watched every handsome line on his face go rigid. Confusion pitched his gray eyes charcoal-dark. He didn't understand. How could he? He didn't know that every few months as a kid she'd been forced to uproot and move on, whether she'd wanted to or not. Town to town. Always wandering. Her mother had never found love, so why should she?

Beside her, Aidan shifted uneasily. He ran a hand through his thick, dark hair, and one side spiked. "Scary how, Allie?"

"Not Halloween scary," she assured him. She didn't want to talk about it, but if she didn't say something, he'd think she didn't feel anything for him. That scared her more. So she opted for the truth. She said in a low voice, "Heart scary."

"You're afraid of getting hurt?"

"This is very hard for me," she said, hoping for

his understanding. "I don't do feelings, and you made me care."

"*Who* cares?" Chris asked, poking his nose into their conversation, which didn't sit well with Pamela. She crossed her arms and pouted. She wanted all his attention.

They had an audience, Allie realized. She hadn't expected the truth behind her departure to surface while sitting around a coffee table in the dark with five other people staring at her.

"No one you'd know." Aidan brushed him off.

Chris shrugged, continued, "The little I heard, I'd say you two have a past and are still hot for each other."

"They make such a cute couple," said Marian Murphy.

"You've got her undivided attention during the blizzard," added Warren. "Go on, boy, court her."

"If the lady is willing?" Aidan offered, meeting her gaze and daring her to commit, to them.

"I might be so inclined." She'd love to have Aidan flirt with her. But first they needed to talk. Seriously. Perhaps they could find a quiet corner while they went shopping for her opera cane.

Allie looked at the coffee table, at the empty teacups and one lone almond cookie, which Chris confiscated. To her relief, no one asked anything more about their brief affair. In truth, there wasn't much to tell. She wasn't sure what had motivated Aidan to make public his interest in her, but she wasn't about to let the matter drop. When the time was right, she'd try to explain to him how she felt.

She shook her head in frustration; so often words failed her.

Across the coffee table, Marian dabbed her mouth with a linen napkin. "That was nice while it lasted."

"Now what?" Chris asked, drilling his fingers on the leather armrest. "Do we sit and stare at the ceiling?"

"You expect entertainment?" asked Sam.

Aidan grew thoughtful. "You could Christmas shop," he suggested. "Find a gift for yourself. Compliments of Dutton's."

That was all Pamela Parker needed to hear. She shot off the couch like a rocket. "We can shop for free?"

"In moderation," Aidan said, wondering if he'd opened a Pandora's box with the name *Dutton* on it.

"You've already chosen two dresses," Sam reminded her.

"My plans are shot for Christmas Eve dinner. Instead I got stuck with tea sandwiches," Pamela said. "I need something fancy for New Year's Eve. I'm hoping for that special invitation to sparkle." She smiled big at Chris, who grinned back.

A match had been made in the middle of a blizzard, Aidan realized. He wondered if he and Allie would be a couple when the sun again shone and the snow started to melt.

"Shop in twos or threes," Aidan said. "Don't wander around the store alone. It's too dark. I don't want anyone getting lost or hurt."

"The buddy system works for me." Chris pushed to his feet. He picked up a lantern off the coffee table, then let his gaze shift to Pamela's chest. "I'll go with Peaches."

Aidan exhaled. Talk about bosom buddies.

"Let's start in formal wear, then go to sporting apparel," Pamela suggested. "I'll help you pick out the perfect golf shirt."

"If this is a free shopping spree, I'm looking at more than a shirt." Chris took Pamela's hand. His next words were meant to impress her. "Maybe a set of Majesty Prestigio clubs and the Damier Geante canvas golf bag."

"Go slow, golf pro," Sam said, raising his hand. "Callaway wouldn't approve."

Chris frowned. "Who's Callaway?"

"Your most recent endorsement on the Tour," Sam reminded him.

"How the hell would you know?" Chris demanded.

"I read an article in *Golf Forum*."

"The *Forum* is the *National Enquirer* of golf." Chris elbowed Pamela forward. "I've not signed with Callaway. Mind your own business." He stormed off, Peaches in tow.

Warren looked at Sam, his expression serious. "It seems you know more about Chris Johnson than he knows about himself."

"From what I know of the man, he's a regular guy on the golf course," said Sam. "Johnson appreciates his fans, supports numerous charities. He's not pushy or a hot head."

"Will the real Chris Johnson please stand up," Allie said. And Aidan nodded.

"Good luck figuring the man out." Warren went on to help Marian to her feet. They each took a lantern. "My wife and I are headed to crystal and fine china. She had her eye on a vase before the electricity failed."

"Get the vase for her birthday along with separate gifts for yourselves," Aidan invited.

"You're good to us, son," Marian said softly. "I'd hate to have the Duttons angry that you gave away store items." She looked at her husband. "We're happy to pay."

"That won't be necessary. I'd be pleased if you'd accept my holiday hospitality," Aidan said. "Would you like assistance upstairs?"

"It's only one floor up. We're quite capable of the climb," Marian assured him.

They moved off, arm-in-arm.

Sam waited until the Murphys were beyond earshot before saying, "I'm warning you, boss, Chris Johnson is bad news. The man's a poser. I feel it in my bones. The Damier Geante is designed by Louis Vuitton. It's a millionaire's French fashion accessory on the green, not a touring professional's golf bag. Chris would leave his competition speechless, and not in a good way."

"Maybe he's a psychological gamer," Aidan said. "Most athletes depend on talent and skill to win, yet there are those who show off and psyche out their opposition with expensive gear. It's like bringing a platinum-covered bazooka to a knife fight."

"Or a buxom redhead to a poker game," Sam added with a smirk. "She'd take the other players' minds off their cards."

Allie looked at Sam, asked, "You think Chris isn't who he claims?"

"Callaway Golf would expect him to be a walking billboard for their gear," Sam said. "There's something about Chris that bothers me. The Chris Johnson on the circuit is gracious. The man with us now is full of himself."

What Sam said made sense, Allie realized. Maybe the guard was onto something. "Why would Chris want to fool us?" she asked.

"He doesn't appear smart enough for identity theft," Sam said. "I'd say it's all about being in the spotlight. Athletes get a lot of attention. He's already attracted Pamela."

"People shouldn't pretend to be someone they're not," Allie said, meaning it. "It's dishonest."

She saw a muscle jerk in Aidan's jaw, and wondered why he flinched. He grew uneasy, pushing forward on his chair, rubbing his palms down his thighs.

"I'm going to clean up, then check on Chris and Pamela." Sam quickly stacked the china in the corrugated box. He held up the bag of ice. "It's melting, but should remain cold for a couple more hours."

Allie eased the Ziploc off her ankle. She wiggled her foot and judged its flexibility. Less swelling, little pain. "I'm better, thanks."

"Take it slow," Sam said, concerned. He then snagged a lantern and looked at Aidan. "My nose is to the ground—I'm tracking Johnson."

"No confrontation or zapping him with the Taser," Aidan warned.

The security guard patted his duty utility belt. "There's always pepper spray." He departed.

Only Allie and Aidan remained. She could barely see out the big window from where she sat.

The snowfall was thick and blindingly white. Three lanterns cast light while the darkness hugged close. The generators sounded like pounding fists, fighting off the storm.

She turned, caught Aidan in profile. She liked looking at him when he wasn't looking at her. She let her gaze wander over his mussed dark hair, the width of his forehead, the arch of his cheekbone, and the sexy curve of his mouth. She could picture him captured in a magazine ad for men's cologne or, even better, ski apparel. He was that handsome.

She cleared her throat, said, "Sam's certain Chris isn't who he claims. Does that matter to you? A person pretending to be someone he's not?"

He visibly hesitated. "Perhaps he has a reason."

"What you see is what you get where I'm concerned."

"I like what I see, when you stick around for me to see you," Aidan said.

She understood. "We're back to Frost Peak Lodge."

"Can we discuss our night together?"

She nodded. "In due time. My opera cane first, our talk second."

"No running away from me this time, promise?"

"I couldn't hop far."

Aidan handed her a lantern, then lifted and carried her down the stairs. The strength in his big body encompassed her. She tipped her head and breathed in against his neck. His scent was spicy citrus. She was fascinated by the pulse at the base of his throat, its beat rhythmically strong. She wanted nothing more than to climb into his shirt pocket and live beside his heart.

She turned slightly in his arms and assisted with the first floor emergency door. He pushed through, walked her to the jewelry counter. In the lantern light, the polished glass shone but the shelves were bare.

A few steps beyond jewelry, Opera Night came to life in a display of black top hats, satin capes, opera glasses, and ornate canes.

"Have you been to the opera?" she asked.

He nodded. "I recently attended opening night of *A Masked Ball* by Verdi."

Allie had seen him naked, yet she could also picture him in a tux. He had a distinctive air about him. He'd be one gorgeous man, all formal and groomed.

She wondered whom he'd taken to the opera, no doubt someone special. Jealousy tugged at her heart. She knew so little about his personal life.

Aidan brushed his fingers across her brow, smoothing its crease. "Jealous?" he asked, reading her mind. "I like that, Allie, but don't think so hard. My parents gave me the ticket to the opera. My mother supports the arts. It was a family night out."

"Did you enjoy *A Masked Ball?*" She was curious. "I don't know the story."

"The king was in love with his best friend's wife and she was in love with him," he told her. "Desperate to end her ardor, she turns to a sorceress for help, but it's too late. Their secret is out and the devastated husband takes revenge."

Aidan shifted her weight, set down, a slow slide of heat and awareness that lit her up like a string of Christmas tree lights. Friction sparked and popped all over her body as her soft flesh pressed up against his hard muscle.

Her nipples went taut, peaked, and heat licked up her thighs. She realized in that moment how much she'd missed him. When his mouth came dangerously close to hers, she parted her lips, hoping he would kiss her. He didn't. Instead, he looked at her with a hunger that promised more than a kiss when the time was right.

Her knees were so weak she could barely stand. She held onto his arms and steadied herself. She didn't want to let him go.

She stood on her right foot, bent her left leg like a flamingo. She didn't want to put weight on her foot. Her ankle ached, but no longer throbbed.

"Pain tolerance?" he asked.

"Bearable," she said. "Time has a way of healing everything."

"So they say," he said wryly. "It's not always true."

She'd never meant to hurt him.

She'd never meant for their time together to go beyond great sex. Yet it had. He'd been under her skin for three long years. The time was close upon her to open her heart and let Aidan in. Dealing with her insecurities was turning out to be more difficult than she'd ever imagined.

Trying to keep her nerves steady, Allie looked around. Even in the darkness, the scent of money prevailed. Aidan definitely worked high-end retail. If she lived in Chicago, she'd window shop Dutton's, but wouldn't enter the store. Its elegance made her feel poor.

"How long have you worked here?" she asked Aidan.

He was slow to answer. "Fifteen years."

"You're the first floor supervisor?"

He nodded.

"What's your advancement? Second floor?"

He grinned at her. "I move around the store as needed. Supervisor is just a title."

"How well do you know the Duttons?"

Again, he appeared indecisive. "They treat their staff like family."

"This is a magnificent store . . ."

"But?" He heard the hesitation in her voice.

"It's too expensive for my blood. I could barely afford the Snow Angels." She sighed. "Do you ever run sales?"

He shook his head. "Sorry, no."

"Your shoppers are loyal?"

"They fly in from all over the world."

"You have job security, Aidan."

"Same as you, Allie. When it snows, you teach skiing."

She lowered her gaze, studied her ankle. "This is my moneymaking season. I hope I can return to the slopes."

"Have you seen a doctor? Had X-rays?"

She heard his concern. And her heart warmed. "I'll see a specialist after Christmas. I would have set up an appointment sooner, but I was in a hurry to get to Chicago to spend time with my sisters."

"Instead of your sisters, you're stuck at Dutton's."

"With you." The words slipped out, soft and sincere.

She sucked in her breath. She wasn't sorry for what she'd said. Her heart raced when she realized he seemed happy to hear them. The sudden seriousness of his expression took her by surprise as well as the intensity of his gaze.

He set the lantern on a shelf next to a pair of French opera glasses, then took to touching her, gently, possessively. Reassuringly. He cupped her chin, ran his thumb along her jaw line. He pressed into the plumpness of her lower lip and drew her close enough to kiss her. Yet still he held back. *Why?*

He went on to slide his fingers down her neck to her throat. The tips came to a rest on her rapid pulse. Hunger darkened his eyes and her stomach fluttered. He wanted her, and she was sensitive to his need pressing hard against her belly. A familiar hardness that promised pleasure.

Anticipation thickened the air.

Silence hovered with indecision.

Aidan eased back and released her. "Your cane." He pointed to a dozen opera canes, their handles looped over velvet hooks along the wall. "Take your pick."

Allie took them in, all highly polished, some richly embellished with jewels. She moved through the display, running her fingertips over the handles. All were works of art, from the blue marble, black pearl, diamond encrusted burgundy leather, to the scrimshaw lion. How could she possibly choose? Every one was out of her league.

"These are too pricey, Aidan," she said. "A simple walking stick would do just fine."

"No trees, no branches, no sticks," he said. "Choose a cane or I'll be forced to carry you."

His carrying her was good; her self-sufficiency

even better. While she appreciated his help, she wasn't ready to depend on him. Trust took time.

"You've spoiled me long enough," she said, then went back to debating the canes.

Aidan Dutton could spoil Allie Smith for a lifetime if she'd let him. Sometime a man just knew a woman was meant for him. Allie went way beyond an Aspen holiday affair.

That's why he hadn't kissed her when she'd looked up at him, her lips moist, her eyes wide. He didn't want to get carried away until they'd hammered out all that was wrong between them. They had baggage.

He watched now as Allie tested each cane before coming to a decision. He smiled when she finally chose his favorite, the one with a crystal-cut rose handle and Lucite shaft. It was a woman's cane, feminine, formal, yet durable, and would give her balance.

She wobbled in a small circle, smiled. "Let the fat lady sing." She then moved slowly down the aisle, away from him.

Aidan watched her fade beyond the emergency lighting. He knew she wouldn't be foolish enough to go far. More than anything, he wanted to discuss their past. Yet given her pleasure in the cane, he decided to let her roam the store at will. *His* store. He would save that confession for later. *Much* later.

She returned to him, slower now, as if her short walk had tired her. He picked up the lantern and went to meet her halfway. Her gaze was bright and her cheeks flushed. She looked beautiful to him.

"I could get used to this opera cane." She tapped it on the black marble floor. "It feels—" she

paused, searched for the right word, and came up
with, "grand."

"I could make you feel grander," he said. "Care
to try on a long gown to go with your cane?"

Her eyes rounded. "Dress up and pretend to go
to the opera?"

"You could pick out long gloves and opera glasses
too."

Her breathing slowed, and her deliberation was
long and significant. She looked ill at ease yet determined when she confessed, "Fancy isn't me,
Aidan. I can't be someone I'm not. I'm more ski
attire than formal wear. I've only dressed up once
in my entire life. That was for a charity event in
support of wildlife preservation."

"How about a new ski jacket then?" he asked.

"The jacket I have is only a year old."

"Ski pants?"

"I have two pair."

He looked to her foot. "You can't try on boots."

"My UGGS will last another season."

"Cashmere cap, deerskin gloves, herringbone
scarf?"

She stared at him, shook her head. "Your sug-
gestions amaze me. You're an unusual mix of ski
stud and retail supervisor. What drew you to Dutton's?"

It was his family's store. He was expected to take
over the helm someday, but it went beyond being a
family tradition with him. Whether in sports or retail, he was a competitive man. At Dutton's, the art
of the sale was in his blood. Engaging the customer, showcasing the best the store had to offer,
seeing someone's eyes light up when he found ex-

actly what the other person wanted. No matter the price. He loved making that happen. But he couldn't tell Allie that. Not right now anyway.

So he shrugged, hedged the truth. "I started out on the loading dock working holidays when I was sixteen. I nearly froze my ass off during the winter months and decided to move inside. I'm not a fashion hound but I do like nice clothes. I've a business degree from Northwestern. Retail seemed right for me."

She looked among the shadows, smiled. "You picked the most famous store in the country for employment."

"I thought so."

"You have the very best of everything at your fingertips."

He nodded. "Pretty much so."

He again caught her mental debate, followed by her sigh. "There's no need to get me anything for Christmas."

He didn't have to, but he wanted to.

She didn't have much and apparently didn't want more.

He pressed on. "Necklace, bracelet, earrings?"

She shook her head. "I don't wear jewelry when I ski."

"You ski year-round?"

"I'm stateside November through March, then I travel to Australia or Argentina. Their winter is our summer. I'm on a mountain twelve months out of the year."

"Luggage, then?" crossed his mind.

"My life fits in a backpack."

His heart sank. There it was again. That gnaw-

ing feeling that she could pick up and leave at a
moment's notice. Here today, gone tomorrow.

Allie Smith was a hard person to shop for.

He had an idea. "How about a gift exchange?
I'll pick out something for you, and you can select
something for me."

"I don't know your likes or dislikes."

"We'll shop together and I'll drop hints." He
grinned at her. "If you don't like what I pick out,
you can always exchange it."

"Let's set a spending limit," she said. "Twenty-
five dollars or less?"

"A little low," he was slow to say. "There's very little in the store for that price."

"How about fifty?" she asked.

He shook his head. "Higher."

"A hundred?" Her brow had furrowed and her
lips now pursed. Allie was frugal and money was an
issue. She wouldn't overspend, even if the gift was
free.

"That's a fair amount," he agreed.

He swung the lantern in a wide arc. The light reflected on Santa's Grotto. Small decorated Christmas trees were displayed near the runners of a
vintage wooden sleigh. The sparkle from the Vene-
tian hand-blown ornaments and Swarovski Crystal
snowflakes shone through the darkness.

Aidan looked at Allie and found her staring at
the small sleigh. "Dashing through the snow," he
said. "Does it bring back memories?"

Her blue eyes rounded. "I can't believe you remembered my sleigh ride story and the fact that
certain couples snuck under the tartan blankets
and fooled around."

He recalled everything of their time together. "You were hard to forget, Allie."

She took two steps, made a concession. "Let's talk before we shop. Join me in the sleigh?"

"You don't have to ask twice," he said, sweeping aside the decorative silver foil gift boxes with their enormous green bows. He made room for the two of them on the front seat. The sleigh was meant for elves, not adults. Aidan banged his knees a couple of times before he was fully settled. Allie sat more on him than beside him, which he didn't mind at all. He liked her on his lap.

She squinted straight ahead. "I can picture reindeer guiding our sleigh tonight."

"Rudolph's red nose would give off more light than our lantern." He hooked the handle of the battery-operated camping lamp over the front curl of the sleigh.

Silence collected, as heavy as the darkness. They sat physically close, yet emotionally distant. He watched her struggle with her personal demons, until finally he couldn't stand it any longer. He had to break down whatever obstacles stood between them.

He rested a hand on her knee, squeezed. "We've three years between us, Allie. Can we close the gap?"

She was intently contemplative, and when she spoke, her words were so soft, he strained to hear them. "Love was a concept, but never a reality for my mom. The richer the man, the faster he'd depart. All my life I watched Margo get hurt. After each breakup, she would curl on the bed and cry for days. My own heart broke for her."

She bit down on her lower lip. "Margo warned her daughters off relationships. My dating was minimal. I never allowed myself to feel, until I met you. I took a chance.

"You were so hot, so confident, so perfect. We had a lot in common. Sex was an adrenaline rush. Our time together was as wild, fast, and free as downhill at daybreak on fresh powder. I really liked you."

She rubbed her chest as if trying to warm her heart. He put his arm around her, as if by doing so, he could bring that warmth to her. Her smile was rueful. "A part of me knew we wouldn't last. I had to leave first, before you showed me the door."

"No door, Allie." Her mother had done a number on her. "I felt the start of something special between us. I wanted to spend New Year's with you. I'd already made a resolution to see you again."

She clutched her hands in her lap. "Instead I acted like a coward and took off."

"Not a coward, Allie, you were acting on instinct." He rubbed her back, his touch accepting of her childhood. "Growing up, you witnessed your mother's mistakes and her pain. Her poor choices in men. You believed relationships were of the moment and that they'd never last. I understand that now."

He ran one hand down his face, pinched the bridge of his nose. Thoughtful. "When you left, I thought you were lost to me. I knew you only as Allie. The hotel manager didn't have anyone at the lodge registered under that name."

"My ski vacation was a gift," she explained. "My room was charged to my sister's credit card. I had no idea you'd try to find me. I didn't have your last name either."

"Three years to the day, you walked into Dutton's."

"Snow Angel was at the top of my sisters' Christmas lists. I couldn't disappoint them," she said. "The scent is romantic. I can close my eyes and conjure up the scent in my mind. It reminds me of a winter wonderland."

Aidan was really in a mess now. How could he tell her the origin of the fragrance was all about her? It had been produced in her memory. The night he'd spent with her was such a powerful aphrodisiac that he couldn't get her woman's scent out of his mind. She'd been sun-kissed snow and melting frost. She was fresh warmth on a cold winter's day.

Snow Angel was all about Allie Smith.

Depending on their destiny, she might never know the truth behind the fragrance. He hoped she'd stay and give them a chance.

She wiggled on his lap, her elbow poking him in the side. "I had no idea you worked here, Aidan."

Worked here didn't really cover the truth. The fact he *owned the store* would scare her silly. "I was upstairs in Security, watching the guards clear the store," he said. "You walked in, and I couldn't believe my eyes."

"You had to frisk me to be sure I was real?"

"I needed to touch you." His voice grew husky.

She lowered her gaze. "I'm glad you did."

He shifted his shoulder and she cuddled against his chest. They were so close, they could've kissed. "What's next? Where do we go from here?" he had to ask. Would she stay or go once the blizzard passed?

She grew so thoughtful, she seemed in a trance. His heart slowed when she got out of the sleigh, her cane in hand. "We've cleared the air and it's time to shop."

Not what he wanted to hear. His hope fell to disappointment. He'd set himself for a fall and this was it. She couldn't see beyond the storm. She could only commit to the next minute. So be it. He'd make every second count.

Chapter Four

"There are seven floors to shop," Allie Smith heard Aidan say as he climbed from the vintage sleigh and collected the lantern. "Where shall we start?"

He didn't look at her, he didn't have to. The tension in the air was taut with uncertainty. She knew that whatever happened next was her move to make. She needed to make it soon.

She stared longingly at the sleigh. It would have been so easy to spend the next hour pressed against this man. Aidan made her feel alive. His warmth slid beneath her skin, making her hot for him. She had liked their tight fit on the front seat. Her breasts pressed up against his broad chest, her bottom pushing into the contours of his groin. The evidence of his erection.

The man was a turn on. She'd been wired from the moment he'd frisked her. They were a perfect sexual fit.

She sighed. Nothing about their situation was simple. Christmas three years prior had complicated her life forever.

She'd always favored the bulk of ski attire on men. Yet Aidan pulled off casual wear. His shoulders were wide, his chest thick. His long-legged stance was sexy. She loved his smile. His kindness. His humor. His sense of style.

After a day in the store, his white shirt showed not a wrinkle and his slacks were sharply creased. Strange, how his tassel loafers and argyle socks made her stomach go soft. Her pulse raced into dangerous territory as far as succumbing to this man was concerned. A man so hot that no patina of corporate shine could hide his rugged appeal. She'd never thought herself susceptible to business types, yet Aidan changed her mind.

She knew him equally as well naked as clothed. He was as physically buff as any athlete on the slopes. The man was a ski stud with a knowledge of retail. He wore the clothes, the clothes didn't wear him.

She liked the mix. A lot.

So why couldn't she commit to this man?

If she read the expression on his face correctly, he wasn't convinced she'd stay with him after the snowstorm. He was giving her his all. She was the one falling short of making the connection.

She'd reach out to him soon. She would find the right moment to slide up close and not back down. She wanted to kiss him, but she hadn't fully lost the fear of rejection. She hoped Aidan was the man she thought him to be, and that she hadn't read him wrong.

She longed to cling to those warm feelings a little while longer in case everything came crashing around her. Burying her like an avalanche.

She wanted to be his Christmas present this year.

She'd let him unwrap her, sinfully slow.

She thought about their future as they moved around the first floor, searching for gifts, playing *Hot and Cold*.

This variation of the kid's game made her smile. *Cold* meant the gift was a pass. *Hot* indicated a definite possibility.

She limped down the main aisle, stopping at stationery, photo albums, and picture frames. She selected a handsome leather bound album, held it up. "Ideal for what my mother used to call Kodak moments."

"*Cold*," he said. "I like art, but I'm not into photography."

Neither was she. She tapped her fingers on a glass display case beyond the albums. "The price is higher than we agreed upon, but how about a Tibaldi fountain pen set?" In white gold, the limited edition set was of exquisite Italian craftsmanship. "This set would make a statement on your desk. You could sign invoices, compose love letters."

He shook his head. "*Cold*. Love should be spoken, not written," he said with a sincerity that surprised her.

"Poetry can be romantic," she insisted.

"Making love expresses the same sentiment."

Yes it did, she had to agree. Aidan was a master of sentiment. He was as tender and passionate as he was raw male animal. He touched both her body and heart. She would soon tell him how much.

At the end of the glass counter, he offered her a sterling silver blade with a ruby encrusted handle. "Letter opener?" he asked.

"*Cold.* I don't receive much mail," she said. "I pay my bills automatically online."

"A box of stationery with your name and address scripted in diamond dust?" he tried again.

Her jaw dropped. "*Cold.* Who buys such stuff?"

"Socialites, actresses, anyone seeking to leave a lasting impression."

She kept her gaze downcast and let that pass. She wanted to tell him that she found such extravagance as diamond dust on stationery a complete waste of money, but didn't share her thoughts. She respected the fact that he worked high-end retail. She would never criticize the store where he earned his livelihood.

"Victorian handkerchief?" He tried once more.

"It's lovely." She'd never seen anything so delicate, so utterly exquisite. The square of ivory linen bordered by rose-patterned lace took her back to turn-of-the-century England. The hankie should be framed and admired on a living room wall, not stuffed in her jeans back pocket. It was an antique.

"But *Cold,* " she said. "Kleenex works for me."

She traced a selection of paisley squares perfectly spaced on the glass countertop. The satin was slippery to her touch.

"Pochettes." Aidan noted her curiosity. "Men's handkerchiefs that fit the pocket of a suit coat."

Allie threw back her head and laughed. "Stuffy, Aidan."

He grinned in agreement.

They moved down the aisle, to beauty and fragrance. He set the lantern on the counter as she looked closely at men's cologne.

She was drawn to Clive Christian, the world's most expensive male fragrance. The Baccarat crystal bottle proclaimed its century-old tradition. She lightly dabbed a drop on her finger, closed her eyes, and let it overtake her. Spice and citrus and pure masculinity.

Aidan's scent. Men who wore this cologne knew their worth. They were worldly, educated, and gentlemen.

She eyed him through lowered lashes. *How could he afford Clive Christian on his salary?* It was the scent of the very rich.

"This is the cologne you wore in Aspen." She'd know it anywhere. "I fell in love with the scent."

"What about the man wearing it?"

"I liked him, too."

"Nice save, Allie."

She wanted to save them both.

She finally had the courage to move beyond her comfort zone. No more misunderstandings. No more waiting.

The time was now.

She drew up close and wrapped her arms about his neck, trying to stand on tiptoe, ignoring the stab of pain shooting through her ankle. Her need for him was far stronger. She traced her finger over his lips, corner to corner.

Three years separated this night from their last

kiss. As her mouth sought his, time melted away to possession and promise. And complete abandon. She gave herself to him, his sexy body turning her on so much she couldn't think of anything else. Not blizzards, or her ankle, or even Santa's eight reindeer who would probably land on the roof at any moment.

There was no more *cold* to their game, it was all *hot* from this point on. Aidan allowed her a heartbeat of sweet and soft and searching before he penetrated her mouth with his tongue. His kisses took her back to Frost Peak Lodge and their night of hot, sweaty sex.

He tucked her close to him. He held her so tight she dropped her opera cane. She heard it rattle onto the polished marble floor, the sound echoing around them like the chain of a ghost from Christmas past.

Her pulse raced, and her intake of breath was sharp in the silent store. He willingly breathed for her, exhaling as she inhaled, the moist heat of his mouth becoming her life force.

He kissed her with three years of suppressed need.

She kissed him back with the urgency of lost time.

She tried to sift her body into his, a merging of two into one. They stood as close as two people could with their clothes on.

Heat spread into her breasts and her nipples hardened. She felt his sex thicken and rise against her belly. She moaned. She sighed. She wanted.

Her insides shifted and melted. She moaned low in her throat. And her entire body hummed.

Aidan touched her everywhere. He traced her shoulders. Cupped her breasts. He ran his fingers over her ribs. Palmed her belly. He spanned her hip then stroked her ass. He felt between her legs and she opened to him. She leaned into his hand.

Overhead, the final slam and shudder of the generators broke them apart. The emergency lights faded. Darkness claimed every corner of the store. The air carried a menacing chill. The ancient machinery had given up the ghost.

Allie clutched his arms, his muscles tensing as their predicament worsened. He blew out a breath, fanning her forehead with warmth. Still, she shivered.

"Scared?" he asked.

"Not of the dark and no longer of you." She lowered her voice, afraid the shadows might have ears. "I don't need a present from Dutton's to be happy this holiday season. I want our gift exchange to be each other."

"Maybe a trip to Aspen to take up where we left off," he proposed.

She smiled, liking his suggestion. He wanted to make future plans with her. To prove he wouldn't leave her. She appreciated his effort. "New Year's sex. There really is a Santa Claus."

"There's also Sam," Aidan observed, noticing the security guard's approach. He was grateful Sam hadn't shown up a moment sooner or his whole life might not have changed for the better. He now knew that Allie wanted him and that was the best Christmas gift he'd ever received in his stocking.

He turned his attention to Sam, packing two

flashlights, a camping lantern, and a deepening scowl.

Sam nodded a greeting to them both, then went on to say, "I need you upstairs, boss. Chris and Pamela have taken advantage of your shopping spree. Their selection of gifts would fill Santa's bag ten times over."

Aidan felt a headache coming on. "I told them one gift each," he said.

"Apparently they can't count," said Sam.

Major mood spoiler, Aidan thought. He and Allie had just found each other, only to be separated by a greedy golfer and money-hungry Broadway actress.

He bent to pick up Allie's opera cane. The cane she'd dropped when he drew her close. Their fingers brushed and he felt a heat at his groin that could roast chestnuts.

"What have they accumulated?" he asked Sam. "Last I heard, Chris wanted a new golf bag and Pamela was looking for a fancy dress."

Sam ran a hand along the back of his neck. "Their spree gained momentum as they went through the store. Chris picked out a new set of golf clubs, golf shoes, then pocketed the TRI Marker." Sam looked at Allie, explaining, "It's a white gold, diamond and amethyst studded marker used to mark ball placement. Chris continues to believe that Dutton's *owes* him for the inconvenience of the blizzard. He's run up six-figures so far."

Aidan stiffened. "How about Pamela?"

"She chose a dozen designer dresses and still has her eye on the red satin stilettos in the front showroom window," Sam said. "Chris convinced her that she needed luggage for her clothes. She went with the Louis Vuitton collection and took all six pieces, including the armoire trunk and hat box. She said the pieces matched Chris's golf bag."

"It sounds like Pamela plans to join Chris on the Tour," Allie speculated.

"The lady's in for a major disappointment," Sam said. "The man's not Chris Johnson. I'd stake my life on it."

Aidan thought Sam was probably right. To get Chris to confess was another matter entirely.

He looked at Allie, who smiled shyly at him. Her hair was mussed, her eyes bright. Her cheeks and chin bore his whisker burn. He rubbed his jaw. He needed a shave.

His chest clutched as he realized how much he cared for her. She was a hot sex partner, but he also felt a soul-deep connection. He knew in his heart Allie was different from any woman he'd ever met. He could be himself around this woman.

She'd yet to know him as the Dutton heir, but that would come soon enough. He'd tell her after the snowstorm, when they had complete privacy. No interruptions.

He would have given her every item in this store, if she had asked. Instead she'd chosen him as her Christmas gift. Lying next to her skin to skin would be priceless.

"Where are the Murphys?" Aidan asked, curious as well as concerned for their safety.

"Sitting happily on the couch like two kids on Christmas morning," Sam told him. "Marian's busy admiring her Waterford vase and Warren's appreciative of his new crocodile wallet."

The guard clasped his hands and blew on his fingers. "It's going to be cold soon. We need to collect pillows and blankets."

"Heat rises," Aidan knew. "Let's move to the sixth floor, to beds and bedding."

"Warren Murphy mentioned his joints hurt," Sam said. "It might do him good to stretch out."

"Bunk beds for Pamela and Chris?" Allie asked, tongue in cheek.

Sam grunted. "Any heavy breathing and I trigger the Taser."

Aidan could picture Allie on the large, draped four-poster bed. A Turkish motif with the finest ivory silk linens, a black cashmere coverlet, and Fez embroidered pillows.

Realistically, they might be warmer in a sleeping bag. Dutton's had several designs. One double-size sleeper had a velvet futon cushioned floor and a thick goose-down lining. The manufacturer claimed it was suitable for Arctic temperatures; it would keep his snow angel warm.

"Let me carry you upstairs." He then swept Allie high against his chest before she could protest. She wrapped her arms around his shoulders and nuzzled his neck. He dropped a light kiss on her forehead.

Sam led the climb, flashlights and lanterns in hand. The stairwell held a foreboding chill. It was time to prepare for the frigid night ahead.

They reached the third floor, and Aidan looked around. Sam had warned him about Chris's and Pamela's stack of expensive gifts. Yet seeing the merchandise piled high made him double blink. They'd clean out his store if he'd let them.

The two sat snuggled together on the leather couch. Their heads were bent, whispering, laughing, carrying on like partners in crime. They appeared more on vacation than stuck in a blizzard.

Three boxes of imported hand-dipped chocolates lay open on the coffee table. Several half-eaten pieces sat sticky on the clear glass. Two wineglasses flanked a bottle of Mouton Rothschild. Pamela and Chris were well into the red wine.

Aidan had every right to be pissed. For Allie's sake, he locked his jaw and held his temper. Said little for the moment.

He set her down gently. Friction sparked. The hot little pinpricks raised his temperature as well as his dick. He turned to the hoarders and said, "I see you two have been shopping."

"We shopped until the electricity failed," Pamela said, pouting. As if the loss of light was Aidan's fault. "It got so dark it was like stepping into a thick bar of chocolate."

"We passed food and wine on our return and helped ourselves." Chris smirked. "Nothing but the best for us. Right, Pamela, honey?"

Pamela waved her hand theatrically. "Snickers are so pedestrian. Life's too short to eat cheap chocolate. *Delicabar* by Bacarr is sublime." She slowly licked her lips, making them shine. "These liqueur truffles are filled with German Robin Brandy, raspberry wine, and Añejo Patrón tequila."

"We ate one entire box looking for the worm." Chris laughed at his own joke. "Then we ran out of wine."

Aidan shook his head. Lack of wine explained

why the candies were bitten into pieces. They'd had nothing to wash the chocolate down.

"Major sugar high," said Pam, cozying up to Chris.

"I'd say the wine chasers helped too," Allie whispered to Aidan.

He agreed. He debated discussing their mountain of gifts with them. Drunks could be mellow or could get mad. He hoped for the former.

He nodded toward their amassed fortune. "What happened to one gift per customer?" he asked dryly.

"A single present doesn't compensate for my time." Chris slurred his words a little. "If I hadn't been stuck here through no fault of my own, I could have attended the charity tournament in Atlanta, I'd have won big money."

Sam stepped more visibly into the lantern light. "How quickly you big shots forget," he addressed Chris. "The winnings don't go to the golfers. The men play for their favorite charity. Yours was St. Michael's Mission. The national organization that houses the homeless."

Chris went so still, Aidan swore he stopped breathing. His features were as tight as his words when he asked, "You knew this how? *Golf Forum?*"

"*USA Today,*" Sam informed him. "I have a copy of yesterday's newspaper upstairs in Security. There's no picture of Chris Johnson, only the mention of his charity. I'd be happy to retrieve the article to jog your memory."

"Shit." Chris cursed under his breath. He looked visibly shaken.

"Care to come clean?" asked Aidan, opening the door for the truth.

Still, Chris hesitated. Aidan swore the man broke into a cold sweat before his eyes.

Pamela scooted to the far end of the couch, distancing herself from the phony golfer. "If you're not Chris Johnson, then who are you?"

Chris swallowed hard, confessed. "I was his chauffer while he was in Chicago this past weekend for the grand opening of his new steakhouse The Nineteenth Hole. My real name's Jay Watts."

"I knew it." Sam puffed out his chest, proud of himself. "Mystery solved."

Jay glared at Sam. "Cut me some slack, will you? I've never pretended to be Johnson until today."

"Why today?" Aidan asked, curious.

"I saw Pamela and thought she was hot. I wanted to impress her."

Pamela smiled weakly and fussed with her hair. She seemed almost embarrassed by his compliment.

"High-maintenance chicks like Pamela won't give a regular guy the time of day," Jay continued. "I wanted to impress her. Professional athletes get a lot of attention. Johnson's always mobbed. Men want to be him. Women want to sleep with him. Everyone kisses his ass."

"You wanted your ass kissed, too." Pamela sighed heavily, as if a burden had been lifted off her shoulders as well. She slowly inched along the couch, back toward Jay. "I have something to get off my chest too," she said, folding her hands in her lap. "I'm not the leading actress in *Peaches*."

"You're kidding." Jay was clearly fooled.

"I'm the understudy in an off-off Broadway production," she admitted. "It's not a long running show either. It's only financed for three months."

Jay shrugged, lowered his gaze to her breasts. "Guess we're both as fake as your boobs."

"My girls are real," she said with pride. "And they're show-stoppers."

Jay's face lit up like the lights on a Christmas tree, all glowy and bright.

Aidan relaxed. Maybe he'd get off easier than he'd expected. In Jay's eyes, nothing Dutton's offered could compare to Pamela's cup size.

"We need more wine," Jay said. "It's freezing in here and I could use the buzz."

"I can't get so drunk I let you take advantage of me." Pamela giggled.

"You'll never be under the influence, babe, only under me," Jay said.

Pamela laughed so hard she nearly fell off the couch.

Allie nudged Aidan with her elbow. "I feel like Alice down the rabbit hole."

"I'm right there with you," he said. "But there's no way out of Wonderland until tomorrow."

Allie laced her fingers with his. "It's funny how things turn out when two people are forced to be honest with each other."

"What do you mean?" Aidan asked. What was she leading up to?

She looked at the two would-be celebrities, laughing and whispering like old friends. "Their department store confessions seemed to bring them closer together."

Aidan kept quiet, knowing he was on shaky ground with whatever he said. Best to let the matter drop. For now. He had his own admission to make. That would happen soon enough.

For the moment, he enjoyed the softness of her palm, the intimate squeeze of her hand. When she shivered, he felt her chill all the way to her fingertips. He tensed. As much as he'd like to believe otherwise, they'd need more than body heat to survive the night.

"Let's move to the sixth floor," Aidan said. "Sam and I will locate battery-heated camping blankets."

"I have sensitive skin and wool blankets can be scratchy," Pamela complained. "I'd rather have a cashmere comforter."

"Our bedding tonight isn't about fashion, it's about survival," Sam said with authority. "We don't want anyone to freeze."

"We have display beds. You can take your pick," Aidan told them.

Jay looked at Pamela, his eyes widening. "Have you seen the Gold Bed?" he asked. "I read about it online. It's the most expensive waterbed in the world. The frame is coated in 24-carat gold, and Swarovski Crystals line the sideboard. We could make some big waves tonight."

Sam shook his head. "No waves. Without electricity, the bed will be a block of ice."

Pamela shivered. "Sounds too cold for me."

"I'll keep you warm," Jay told her.

"I'll help Sam gather what's needed so we can all keep warm," Aidan said to Allie. He bent, lightly brushed her lips with his own. He would have enjoyed deepening that kiss. Wrong time.

Wrong place. He didn't want his woman to freeze on the spot. "I'll be right back. Then we'll head upstairs."

He returned in record time, not wanting to leave Allie alone longer than was absolutely necessary. With him he had battery-operated blankets that were thick, durable, and meant to sustain sub-zero temperatures.

Tonight was all about warmth. Not sex.

The sleeping bag for two was his personal favorite.

Spooning was his position of choice.

Sam assisted the Murphys to the emergency stairwell, making sure they had plenty of light to guide their way. They began their climb. Pamela and Jay scooped up the leftover chocolates. Lanterns in hand, they weaved unsteadily across the room, making Aidan wonder if he should follow them to keep them out of trouble. Their laughter echoed eerily through the darkness.

Allie nudged him, offering to carry the blankets and sleeping bag, if he carried her. He hooked her opera cane over her left wrist, lifted her easily. He swiped the last lantern off the coffee table.

"Are you hungry?" he asked. "We can make a quick stop on the fifth floor. Food and wine can provide dinner."

"Sounds like a plan." Allie smiled back. "We could pick up something for Sam and the Murphys too," she suggested. "Pamela and Jay are having their own private party."

Aidan swung the lantern wide on their departure. There were so many items to be returned to their regular departments. At that moment, he didn't much care. Getting through this bitter cold night was his number one priority.

He held Allie close. So close, he couldn't tell where her body left off and his began. It felt right to have her in his life. Three years of missing her now melted like an ice cube. She warmed him with a look. A touch. A smile.

Food and wine produced sweets for everyone. Aidan topped the blankets with a holiday tin of orange-pecan biscuit thins and a sticky toffee pudding. Eau de Sucre was his favorite gourmet microbrew soda, served in aqua mosaic bottles. His tastes ran to maple syrup root beer, while Allie wanted to try both chocolate lavender and black lemonade.

She was soon completely covered with blankets and food. He could only see the top of her blond head. He could, however, feel her curves, as one of his arms supported her bottom and the other crossed her back. They proceeded to the emergency exit.

Sam came quickly and unburdened Allie once they reached the sixth floor. The guard spread the biscuits, pudding, and sodas on a mahogany nightstand. The Murphys came to serve themselves. Luckily the pudding came with plastic spoons.

"Any particular place you would like us to sleep?" Warren asked Aidan, stifling a yawn. "I'm tired and would like to stretch out soon."

Aidan pointed to a row of Sweden by Hastings beds. "The beds are all made up. The mattresses are like sleeping on a cloud," he said with just the hint of a sales pitch. "Sam will put batteries in the camping blankets and you should stay warm throughout the night."

Marian Murphy slipped into her winter wool coat. She wrapped a scarf around her neck, then donned her mittens. "I'm all for being toasty," she said, hunching her shoulders and rubbing her gloved hands together.

"I'm all about heating the sheets," Pamela said from two aisles over. She pulled back the comforter on a queen-size bed and began to stroke the top sheet as if it was a lover. The little sound of appreciation she made was almost sexual.

She grabbed the price tag off the bed and her eyes popped. "Only Midas could afford these linens. It says here they're handmade merino wool backed with thousand-count Egyptian cotton. They're also threaded with gold."

Jay came up behind her. "I've never slept on gold."

"That bed's strictly for show," Sam interceded before the two could crawl under the covers. "Pick another one."

"Party pooper." Pamela sniffed.

"Forget him," Jay said, slipping his arm around her. "We'll try out all the beds until we find the right one."

"Just call me Goldilocks," she giggled.

Aidan and Allie watched as the couple sat, bounced, and flopped on a dozen display beds before settling on an ornate brass one in the far corner. They picked out orthopedic pillows and thick down comforters. Sam left two camping blankets on their nightstand in case Jack Frost nipped their noses.

The Murphys chose a double bed and Sam saw to their comfort, making sure they were snug under the covers. Sam settled onto a juvenile boy's single near the emergency exit. Aidan knew he took his security job seriously. He would safeguard their sleep from a bed designed as a race car.

Aidan finished off the biscuit thins and Allie sipped the last of her soda. They looked at each other, Allie biting down on her lower lip, Aidan trying to keep his libido from getting out of hand. He restrained himself from licking off her chocolate lavender soda moustache. Instead he pressed the cuff on his shirt to her upper lip. It was time to turn in.

Never in his wildest dreams had he imagined taking Allie to bed at Dutton's Department Store in the middle of a blizzard. Yet here they stood, looking over the displays, ready to make a decision on their bed for the night.

"Sleigh bed? Round one?" he asked her.

"I'd be waiting for Rudolph all night in the sleigh bed," she said with a smile. "The round one reminds me of a marshmallow."

"Four poster?" He grabbed the sleeping bag, took her by the hand, and led her down the aisle. She limped beside him. He brought her to a luxury bed with a sheer nude fabric canopy and matching sheets. It was a bed where naked bodies could blend with the bedding. Sex would get all wrapped up in an intimate heat.

No lovemaking tonight, it was too public. Aidan focused on the cold that settled around them. Tonight was all about survival.

"The bed looks inviting," she agreed, letting out a long, slow breath as if she could read his thoughts.

Aidan spread the sleeping bag over the sheets.

He unzipped one side to give her easy access. She rested her cane against the headboard, toed off her right boot, and climbed inside.

"Feels like a furnace," she said.

Aidan took off his loafers, eased in behind her. He positioned himself against her back, careful of her sprained ankle. Her head rested on his upper arm, and her shoulder pressed his chest. Her bottom curved against his groin. The slide of the sleeping bag zipper locked them in for the night. She pushed back, snuggling tight.

The lady was exhausted.

She softened in his arms.

He hardened against her ass.

He counted close to a million sheep before he fell asleep.

Chapter Five

"**A**idan, Allie, wake up."

Allie Smith opened one eye and yawned. Someone was shaking Aidan's shoulder so hard it awakened her too. She tried to stretch, but found herself confined between man and sleeping bag. She smiled, remembering how cozy she'd felt all night with his arms around her and what she guessed was his erection pressing against her behind.

She located the zipper at the top of the bag and tugged it down the side. Unfortunately their sexy sleepover had come to an end. The light from the overhead fixtures nearly blinded her. The electricity was restored.

Sam stood over them, his expression wary.

Directly behind the security guard was a uniformed policeman. His badge read OFFICER LINK. The cop stared at her for a long time, making her self-conscious. She knew she looked a mess. Bed head and wrinkled clothing had her wanting to zip the sleeping bag back up.

Aidan stirred beside her. He pushed up on one elbow, blinked against the brightness. "Officer," he acknowledged, his voice hoarse. "Emergency services must have worked quickly to restore electricity."

"State Street is up and running, Mr. Dutton," the officer stated.

What did he just say?

Allie started, tried to clear the cobwebs from her head. She must still be asleep. The law enforcement office had address Aidan as *Mr. Dutton.*

"We're assisting those trapped to leave the building," the cop continued. "We'll provide police escort to their homes. The street is almost cleared. We found vehicles buried at the curb. It's been slow-going for the snowplows."

"Any further problems, Officer Link?" Aidan asked.

Allie noticed he avoided her gaze. They'd just spent the night pressed together like puzzle pieces and now he wouldn't even look at her? *What was up with that and the "Mr. Dutton" business?*

The officer cleared his throat. "Law enforcement is canvassing the area now. We're making certain there weren't any looters. Down the block, Lacy Antoinette's has a broken front window, no doubt from the blizzard. Unfortunately, racks of lingerie were stolen. I found a red bra on the sidewalk."

Sam shook his head, muttered, "The thieves must have escaped on snowmobiles."

Allie wasn't concerned about criminals or red bras. She mentally backtracked to the policeman calling Aidan *Mr. Dutton*. Surely the cop had made a mistake.

"Your parents were concerned for your safety, Mr. Dutton," Officer Link said. "They would appreciate a call once the phone lines are restored."

Again, "Mr. Dutton." She might be sleepy-eyed, but her hearing was acute. Her man radar told her Aidan was hiding something from her. Something important.

The officer tugged the flaps on his winter cap back over his ears then nodded to the security guard. "Good job, Sam. Looks like everyone survived at your store. Others in the city weren't so lucky."

"That's my job, Officer Link," Sam said with pride, "and I try to do it well in any kind of weather."

"Good to see you again, Mr. Dutton," the policeman said on his departure. "Those of us at the thirty-ninth precinct always appreciate your generous donation of Trees for Tots. We gave away two hundred decorated evergreens this year. The children went nuts. Kids believe they must have a tree for Santa to leave presents."

The third *Mr. Dutton* couldn't be a mistake.

A bitter chill raced up and down her spine, his betrayal making her numb. She couldn't feel, couldn't think, couldn't move. Every nerve in her body was stretched taut. If she so much as took a big breath, she would explode into millions of tiny particles. And she'd cease to exist. Her heart broken.

The richer the man, the faster he leaves. Her mother's words rang in her ears, loud as an alarm.

A shudder racked her body, breaking the spell. Pain stabbed her insides. It hurt. Hurt bad. This couldn't be happening. Surely Aidan hadn't played her.

She knew deep in her heart he wasn't a mean man. She'd seen firsthand how he took interest in the welfare of the Murphys, how Sam looked up to him with respect, even the way he handled the phony would-be celebs. With firmness but compassion. Still, she couldn't deny he hadn't been honest with her.

She silently fumed. The man knew her body as well as he knew his own, and he couldn't let her in on what the entire police department already knew?

Of all the failures she'd endured with men, this was the worst yet. There was no room in his privileged lifestyle for a broken down ski bunny who could barely hop.

Whatever excuses she made, she couldn't deny the awful truth. She'd fallen in love with the first floor supervisor, only to be told he *owned the store.*

Merry Christmas from the Grinch.

Allie Smith had just found coal in her Christmas stocking.

She pushed to a sitting position against the headboard, glanced at the man she now knew as Mr. Dutton. His hair was mussed, his gray eyes were heavily lidded. He looked uneasy. Worried. His lack of self-assurance made her own confidence wane.

They were momentarily alone. Sam walked with the police officer to the emergency exit. The Murphys, Pamela, and Jay had yet to rise.

"*Mr. Dutton?*" The words stuck in her throat. She waited for his answer. It didn't come.

His silence gave her pause. His jaw muscles worked, bunched, and his face looked hard. He seemed cautious, as if whatever he said wouldn't make up for what he hadn't told her earlier.

"I can explain, Allie—" he said finally. But he didn't. It was as if he couldn't find the words.

Or didn't want to.

She chose to believe the latter.

"I'm sure you can, Aidan Dutton," she repeated, afraid to let the stillness overtake her, to bury her so deep she'd never dig her way out and find herself again.

She went into escape mode. Time to exit gracefully. If she could with this bum foot of hers.

She swung her legs over the side of the bed, then located her opera cane. It was within reach. She could grab it and hobble out of his life in a heartbeat.

But first she had to ask him, "Why didn't you tell me who you were?" Her heart went cold, shivered in her chest.

She waited for the answer she didn't want to hear, that she was great on the snow and in the sack, but only as a distraction. The blizzard had passed. And so had their fantasy date.

He ran one hand down his face. He looked sad and resigned, as if he was about to suffer a great loss.

That wasn't what she'd expected. She'd thought he would show her to the emergency exit.

"I hated the pretense, Allie."

She let go the deep breath she'd been holding.

A part of her believed him. A second part was already looking for her discarded UGGS. There'd be no retreat without her winter boots.

"You could have confided your secret identity," she accused, tapping her good foot nervously, "and not acted like a department store ass."

"I'm a wealthy man," he explained, looking self-conscious, almost apologetic. "What I did was wrong. No excuse. But when I saw you again, I could think of only one thing: keeping you here until I found out why you bolted in Aspen."

She blushed. "I guess I'm no snow angel either, running out like I did. But I was always up front about *who* I am, a skiing instructor with a dysfunctional family." Her gaze swept the sixth floor. "Not heir to an exclusive department store that rivals Harrods."

"Dutton's was started by my great-great-grandfather," Aidan said without apology. "The store will be mine someday."

A significant pause, as he rolled out of bed. She stared at him. He looked the same, yet different somehow, now that she knew who he was.

He stood across the mattress from her, his shoulders broad, his stance wide. His white shirt still looked pressed and his slacks remained creased. The rich never looked rumpled.

"When we met, we were two people on a ski holiday, out for a good time," he said. "I liked the fact you knew me as a man, a friend, then a lover before you learned my bank balance."

Allie took offense. She was no fortune hunter. Yet there was no denying the man was worth millions.

A man like that needed a woman who could fit

into his crowd. Smile with perfect teeth. Make polite conversation in social situations. Wear basic black and make it look like spun gold. She was none of that.

Allie took it all in. This opulent, luxuriant, seven-story department store was Aidan's heritage. He'd grown up with wealth and privilege whereas her youth was spent apartment hopping and hoping for a meal.

No matter how she looked at it, the truth was she didn't belong here. They were just too different. He was designer sheets. She was irregular markdowns.

"Your life is so"—she searched for the right word—"*large*." The words hurt her as much as they would Aidan. "My paycheck barely covered two bottles of Snow Angel cologne."

"The cologne is all you, Allie." He gave her a moment, allowed his words to sink in. "Snow Angel is the fragrance of you on the mountain, of you in my bed. I hired a French perfumery to produce the scent of a woman I'd met on holiday."

Aidan Dutton had created a cologne for her.

The fragrance was clean, fresh, and romantic. One whiff and she was wrapped up in Aidan's arms all over again, blending the pink-cheeked coldness of downhill with the blush of heated skin on silk bedsheets.

She felt a moment of hope, only to have reality hit her broadside when she looked down and spotted her UGGS. Battered, worn. Like her. Wincing, she pulled on her boots, one at a time. She had to accept that the scent was Aidan's creative imagining of who he believed her to be. She wasn't the woman behind the winter wonderland mystique. She was plain old Allie Smith.

She'd never been to the opera. She wouldn't have set foot in Dutton's had it not been for the Snow Angels. She'd never planned to lose her heart to a man with a clothes closet bigger than her whole apartment.

She flexed her ankle. The pain was minimal. She had some run in her today. She pushed off the bed, retrieved her cane. She took her first step, her knees weak and her steps wobbly.

"I have to go," she said, avoiding his gaze. "I need time."

"How much more time do you need?" His tone was desperate now. "We've had three years apart."

"I don't know you, Aidan," she said, meaning it. She rubbed her forehead. "Please, don't try to stop me. It's all so confusing."

"Bullshit, Allie." His tone called her on the carpet. "You're making excuses for something you don't want to face."

"What is that supposed to mean?" she shot back.

"You think you're like your mother because she couldn't hold onto a guy. You believe all men leave. Especially the rich ones."

"How dare you talk about my mother like that—"

"It's true, think about it," he said with urgency. "All your life you were afraid if you found the right guy and he made you happy, your mother's prediction would come true: he'd up and leave you too. So you left first to stop that from happening. You also didn't want to hurt your mom by finding a man of your own when she remained alone."

"That's not true—" *Or was it?* She stopped

abruptly. Tears stung her eyes. She refused to cry. Could he be right? Was she so afraid of hurting her mother that she sabotaged her own relationships with men? Even if it was true, Aidan had no right to say it.

She turned to leave, her breathing labored. She didn't want to hear any more. Not another word. Especially on the subject of her mother.

Before she got more than a few steps, Aidan grabbed her cane and pulled her back to him. He turned her around, held her close. His expression was fierce. "Your mother was wrong about men, Allie. Dead wrong. Let me prove it to you."

"No, please, let me go—"

"Not until you listen to what I have to say," he forced out. "You liked me as a skier, and again as the first floor supervisor. All I ask is that you find a place in your heart for Aidan Dutton."

"I'm trying."

"*Try harder.*"

"I can't change how I feel," she insisted. "Not without taking some time to think things through— what you said about me, about us."

She was doing the best she could, but apparently that wasn't good enough for him. He laid down his ultimatum.

"I won't beg you to stay, Allie Smith, but somewhere, somehow, you need to find your own happiness. You've followed in your mother's footsteps too long."

Sadness slipped around her heart. "Aidan, I—"

"You need to face your future, with or without me." He released her, but held her gaze. "If you decide to give us a chance, I'll be in Aspen on New

Year's Eve. There'll be champagne and fireworks,
big fireworks. They go off at midnight."

Frost Peak Lodge
New Year's Eve

It was 11:15 P.M. when Allie Smith entered Aidan
Dutton's suite. He'd left a room key in her name at
the registration desk, hoping she would show. She
had. That was the easy part. Now what?

Her practical side still questioned her sanity.
What was she doing here? Her face-the-future side
seduced her with the idea of hot, crazy sex with a
man who claimed to love her. Still, that hadn't pre-
vented her from spending the past ten minutes
pacing up and down the hallway, getting up the
courage to let herself in.

She was in now. She broke into a cold sweat and
her hand shook when she closed the door behind
her. The lock clicked, and her insides tangled. Her
stomach was one big knot.

She lowered her backpack to the carpet,
dropped her opera cane alongside it. She shrugged
off her winter jacket then looked around. A hundred crystal candle holders held snow-white vo-
tives. The tiny flames danced, and vanilla scented
the air. A romantic glow tinted everything in the
room gold. The playful shadows beckoned her to
stay.

A bottle of Snow Angel sat on the coffee table,
his gift to her. She laid the card key down and
picked up the cologne, spritzed lightly behind her

ears and at the pulse point at her throat. She loved the scent.

A dinner cart sat off to the side, yet to be removed. The service was for one, she noted, relieved. Aidan had eaten his meat and potatoes but left his vegetables. He apparently didn't like asparagus.

There was no immediate sign of the man. What if he'd gotten tired of waiting? She was late, but she'd had no choice. She'd seen an orthopedist that very day. His diagnosis: a hairline fracture. He recommended rest, ice, and elevation of her foot. No skiing for at least six weeks.

She smiled. With any luck, she'd be recuperating between the sheets in Aidan's bed. She'd even purchased a lacy bra and satin thong for the occasion, which she wore beneath her jeans and sweatshirt.

She moved toward the master bedroom, relaxed when she heard the shower running. The bed was turned down. A mint sat on his pillow. It looked small and lonely. Like she'd felt all her life. Not tonight. She was here and that was all that mattered. She had every intention of welcoming in the New Year with this man.

Movement near the bathroom door caught her eye. She cut a glance left, found Aidan leaning against the doorjamb—naked, damp, buff. A calendar hunk come to life. And that stare of his was positively lethal. He crossed his arms over his chest, fixed his gaze on her.

She stared back so intently, she aroused him. He

grew stiff. His sex soon lay flat against his abdomen, reaching almost to his navel.

He was one superb man.

Her heart lodged in her throat and her voice went tight. "Happy New Year, Aidan."

"You're late, Allie Smith," he said, his voice low, concerned. "By six hours, fourteen minutes, and eight seconds."

"How did you know I'd show up?"

"I made a bet with myself that you would."

"And if I hadn't?"

"But you did, babe."

She detailed her day. "An afternoon doctor's appointment forced me to change my flight."

"How's your ankle?"

"On the mend." She would give him the details later.

His jaw worked. "What got you here, Allie?" He needed to know. "What changed your mind?"

It was her moment of truth. She opened her heart and told him how she felt. "It's simple, Aidan. I love you. I was lonely without you."

He sniffed the air, got a whiff of her scent, and smiled. "I missed you too, Snow Angel."

He pushed off the door frame, came to her, a human sculpture, all water slicked and generously proportioned.

Inches separated them as she made the first move and placed a kiss over his heart. "You're a man of strength, courage, and immense patience," she murmured appreciatively. "You protect the pride of your security guard and show kindness to snowbound shoppers."

"Sam sends his best, by the way," Aidan relayed.

"Jay, Pamela, and the Murphys requested invitations to our wedding."

Marriage. Had a nice ring to it.

She scrunched her nose. "I'm not very domestic."

"You're a free-spirit," he said. "I envy you that."

"You do?" This was the first time anyone had said her offbeat lifestyle was something desirable.

He grinned at her. "You fly down mountains, enjoy hot buttered rum, wear red sunglasses, and travel light. You moan low in your throat when we make love. And when you sleep, you hog the covers."

"You always sleep on your right side."

"You noticed?"

"That, and the fact you snore."

The bedside clock softly chimed the quarter hour. It was eleven forty-five. He took her hand, gave her fingers a squeeze. "You're overdressed for New Year's Eve."

He stripped her in under a minute. Her red sweatshirt and jeans soon pooled at her feet. His gaze heated on her bra and panties. "Nice. Very, very nice," he admired as he removed them.

He had fast hands when it came to getting her naked.

Slow hands when it came to making love.

She wrapped her arms about his neck, leaned into him. She so loved his body. Her hands grazed his strong back. His chest tensed when she rubbed her nipples against his skin. His leg muscles tightened when she leaned into his groin. She fit so perfectly between his thighs.

He lowered his head and she lifted her lips for his kiss. He changed the angle of his mouth, and deepened their intimacy. His tongue penetrated, then retreated, leaving heat and longing in its wake. She never wanted the kiss to end. She stretched her body in pleasure to be closer to him.

He walked her backward until her thighs hit the side of the bed. Then he lowered her to the mattress. Slowly. And he followed her down.

He fondled her breasts, ran his hand over her flat belly, moved down between her legs. She loved the touch of his hands on her inner thighs. He opened her. Stroked her. Coaxed her. She went hot, soft, wet for him.

She was gasping, panting, aching for him to fill her when he snagged a condom from the top drawer of his nightstand and slipped it on.

He came back to her, his mouth fastening on her sensitive nipple, his hands closing around her waist. Her heart slammed as he moved over her more fully, then spread her thighs and claimed her.

He felt huge inside her. She felt every thick inch of him. He rocked his hips, slow, deep thrusts; steady and prolonged. Heat pooled between them, a fiery friction.

She moaned, gasped, let her need overtake her. He knew how to touch her, just how hard and how soft, to keep her on edge. The pleasure was so blinding it was almost painful. She was burning up.

She arched herself even more tightly against him. She rubbed her nipples against his chest, rotated her hips, curled her fingernails into his back.

She clawed his shoulders as her body climbed higher. His flesh was deeply scored by the time she climaxed.

She looked deeply into his eyes when she came. They were joined in every way a man and woman could be joined, sex to sex, heart to heart, gaze to gaze.

They shared a hot breathless kiss as they reached completion. Their shudder should have shattered them both.

With an expulsion of air, they collapsed, their energy spent, their bodies wet and hot against cool white sheets.

She didn't want it to end. She'd waited such a long time. Only after she let go and allowed herself to love him did everything fall perfectly in place.

He now lay on his back, still semi-erect. She liked a man with staying power, in both her life and in her bed. She'd been such a fool not to trust Aidan, and because of that she'd almost lost him. Now she was here, unafraid to show him how she felt. And she felt plenty. She would never tire of looking at him, feeling him. They would make love all night.

A loud pop echoed outside their bedroom window. Allie propped herself up on her elbows in time to see gold, red, and orange fireworks flaring, then brightening the night sky. One year had come to an end and another had just begun. She couldn't believe everything she'd ever dreamed of was now hers. She had a man who loved her and wanted her in his life. Always.

She kissed him long and sweet and loving, committing herself to him. He hugged her close, in an embrace never intended to end.

He was her man.

She was his snow angel.

Can't get enough holiday spirit? Try
JINGLE BELL ROCK!

*Skip the mistletoe—you won't need it after you indulge
in these six tempting tales of romance filled with the sort
of naughty-but-oh-so-nice men who make the season so
bright it's downright hot . . .*

He Sees You When You're Sleeping
LORI FOSTER

Baby, It's Cold Outside
DONNA KAUFFMAN

Turning Up the Heat
SUSAN DONOVAN

All She Wants for Christmas
JANELLE DENISON

A Blue Christmas
ALISON KENT

The Nutcracker Sweet
NANCY WARREN

Now available from Kensington!

Thrilling Suspense from
Beverly Barton

Available Wherever Books Are Sold!

Visit our website at www.kensingtonbooks.com

More from Bestselling Author
JANET DAILEY

Books by Bestselling Author
Fern Michaels

___**The Jury**	0-8217-7878-1	$6.99US/$9.99CAN
___**Sweet Revenge**	0-8217-7879-X	$6.99US/$9.99CAN
___**Lethal Justice**	0-8217-7880-3	$6.99US/$9.99CAN
___**Free Fall**	0-8217-7881-1	$6.99US/$9.99CAN
___**Fool Me Once**	0-8217-8071-9	$7.99US/$10.99CAN
___**Vegas Rich**	0-8217-8112-X	$7.99US/$10.99CAN
___**Hide and Seek**	1-4201-0184-6	$6.99US/$9.99CAN
___**Hokus Pokus**	1-4201-0185-4	$6.99US/$9.99CAN
___**Fast Track**	1-4201-0186-2	$6.99US/$9.99CAN
___**Collateral Damage**	1-4201-0187-0	$6.99US/$9.99CAN
___**Final Justice**	1-4201-0188-9	$6.99US/$9.99CAN
___**Up Close and Personal**	0-8217-7956-7	$7.99US/$9.99CAN
___**Under the Radar**	1-4201-0683-X	$6.99US/$9.99CAN
___**Razor Sharp**	1-4201-0684-8	$7.99US/$10.99CAN
___**Yesterday**	1-4201-1494-8	$5.99US/$6.99CAN
___**Vanishing Act**	1-4201-0685-6	$7.99US/$10.99CAN
___**Sara's Song**	1-4201-1493-X	$5.99US/$6.99CAN
___**Deadly Deals**	1-4201-0686-4	$7.99US/$10.99CAN
___**Game Over**	1-4201-0687-2	$7.99US/$10.99CAN
___**Sins of Omission**	1-4201-1153-1	$7.99US/$10.99CAN
___**Sins of the Flesh**	1-4201-1154-X	$7.99US/$10.99CAN
___**Cross Roads**	1-4201-1192-2	$7.99US/$10.99CAN

Available Wherever Books Are Sold!
Check out our website at **www.kensingtonbooks.com**

Romantic Suspense from
Lisa Jackson

See How She Dies	0-8217-7605-3	$6.99US/$9.99CAN
Final Scream	0-8217-7712-2	$7.99US/$10.99CAN
Wishes	0-8217-6309-1	$5.99US/$7.99CAN
Whispers	0-8217-7603-7	$6.99US/$9.99CAN
Twice Kissed	0-8217-6038-6	$5.99US/$7.99CAN
Unspoken	0-8217-6402-0	$6.50US/$8.50CAN
If She Only Knew	0-8217-6708-9	$6.50US/$8.50CAN
Hot Blooded	0-8217-6841-7	$6.99US/$9.99CAN
Cold Blooded	0-8217-6934-0	$6.99US/$9.99CAN
The Night Before	0-8217-6936-7	$6.99US/$9.99CAN
The Morning After	0-8217-7295-3	$6.99US/$9.99CAN
Deep Freeze	0-8217-7296-1	$7.99US/$10.99CAN
Fatal Burn	0-8217-7577-4	$7.99US/$10.99CAN
Shiver	0-8217-7578-2	$7.99US/$10.99CAN
Most Likely to Die	0-8217-7576-6	$7.99US/$10.99CAN
Absolute Fear	0-8217-7936-2	$7.99US/$9.49CAN
Almost Dead	0-8217-7579-0	$7.99US/$10.99CAN
Lost Souls	0-8217-7938-9	$7.99US/$10.99CAN
Left to Die	1-4201-0276-1	$7.99US/$10.99CAN
Wicked Game	1-4201-0338-5	$7.99US/$9.99CAN
Malice	0-8217-7940-0	$7.99US/$9.49CAN

Available Wherever Books Are Sold!
Visit our website at **www.kensingtonbooks.com**